HOUSEBROKEN

HOUSEBROKEN

LESLIE J. SHERROD

Write On Time Publishing

Housebroken © 2024 by Leslie J. Sherrod
Write On Time Publishing, LLC
Baltimore, Maryland
www.WriteOnTimePublishing.com

ISBN: 979-8-218-10736-9 (Digital)
      979-8-218-10735-2 (Print)

All rights reserved. No part of this book may be reproduced in any form or by any means including electronic, mechanical or photocopying or stored in a retrieval system without permission in writing from the publisher except by a reviewer who may quote brief passages to be included in a review.

First Write On Time Publishing, LLC trade printing
Manufactured and Printed in the United States of America

Scriptures taken from the Holy Bible, New International Version®, NIV®. Copyright © 1973, 1978, 1984, 2011 by Biblica, Inc.™ Used by permission of Zondervan. All rights reserved worldwide. www.zondervan.com The "NIV" and "New International Version" are trademarks registered in the United States Patent and Trademark Office by Biblica, Inc.™

This is a work of fiction. All the characters, organizations, and events portrayed in this novel are either products of the author's imagination or are used fictitiously.

Cover design by Brian Sherrod.

Acknowledgments

The journey continues. Sending special thanks and gratitude to the people who support me most: my husband Brian and our children, my mother and sister, my "in-loves" and all my extended family, close friends, writing buddies, and everyone who's read my work, shown up, or shared an encouraging word. Special thanks to Angela, Charese, Yolonda, and MaRita for your friendship, and Zukeila, Tyronnia, Dana, Victoria, and Janice for your feedback. Additional special thanks to Chandra Sparks Splond for your patience, insight, and masterful skills with editing. You are phenomenal.

Obieray Rogers, I publish in your memory, grateful for your feedback and words of encouragement.

Dear Reader, you are valued and appreciated beyond words. Thank you for supporting my work. I hope you truly enjoy these pages. Connect with me at www.LeslieJSherrod.com.

All praise and glory to God.

I'm grateful.

*...first comes love,
then comes marriage,
then comes the baby in the baby carriage.*

I

The Rehearsal Dinner

Listen, I told them to just say no from the get-go, but I was only seventeen at that time, and they were the parents.

"Don't buy it," I'd begged. "This house is too damaged and broken. There's too much that needs to be done."

But, nope, my desperate pleas for common sense to take the wheel were not heard, and they zoomed full speed ahead, crashing right into my current catastrophe.

I'd tried my best to appeal to my parents' better judgment back then. When we first viewed the house in 2010 or so, I'd pointed out the stained brown carpet that covered the main floor like a sewage spill and the exposed subfloor that ran through the rest of the home. Rotten wood beams framed and filled the kitchen and dining room. The living room floor moved as you walked on it, and when you turned on the light switch in the foyer, a motor rumbled somewhere in the basement. Watermelon-sized holes riddled the walls and ceilings, and there was even a hole where an entire bedroom was supposed to be. A collection of dollar-store foil pans filled the space where a bathtub and sink should have been, and a shower head jutted meaninglessly from a hallway wall.

And those were just the things you could see at first glance. I'm not even going to get started detailing the busted pipes, the exposed wires, the rust, the cracks, and the termite damage.

The list of horrors went on and on.

"Seriously, Ma, Dad, you can't just binge-watch shows on HGTV and think you know how to renovate houses," I'd said.

Like I said, though, I was seventeen at that time, and they were the parents. They had already taken out a personal loan to purchase the abandoned home outright.

Fifty thousand dollars cash.

"Selena, this is called investing," my father had lectured.

The other townhomes in the development averaged $250,000. That should tell you all you need to know about the value and condition of the home they'd found online.

My parents were determined to make it work based on some seminar they'd attended at a two-star hotel in downtown Baltimore.

Marlene and Clarence Tucker were the queen and king of infomercial spectators when I was growing up in the nineties and early two thousands. Every $19.99 deal that flashed on TV seemed to end up in our home, and every nearby self-help symposium had their names as registrants. The year they bought the house was their year of investing. Name it, claim it, sow it, reap it—a revival they'd attended at a friend's church sealed their decision to move forward.

"We're listening to the Lord, Selena," my mother had explained as she'd thumbed the latest brochures on investment properties she'd ordered and received in the mail. "He has blessings waiting to rain down on us."

"But wouldn't the Good Lord tell us to get some of the basics fixed before we move in, you know, like, make sure water doesn't rain down on us from a leaky roof?" I remember scowling as we moved our meager belongings and our rent-to-own furniture from our place in East Baltimore into the fixer-upper in Randallstown. "Is it even legal to live like this?"

They—Ma and Dad—had looked at each other and laughed as they unpacked.

"Getting a home at this price in western Baltimore County is a blessing and a bargain," my father had asserted. "This is our slice of the American dream pie."

"It's an end-of-group townhome with a wonderful view of trees," my mother had chimed in.

"Trees." They both had sighed, smiling, like I should have stopped right there on the unsteady living room floor and started a holy dance and shouted like Sunday morning. We didn't have trees in our old backyard, and I'm sure they meant to inspire me as they reminded me of the block of cement that separated our former backdoor from the trash-littered alley. It wasn't quite what you'd call a yard, but it did offer a nice view of what my college professors so poetically termed "urban blight."

Anyway, they were rejoicing over trees and birds' nests and blue jays and assuring me Daddy's handyman friend Kunta X (don't ask) would be helping him start all the repairs as soon as he returned from his reparations conference.

Now, either that conference was on some serious CP time or Mr. X was waiting for his reparations check to come in the mail to buy supplies because here we are today, six years later. The house is nearly in the same condition as it was the day my parents bought it.

Okay, Ma tried to make the place home-worthy with some new curtains and some splashes of paint on the walls, but ain't enough Morning Mist (or whatever color blue that was) in the world to make you miss foot-wide holes, flaking plaster, and water damage.

They both tried to make it work. Some projects were started, some patchwork completed here and there. My father had a sump pump installed that reduced the basement flooding. But, as anyone who studies HGTV should have known, one new project leads to another—one wall torn down led to more discoveries. The very foundation of the home was unstable. The stripped bare and exposed horrors of the house meant we lived back and forth between there and the functioning home of my Grandma Verdine my senior year of high school while my parents outlined what to tackle next. There was nothing more I could say or do, my voice an empty echo on forlorn walls and damaged ceilings.

However, sometime during my freshman year of college, while I was working hard to maintain my full ride at Bowie State University and after Grandma Verdine moved on to her golden mansion in the sky, Ma and Dad had a "discussion" about the exponential costs of repairs and materials, the mounting debt, and the ongoing absence of my dad's handyman buddy, Kunta X.

The result of their exchanged words? My father took the last of the money he'd saved up for renovations and used it as a deposit for an apartment in Lochearn, just blocks away from the Baltimore City line. Ma joined him ten days later, using the excuse that I, the youngest of their two children, was almost out of their house and they didn't need that much space anymore. That, and also, the Lord had "moved them on to a new season."

They put the house on the market, and—surprise—it did not sell. Desperate, they tried to talk some of our neighbors from around the old way into buying it, but they all had more sense than to take on a money pit from hell.

They even attempted to get my older brother, CJ, to stop sofa-surfing at his friends' homes and accept a transfer of the deed.

"You can keep the house for yourself. It's paid for," my mother had said to him. "All you'd need to do is fix it up and pay the property taxes."

That should have been the red flag for me. I should have realized it then, the day I overheard Ma pleading with CJ, of all people, on the phone they were trying to free themselves of the house by any means necessary. I shouldn't have snickered to myself and shook my head at their pitiful choices and miserable fate.

Nope. I missed it. I missed the moment the tide changed and roared in my direction to knock me off my feet and leave me sputtering for breath in its merciless wake.

See, now, six years later, after time, money, and sacrifice were wasted on a place that should have remained abandoned, the tables have turned, and my parents' missteps have become my misfortune.

And, as would seem fitting for me, the tables have turned—crashed down, really—on the very day before I'm to be married. I should have fought harder to be heard at seventeen because here I am at twenty-three about to battle the brawl of my life.

*****

"So, Evan, babe, this is it."

It was a Thursday evening in late April, my wedding eve. I was standing in the living room of "the house," as my family calls it. Well, technically, I was balancing precariously on the living room floor. My fiancé, Evan Wayland, stood next to me.

We both should have been at the intimate banquet hall his parents had rented for our rehearsal dinner, finishing the petit fours, or whatever the heck they're called, that his mother ordered from a local French bakery. Everyone else was there, including my parents, enjoying the delicacies and reveling in the elaborate celebration. We were not with them. We left. We were standing here taking in the madness of my parents' money pit.

Let me just say this: I gave Jesus my heart when I was eight years old, and I figured we've been pretty tight through the years. You know, when the praises go up, the blessings come down, and all that? *So, Lord, you could have at least given me a heads-up on what my parents were about to pull on me.*

Evan's mother, Mrs. Wayland, had a catered seven-course, southern France–inspired meal for our rehearsal dinner. I'm talking real linen, silver, crystal, gold, and food I'd never heard of nor will ever be able to pronounce. The queen of socialites and the unmatched planner of charity balls, she'd even used her connections to surprise us with a personalized taped performance by the legendary Razi to serenade us with one of his chart-topping soulful ballads.

I'd wondered at the sixty-five-inch flat-screen TV at the dinner, framed by red velvet curtains and hoisted on a wall near the head table. I'd thought Mrs. Wayland was preparing to play a video montage when she dimmed the lights and used a remote to turn it on. I'd braced myself to see pictures of a ten-year-old snaggle-toothed me set to one of Mrs. Wayland's favorite Motown oldies. Instead (and thankfully), there was the smooth-as-black-silk Razi smiling and winking from a bench in front of a shimmering black baby grand. The Johannesburg nighttime skyline glittered in a window behind him, a stop on his ten-city world tour.

"Hey there, Evan and Selena, this is for you." His tenor voice rippled through the speakers. I'd watched in awe and disbelief as the local Maryland legend turned international R&B superstar—who'd actually said *my* name—crooned his hit love song to me and my beloved through a TV screen at our wedding rehearsal. "Best wishes to the beautiful bride and the lucky groom," he'd ended, blowing a kiss to the camera.

That should have been the highlight of my evening, the sole significant moment from my special night that would be sealed in my memory bank forever, right?

I mean, half an hour ago, Evan and I were at the dinner with everyone else, swooning and swaying along with the vocal runs and smooth vibrato of the one-named wonder. Razi belting out his sultry melody at my rehearsal dinner went beyond any dream I'd ever had, making what happened next the monster of all nightmares.

Right after the television went dark and the room went back to full brightness, my parents stood and made their big announcement. Mrs. Wayland was frowning because of their timing. I was frowning period.

"Excuse us," my father's bass voice had cut through the rousing applause of the sixty or so guests who were still applauding the surprise serenade. I glared at my mother furiously when I saw Mrs. Wayland look up from her typed and laminated program, her perfectly arched eyebrow raised at the interruption in her carefully scripted affair. My glare turned to horror when I noticed the snicker on CJ's face. I knew immediately it was not going to be a good announcement.

"God has blessed us with a wonderful daughter." My father smiled too hard. "I'm happy that the Waylands were able to *present* the illustrious Razi for this special night. However, God has blessed my wife and I with the perfect *present* for our daughter and our new son that will last for many days and nights to come. Stand up with me, Marlene." He beckoned to my mother. As she stood beaming, my father took out an official-looking document and held it up for us all to see.

"Selena, you and Evan don't have to worry about paying for that little overpriced studio you rented downtown because your mother and I are giving you our house… Signed, sealed, delivered, it's yours." He had sung the last words in an off-key falsetto, the tiny diamond stud in his ear sparkling in the crystal chandelier light. "Y'all didn't know you were going to get a little Stevie after the Razi, did you?" He chuckled.

The crowded *oohed* and clapped again. Both Evan and I were overcome with tears, except Evan had never seen the house, and his tears were happy ones.

Early in our relationship, I'd mentioned to him in passing that my parents owned a house they were fixing up. The shame and pain of the whole story was too much for me to have provided him further details.

I wished I had.

"Wow, amazing!" Evan gushed. "Thank you, Mr. and Mrs. Tucker. That's so generous of you. Thank you so much."

I wondered then how thankful he'd be when he saw what we were getting, especially knowing what we'd have to give up. The "little overpriced studio" downtown my father mentioned was on the top floor of a new development near glitzy Harbor East. My parents weren't aware that Evan's parents had insisted on helping with the high rent. The building was near Evan's job at a law firm, and the address was trendy enough for Mrs. Wayland to name-drop to her circle. Evan had been commuting from his parents' home in Bowie, and I'd made my parents' sofa my home since I'd graduated from college last spring. (Look, there is no shame in taking five years to work my way through school after my scholarship collapsed.) So, what I'm saying is the move to the fancy studio apartment felt like a glamourous step forward and the beginnings of my dreams come true.

"I didn't know your parents owned a house," Mrs. Wayland had whispered loudly to me over the applause and hugs and kisses. A spidery web of deep scarlet found a way to inch up her almond-brown face.

Mrs. Wayland didn't like surprises involving her baby boy that had not been okayed by her first. There were standards to be held, and she was the God-ordained standard checker. Said so somewhere in the Bible. In bright red letters. Mrs. Madelyn Ernestine Wayland was sent to make sure the world was doing right by her only begotten son.

Anyway, that's how Mrs. Wayland surely acted and what she

most certainly believed. Imagine what happened when Evan first introduced me to her and the good doctor. But that's another story for another day. Back to the house.

I knew I had to get the house out of our hands before she saw it and before my Harbor East fantasy collapsed. That's why I immediately whisked Evan away from our lovely little wedding rehearsal dinner with the petit fours.

That's why we were there right now looking at holes in Morning Mist painted walls.

"Look at this house. So much potential." I smiled as Evan fingered the kitchen island that was literally a piece of untreated lumber some fool had nailed to the vinyl floor. I had to let Evan believe giving back the house was his idea. My mother told me making a man believe he'd come up with a plan that his woman had subtly planted in his head was the best trick in the unwritten code of wife ethics. Trickery would build his esteem and keep the peace, my momma said.

Maybe believing and acting on this myth was the traceable moment my disaster began.

Sidenote to mothers: Please don't lead your daughters astray with false relationship advice and bad marriage tips. Tell your daughters their voice matters. Presentation is everything, and silence is not always golden.

But I didn't know any of this. Yet.

"See the trees," I continued with Evan as I pointed out of the patio door. "Can't you imagine all the birds that will come to the birdfeeder we can hang out there? And look, the deck. We can host our own cookouts this summer. Can you say barbecue?"

I actually called it a deck. The wooden beams that weren't missing were splintered and rotten. I wouldn't even try to balance a bottle of ketchup out there, forget a charcoal grill.

I looked over at Evan who stared intently out the glass. A frown tugged at the corners of his lips, and his deep brown eyes had that serious look of concentration I'd seen him give his thick law textbooks during his Georgetown years. When he turned to face me, he was rubbing his chin like an old man contemplating his next chess move.

"What's wrong, baby?" I gently massaged the wrinkles on his forehead with the tips of my fingers.

"Oh, nothing. I mean, it's something we can figure out together." *Checkmate.*

This marriage thing was going to be a breeze, I believed in that moment.

"I know my parents meant well." *Yeah, right,* I thought. "But if we sit down with them after the wedding and explain—"

"It's the trees. Not all of them." Evan pointed. "Just that one big oak tree in the center of the yard. We can get that cut down so the pool will fit."

"Exactly. I'm sure my parents will understand that we... Pool? Did you say something about a pool?" I think I was too shocked to believe what I was hearing. He was making plans for the house.

"Yes. A pool would be perfect to go along with those backyard barbecues. And I love the trees. We'll just get rid of that one right there." He pointed to a massive oak that sat in the middle of the sprawling yard before turning back to face me with a smile. "Otherwise, the house is perfect. Sure, it needs some work, but your parents did say they're gifting their contractor friend so we can make this home our own."

Kunta X comes with this package deal? I'd missed that. I must have blacked out after my father held up the deed.

"We can make this house whatever we want it to be." Evan was still talking. "I'm thinking out in the backyard..."

He continued with his own fantasy, but I didn't hear the rest of anything he said.

I was stuck on the tree he'd pointed to.

"Trees," my parents had said, smiling the first time they'd shown me the house years ago.

"I love the trees," Evan had just echoed in.

I officially hated trees.

"Well, the big day is tomorrow." Evan was saying something or other about the wedding. "We need to get back to the party so we can end the day and get some rest. CJ said his gift for us is to move our furniture from the studio to here while we're on our honeymoon. I think that's a great gift. And don't worry. My parents will take care of us backing out of our lease at The Wharf Warehouse, I'm sure. One less thing to figure out." He kissed my hand and led me to the door.

"*Ummm,* Evan, do you think it's actually safe to live in here?" Where did I even begin? My feet felt like weights had been added to them as I followed him out of the house. The last time I'd spoken out about this place, my words had led to nowhere. What would change now?

"You're so funny, Selena." He laughed. "Your sense of humor is one of the things I love about you. I know your parents would never put us in danger."

"You don't know my parents," I murmured. Then, seeing the slight confusion on his face, I threw in a loud laugh that ended with a snort.

"Well, maybe you don't know me, Selena." He joined my forced chuckle. "I'm going to get everything perfect for you. For us. I'm certain I can do that." He nodded like a madman.

"Of course, you will, Evan—" I reached for his hand and squeezed it— "because you are absolutely perfect."

And, he was. Absolutely. Perfect. My groom was a delicious looking black man from a well-to-do family, with a law degree and a winning smile. He'd joined my church the first time he'd visited and even volunteered to set up the tables for our annual church picnic held that same day. He towered over my five-seven frame at six feet even, and he got me to join a gym with him, and he watched reality TV shows with me. He had smooth hazelnut skin, a trimmed mustache and goatee, clear brown eyes, and charming dimples.

What more could I want or ask for?

He leaned over and pressed his lips on mine, and then, still holding my hand, led us both back to his car.

And that was that.

Tomorrow is my wedding day. My marriage, my life is not about this house. I am marrying the man of my dreams, and he will fix all the brokenness my parents gifted me. This is what I repeated to myself all the way back to the banquet hall.

"Wait until my mother sees this place." Evan was giddy.

His mother. My spirit groaned.

"Yes, won't that be nice?" I mean, what was I supposed to say? "We'll have your parents over for dinner once we get settled." Once we get a stove that works. And plaster on the dining room walls. And a refrigerator that doesn't sound like it's speaking in tongues. And I still haven't figured out why there's an "N" where the "H" should be on the kitchen sink faucet.

"The first thing we need is a brand-new welcome mat." Evan chatted endlessly.

"That was my first thought exactly." I rolled my eyes out of his view as an unspeakable fear of the future threatened to put a damper on my pre-wedding glow.

A big, brand-new welcome mat is exactly what was needed to make the house welcoming. A big, brand-new mat that said "Welcome to My Happily Ever After. Watch Your Step."

2

The Wedding

It was a Friday evening wedding ceremony with just enough sunlight left to easily showcase the blooming late April colors of the Cylburn Arboretum. I originally wanted a good, old-fashioned church wedding with an organist and heavy wooden foyer doors that would open dramatically at my entrance. You know that moment: The old man at the pipe organ plays those unmistakable first notes of "The Wedding March," and everyone in the sanctuary stands and *ooh*s and *ah*s at the woman in satin, pearls, and lace who magically appears at the top of the aisle.

Anyway, that's what I immediately envisioned the day Evan popped the question. We were standing in line at the grocery store, picking up some last-minute items Ma needed for Easter dinner. Evan, being the ever-so-kind gentleman that he is, offered to pay for the groceries, and as he pulled his wallet out of his jacket pocket, I noticed a small black box landing next to his left foot.

In retrospect, I should have instantly realized the box came from Evan's pocket and he was planning to make his first Easter dinner with my family an event for both of us to forever cherish. I should have acted like I never noticed him slowly reaching for the velvet box, and I should definitely not have asked the drunk man with the can of sweet potatoes standing behind me if he'd dropped something. But I can be a little slow at times.

This was one of those times.

To make a long story short, I was proposed to in the express lane of Shop-Rite, holding a pack of brown-and-serve rolls and some mix for grape Kool-Aid. Not exactly the picture I had in mind when I used to stand in front of my dorm room mirror and practice my "Yes, Evan, I will marry you" speech. The biggest romance of the moment came when the cashier, who was squealing like Evan had just offered her the one-and-a-half carat ring, gave me a free bouquet of red roses and joined the tear-filled group hug between me, Evan, and the drunk sweet potato man.

Now that I think about it, that was probably the most appropriate way to begin my fantasy-crushing twelve-month journey to the altar. Did I say journey? *Circus* is a better word. Three-ring to be exact. Mrs. Wayland was the ringleader, most of the bridal party were the clowns, and Evan was the spectator munching on corn dogs and clapping at the poor dancing elephants. Me? I was the fool sticking my head in the tiger's mouth.

I must admit, Mrs. Wayland and her right-hand lady (Evan's godmother, the Honorable Judge Vanessa Grant) planned everything beyond anything I could have ever imagined. Mrs. Wayland had big dreams for her son's wedding day, and neither my parents' limited checkbook nor my pint-sized, needs-new-carpet home church were part of her vision.

The arboretum was his mother's idea, and to keep the peace, I accepted it as a church whose walls were made of sculptured green and whose floors were lined with sweet-scented blossoms. The heavens were our canopy. White clouds and angels filled the balcony, and God Himself set the mood in the quiet breeze that stirred our love.

*****

"It's almost time, Selena."

Neeka Mack has always been good at snapping me back into reality. I smiled at her, unable to speak, realizing I'd been holding a breath of air in my lungs for too long. My hands were turning pale from gripping my bouquet so tightly.

"Exhale," Neeka said, and then, filled with excitement and joy for me, she couldn't say anything else. She squeezed my wrists before turning to join the lineup for the processional.

Neeka was my best girlfriend and my maid of honor. I watched her disappear behind the bushes and stand with my other four bridesmaids. Evan and Pastor Knight from my church waited in the center of the courtyard at the specially designed fountain Mrs. Wayland had commissioned for the event.

Floating candles filled the fountain's base, and candle lanterns were scattered throughout the gardens. It was just enough candlelight to fill in the gaps left by the closing day. I liked the colors cast by fire and sun and made a mental note to never forget this moment.

A hundred or so guests were seated in white chairs that encircled the fountain, and a string quartet played from a nearby gazebo. I listened to the violins, viola, and cello serenade Neeka, my cousins, and Evan's sisters as they walked down multiple aisles to where Evan and Pastor Knight stood. My bridesmaids were dressed in black silk gowns. Flickering lanterns were part of their bouquets, adding to the intrigue and dance of shadows and lights. A bird somewhere in a neighboring treetop joined the quartet's melody as the three flower girls—Evan's twin nieces and my baby cousin D'Tonya—showered the air and aisles with petals. Red rose petals.

In honor of my impromptu proposal at the Shop-Rite, every single flower in my wedding was a red rose.

There was a crescendo in the music, and my father took my arm. This was it.

Now, y'all should see me in my wedding gown. It was a sleeveless organza ball gown masterpiece with a charmeuse bodice covered with vintage rhinestones. For that one frozen moment when Evan first saw me at the start of the rose-covered path, for the look on his face, *for the look in his eyes*, I will swallow my pride wholeheartedly and thank Mrs. Wayland for insisting I wear the designer gown she got through some nameless connection she had in New York. I looked good, and for once I knew it. Everybody there knew it. I was seriously wearing my hard-earned white.

For the record, I'm thoroughly convinced the whole processional down the aisle is a fashion show in its purest form. Think about it: There's all these designer clothes and fabrics, a walkway, accompanying music, flashing cameras, and onlookers making mental notes of every detail head to toe. The only thing missing is an emcee.

But the fashion show is not necessarily a bad thing. Any woman, no matter how tall or short, flat or fluffy, looks beautiful on her wedding day. For those brief moments, you are the center, the queen, the picture of perfection; and at the end of the aisle is a vowing mate who is promising to keep seeing you as all these things, even when the show is over, the lights have stopped flashing, and the clock has struck twelve.

That's how Evan makes me feel.

That's why when Pastor Knight gave me the words to say, I could speak them with my mouth and mean them from my heart. Evan looked like he was thinking about every vow he was making to me and God. You could almost see the aha moment in each promise he declared. "Aha, this is the moment I've been waiting for since I met you. The moment you would know without a doubt that I will love and cherish you no matter what, no strings attached, no conditions applied. The moment when you know that I'm so serious about you that only God Himself can end our union."

He didn't say these words out loud, but I heard him loud and clear. His commitment was placed on my finger with a ring, sealed on my lips with a kiss, and later that night...

Okay, there are some things you don't need to know.

But I will say this: Everything that happened during my yearlong circus (I mean, engagement) and the four hours that made up my whole wedding thing did not always go according to my sixteen-year-old—okay, twenty-three-year-old—fantasy. I'm not going to talk about how the limo was late and got lost; how CJ forgot to pick up his tux and showed up in his best streetwear—designer hoodie, jeans, and Jordans—thinking he'd be the cool usher before my father made him wear his old (translate 1989) tux. I won't even bring up the fact that the wedding cake was not the flavor I ordered. (I understand now why a lady brought some caterer to one of those TV judges to sue over chicken.)

But I took a lesson with me that I picked up at a friend's little sister's wedding. Their flowers never came, the pianist never showed up, and for some reason, there were no forks at their reception. There were no designer names, posh venues, fancy decorations, bell ringers, or flying doves. All the bride and groom had was each other, and it was obvious to every attendee that was all they needed.

Today was my wedding day. Was it the wedding of *my* dreams? Maybe, maybe not. Either way, it was perfect.

3

The Honeymoon

The water of the Caribbean was so clear I could see the raspberry nail polish on my pinky toe. Evan thought I was out of my mind for wanting to sit my beach chair in two feet of water, but I was simply amazed at how vivid everything showed up below the surface. Couldn't do this in the Inner Harbor back home.

Besides, I was still getting used to wearing a bikini. I usually stayed away from the two-piece swimsuit collections at department stores, but I figured this exclusive resort in St. Martin was far enough away from people who knew me to peek and laugh. So here I was, hiding—I mean sitting—in the ocean, trying to look like a size sixteen Victoria's Secret model.

"You look amazing, Lena." Evan kept telling me the black string thingy (I don't know what else to call it) looked good on me, so for him—and for me—I kept telling myself to be confident and strut my stuff like I had stuff to strut. I'm one of those pear-shaped women who's tiny at the top and all round at the bottom. Too round at the bottom. But I was working my roundness today. There were too many *topless* sunbathers on this beach, and I wanted Evan to keep his eyes on me.

Maybe that's why I had him sitting next to me in chest-high water, faced away from the sandy shoreline. I'm sure we looked like two seals with our heads poking out of the water. And to top it off, we had nerve enough to be the only black people out there sitting like this. I could almost hear all the white people going back to their hotel rooms now saying, "John, darling, did you see those two black seals in the water?"

Evan tells me all the time I'm too race conscious and afraid of how people view my skin, and maybe I am. But right then, I felt too *self*-conscious and like a chubby seal, and I thought how Victoria's Secret models don't sit on beach chairs with their heads sticking out of the water. They walk around the seashore and grab cliffs and stick their butts in the air and twist their eyes and mouths around like they're having convulsions.

If we saw someone acting like that on a beach in real life, we'd probably all move our blankets, towels, and umbrellas to another area and go home talking about the weirdo we saw groping the beach.

But right then, I felt like I needed to look like that because I was on my honeymoon and looking seductively delicious was an unspoken requirement.

"Evan," I said, "the sun's almost gone. Why don't we go take that walk along the beach like you've been wanting to do? We could take some pictures. Splash in the waves." I felt more confident striking a sexy pose in the dusk of the day.

He began a soft kiss on my shoulder that ended on my lips as a reply, and I knew he wanted to take a walk back to our honeymoon villa suite and tread water of a different kind. But I was still in my Victoria's Secret swimsuit posing moment. I stood and grabbed his hand to start walking barefoot toward the postcard-perfect horizon.

Evan was quiet as we walked. I tried to think of something to say about how beautiful the purple and orange sky was and how the sun looked like it was melting into the crystal water. Only God could paint a picture like that. I looked at the water and how calm it was, and I remembered why I was so excited when Dr. and Mrs. Wayland told us they were sending us here as a wedding gift.

Wedding gift.

I pushed back the sinking feelings that came with the thought of my parents' "wedding gift." Evan and I hadn't talked about the house since we saw it the night of our rehearsal dinner. I didn't know how to even bring it up or tell Evan how I felt. I willed myself to focus only on the tropical view in front of me. The rippling waves and clear water made it easy for me to forget the trouble waiting back home—the house, the fears, the inward freeze that trapped me.

I love water. I love large bodies of water where you can't see the end and sailboats look like they'll fall off the edge and land in the sky. I looked at the water and thought of all my clouded dreams. Unspoken dreams I'd sent up to God in silent prayers like so many sailboats pushed out into the unseen unknown. Undefined dreams I had unanchored and whispered Godspeed to, hoping they docked at ports of call named Purpose and Fruition.

When I was ten, I told my fifth-grade teacher I was going to be something nobody had ever been and do something nobody had ever done. She'd asked our class what we wanted to be when we grew up, and I felt this ripple inside like I was going to grow to be someone great, but I wasn't sure exactly in what way.

I asked my mother and then my Sunday School teacher back then what this feeling was, and they both said it was the Jesus in me trying to push His power out, and if I listened real hard, He'd tell me what He was powering me up to do. I wanted to make sure I heard Him correctly, so I listened hard for three weeks, cocking my ear to every conversation passing by me, listening for something different in the wind, straining to make sense out of any bird chirping or dog barking.

But all I heard was the latest gossip about the new choir director at church, some recipes for fried pork chops and biscuits, and, well, birds chirping and dogs barking. I decided then to just spend an hour a day listening hard with a Bible in my lap. That hour shrunk to thirty minutes to fifteen minutes to just barely over five minutes every few days by the time I reached college. I guess I reasoned God would tell me what great thing I was supposed to do when He was good and ready to let me know.

In the meantime, I simply packaged all my big dreams of becoming the first black woman president of the United States or the doctor who found the cure for AIDS or cancer, or the inventor who made the first run-less pantyhose into a neat knot and left it floating somewhere inside of me.

I majored in communications in college, and after bouncing around a few retail jobs after graduation, I finally had a job in my field waiting for me to start when we get back home. Evan's older sister helped me get a foot in the door at a local AM radio station as a production assistant. I reasoned I could help someone else get their message out on the airwaves as I figured out what messages I needed to sort through in my own life.

"You still up for ziplining tomorrow?" Evan finally broke the meditative silence.

"Sure," I said, remembering to stick my padded-bra-still-ain't-helping chest out in full Victoria's Secret mode. Evan noticed because the grin that curled onto his lips told me his planned itinerary before he even announced it.

"Well, the sooner we tuck in for the night, the sooner tomorrow will get here." He let out a playful stretch and yawn.

The brother *did* wait for a long time. No need to continue in that effort. We headed back.

I took one last look at the water from the balcony of our beachfront suite. The view of the quiet waves disappeared with the setting sun. The horizon was nearly gone, but I knew there were still some boats out there drifting lazily away.

"Are you finding what you're looking for?" He wrapped his arms around me, and I felt myself giving in to his embrace.

This marriage is going to be perfect.

"Yes, you. I found you." My voice faded as his lips pressed on my neck and his arms held me closer.

As I closed the balcony doors, I knew some boats had already entered safe harbors. Others still tossed and turned on open seas.

4

The Threshold

We weren't home five minutes before my phone started ringing. I use the term *home* loosely because the place still looked like a condemned wasteland. I wasn't going to answer the phone at first because Evan was still in full St. Martin mode, wanting to carry me over the threshold of our bedroom door. Wasn't that difficult as there wasn't a door.

CJ had managed to move all our furniture into the home as promised, but the only piece that was in the right place was our bed. That's it. Everything else was crammed into the basement. The furniture that filled the rest of the home was the leftover hodgepodge of items my parents had abandoned years ago. I guess even CJ didn't want to sort through that mess. I could tell my mother had come in along with him. The floors were swept, and my parents' old furniture had been dusted among the ruins. And our bed was made—comforter, mounds of pillows, and all.

Evan seemed not to notice any of this, focused only on the fact that our bed was there and ready to be christened by our love. After the fifth deluge of vibrating rings coming from my phone, just as Evan dropped me on the king-size bed and reached for my shirt strap, I couldn't take it anymore. I answered my phone.

I swatted Evan's hand off me and sat up. "Hello?"

"I drove by the house on Tuesday. I had assumed when I heard it was in Randallstown the house would be acceptable, but I fear I was mistaken. I just want to know, does it look as bad inside as it does outside?"

Evan's mother.

No hello, congratulations, how was the trip, none of that.

"Well, it's definitely a fixer-upper, but we'll have it looking good in no time." I peeked over at Evan and fixed my shirt as if his mother could see me through the phone. He gave me a reassuring smile. "My father's contractor friend will have everything repaired and updated soon." I wanted to believe this. I needed to believe this.

"Your father's friend will fix...this." There was a pause and then a heavy sigh before she continued. "Let me speak to Evan."

I passed my phone to him.

When Evan took over the call, there must have been a serious turn in conversation. I watched his face light up as he began describing in select detail the happenings of our honeymoon, the blissful scenery of St. Martin, the perfection of our wedding. When he handed my phone back to me, smiling, I was sure the storm was over and the sun was out to shine.

"Hello, again, Mrs. Wayland." I smiled.

"I did not raise my son in an estate that was featured in *House & Studio* magazine for you and your family to transport him to a shack that wouldn't keep a rat satisfied. I should have known to inspect your place before we cancelled the lease for the apartment downtown. You have three months to get it together before I ask your parents to repay the tremendous cancellation fee my husband and

I were responsible for. This is not acceptable. Three months." Then, the line went dead.

No, the lady did not just hang up on me.

And, no, my parents would never agree to pay that fee. The thought of even mentioning this to Charles and Marlene Tucker sent me shuddering.

I slowly laid my phone on the floor, blinking hard, still smiling. What else was I supposed to do? Call her back? Call my parents? Talk to Evan? (Who, by the way, had left the room to enjoy some puffy-looking dessert a man in an apron had just delivered to our front door. Courtesy of his mother, of course.)

I needed to talk to Jesus, but then my best girl Neeka called, so I talked to her.

"She said *what*? Oh no, girl! We need to drive right out to Bowie and slap the—"

"We'll deal with this tomorrow." I cut her off before she could continue. I knew she was joking—well, kind of—but this was not the way to start my first moments home with my new husband, scheming on the phone to put his mother in her place.

I could hear Evan's whistles downstairs getting closer. He'd be ready to pick up from where we'd been interrupted. I hurried to end the conversation. "I have to go."

"Not so fast, Selena. You know the real reason why I called."

I groaned, kicking myself for not just talking to Jesus like I should have.

"Well?" Neeka was grinning, I could tell. She'd been waiting to make this phone call since she knew me.

See, unlike Neeka, I had no issues with being a virgin for the first twenty-three years of my life. She, on the other hand, quickly discarded that title from her résumé on her sixteenth birthday. From then on, *it* became a long-standing debate between the two of us that only worsened when I met Evan.

"A pretty man like that ain't going to wait but for so long," she'd told me when I first brought him home to meet my parents. She was sitting in their apartment living room with this phony innocent smile on her face that made me wrap my fingers around his hand even tighter.

Not that I didn't trust my best friend. I mean, she *did* gain quite a reputation as a man-stealing, goody-giving girl in high school, and she only added to her credentials when I went away to college. Or so I heard. But we were girls, and although nobody (my parents included) could understand how the two of us could be so close, I knew I could trust her with the secrets and the people most important to me.

That being said, I still found myself clutching on to Evan the entire evening when Neeka first met him, until he got into his car to drive back to his apartment near Georgetown.

Neeka used to tease me and tell me that I was afraid of sex. She constantly told me I would never be able to keep a man without giving some away. What she didn't understand was that fear had nothing to do with it. Contrary to what she believed about me, I didn't think sex was dirty and something to be avoided like the plague.

Truth be told, I valued sex so much that I only wanted to have it with someone who valued it as much as I did. I wanted my first time to be with a man who could declare to me privately and publicly I was worth being his one and only. His wife. If a man didn't view my body as the sacred temple God said it was, I had no problem letting him go. He was not "The One."

Neeka thought I was out of touch with reality. Completely. "Men don't come like that anymore," she said. "Those prayers are pointless."

Don't get me wrong. Those twenty-three years of waiting were difficult. Okay, grueling. I went through adolescence and all that just like any other girl on my block, but I figured if I believed sex was that precious and my body was that valuable, it was worth the sacrifice.

And Jesus did say He'd give you what you want if you commit your way to Him. I read that somewhere in Psalms once in one of my five-minute Bible studies. Now, Jesus wouldn't lie, would He?

"Selena, you got to tell me something," Neeka was pleading. "Inquiring minds want to know. Did you get what you've been holding out for all these loooong years?"

I thought about it and wasn't sure immediately what to say. How could I explain to her that when I laid down with a man for the first time, I wasn't afraid of getting up with some disease I hadn't asked for or getting up to see him gone and a part of myself with him? How could I explain to her the oneness I celebrated with a man—*the* man—I was truly one with? How could I explain to her that the first time I had sex, I knew God was in the room smiling (okay, laughing) and the angels were holding their breath in awe.

No shame, no sorrow. And we both woke up smiling. Again, and again and again. That was the privilege—the freedom—I got the moment I said, "I do."

I mean, what could possibly go wrong with this level of perfection? (Y'all, I ain't know. Yet.)

"Selena, are you there? Tell me, were the islands good to you, girl?"

"Neeka, I'll just say this: The pure freedom I felt was beyond anything I imagined. *Good* ain't even the word. Girl, it was *mmm, mmm* great."

Neeka laughed, but before I could join in the laughter and enjoy the sweet sincerity of the moment, before I could sigh that cleansing sigh you give when the world for once is at peace and life feels just right, Evan was tapping on my shoulder with news that had him gleefully grinning from ear to ear.

"Guess what, Lena? My mom and my godmother are here. Mom's parking the car right now."

5

The Mother

They had just come back from a shopping trip, they said—a several-thousand-dollar shopping spree in Tysons Corner, Virginia, to reward their hard work for our wedding. They'd also raided a gourmet food store to ensure we had initial groceries for our return home. Mrs. Wayland had "forgotten" to mention their "impromptu" visit when she called on her cell phone half an hour ago. Don't think I missed she'd probably only called to make sure we were home and available for their surprise visit.

"We thought we'd drop in to make sure you didn't need anything. We won't be here long." The godmother, Judge Grant, scanned the downstairs with a hard frown and then set herself on unloading a Nordstrom's bag on the dining room table. She threw a smile on her face, but the corners of her mouth wobbled like the table teetering under the weight of the crystal vase she was balancing on it. That vase probably cost more than the entire oak dining set and the curio cabinet that matched it.

My mother had found both, unfinished, at a yard sale, along

with a claw foot bathtub. All three pieces, including the tub, were the highlights of the dining room décor and were among the many projects my mom had started and never completed. The curio was still filled with the yard sale owner's ceramic dog collection. And, now, it also held a plate inside of it that Mrs. Wayland picked out for my wedding registry. (Yes, I mean a plate, as in one plate. At Mrs. Wayland's insistence, I'd registered for an entire eight-piece set of platinum-rimmed plates crafted in a quaint town in Italy. An old neighbor was actually kind enough to buy one and present it to me at my bridal shower, a month before the wedding.) CJ or my mom had been kind enough to place the single plate inside the newly dusted cabinet.

Anyway, Judge Grant was stooping eye level with the table while Mrs. Wayland went through the rest of the kitchen, stepping over and around raw beams and poles, opening the cabinets and fixtures that still had doors, turning the faucets on and off, when Evan had a bright idea.

"Mom, Ms. Nessa, since you're here, why don't you stay for dinner? I'm sure Selena can whip up something from this food you bought, so we might as well make it a small feast and have our official first dinner at home." He rustled through the paper bags of fine foods scattered on the kitchen floor. "*Mmm*, truffles."

"What a wonderful idea. See, Vanessa, I told you these place settings would come in handy." Mrs. Wayland took out seven dinner plates identical to the one in the curio cabinet, along with eight each of matching salad plates and soup bowls. She gave the kitchen another scan, as if a proper place to put the elegant dinnerware would suddenly appear. She settled on the untreated block of wood serving as a cooking island. "Selena, what do you have in mind to prepare tonight? I'll be glad to help you."

The horror on her face said otherwise. Especially considering the stove looked like it was from 1981 and a box of matches sat next to it to help get the single-functioning burner started.

But there was another, bigger issue here.

Maybe the man thought this was some kind of Cinderella story where with the wave of a magic wand your dreams come true. What was he thinking? Evan knows I can't cook.

I come from a long line of women responsible for bringing only the cups and plates and maybe a dessert—if it was store-bought—to potluck dinners. Saying "I do" days ago has not changed that fact. And his mother pulling an apron, cooking mitt, and ceramic cookware out of another bag has not changed that fact. Not to mention the stove still only had one working burner. I give Evan a good look in the eye, suddenly realizing we haven't spent twenty minutes alone since we left St. Martin. Suddenly realizing this man thinks—expects—that I really know how to put a dinner together for him, his mother, and the Honorable Judge Vanessa Grant with the packages of truffles, fig chutney, chicken liver pâté, and quail legs they'd brought into my home. Nope. I had not signed up for a newlywed version of The Food Network's *Chopped*, the show where contestants compete to make fancy dishes from random ingredients in a fast-moving thirty minutes.

I wished I had some of that magic sparkle dust Evan's obviously been snorting to poof a meal on that wobbly table. *Jesus, tell me what to do*, I prayed.

Forty minutes later, the three of us were sitting around my mother's yard sale find eating the Saturday night delivery special from Bamboo Express. Conversation was at a minimum as the two ladies, dressed in their tailored suits and gemstones, sloshed beef lo mein noodles and egg foo young in the soy sauce that puddled in clumps on the platinum-rimmed plates. The sterling silver forks and knives looked particularly elegant on the linen napkins Mrs. Wayland insisted we use to complement the flower arrangement the judge finally balanced in the center of the table. I was praying nobody noticed the table slightly shifted every time one of the wineglasses filled with cherry cola was lifted.

Yeah, the wineglasses were the only option for the cola.

"Well, this is quite...lovely." Judge Grant spurred some dinner conversation as we finished. "I do have some exciting news to share." She put down her fork. "Evan, I had a chance to speak with Razi's manager when your mom contacted his team to thank him for the video he did for your rehearsal dinner. His manager disclosed that Razi is dealing with a minor copyright issue related to the lyrics of an unreleased song. I convinced him to seek the services of your law firm. While you were away on your honeymoon, I confirmed the partners of Wernowski & Associates are going to have you represent him. This is a phenomenal opportunity for your entertainment law goals. It's a pretty easy open-and-shut case, and having Razi as a client will only open amazing doors for you."

"Wow," I blurted, "you really are a fairy godmother, Judge Grant. Who needs a magic wand when Evan has someone like you on his side? That's awesome, Evan. Razi? You'll actually be representing the one and only Razi?" I playfully patted my new husband's shoulder. He took a sip of cherry cola from his wineglass, quiet.

"It's not magic and mysticism that has brought my son his continued success, Selena." Mrs. Wayland's tone scolded as she dabbed soy sauce from her lips with her linen napkin. "It's hard work—and the right connections." Her face broke into a soft smile. "You are truly amazing, Vanessa. Well done. Imagine, my son, Evan Wayland, the soon-to-be world-renowned entertainment lawyer."

"Yeah, entertainment law," Evan mumbled as he scraped some noodles from his plate and then sighed. "By the way, speaking of entertainment, I learned about this pro bono group downtown that helps creatives with legal consultations. Local artists, writers, and start-ups looking for help, that sort of thing. I'm thinking about volunteering to—"

"Volunteer to serve on the board," his mother interrupted flatly. "You'll go further in your career taking on roles of leadership and power than just settling to get mixed up in the minor squabbles of lost dreamers. Be a decision-maker at the table where your ancestors fought to give you a place. Aim high, Evan. You have such a good heart, but you also have the wisdom of your mother to help keep that good heart of yours connected to the proper circles." She turned to Judge Grant and waved at him dismissively. "Just think, if it weren't for me, he'd be working as a public defender, going in and out of dirty city jail cells, proclaiming the innocence of low-level drug dealers and two-bit hustlers." She frowned.

"Mom, you always bring that up." Evan sat back in his seat. "That was a short-lived idea I had during law school. I know the entertainment industry is the best route for me, financially and for the brand I hope to build. I've listened to you every step of the way."

"And I've never led you astray." She beamed.

"No, you haven't. Ever." His pursed lips melted into a smile, and he slowly nodded. You've always led me on the right path. You're the greatest. Thanks for that, Mom."

"That's so beautiful. You've listened to your mom and now look where you are, Evan." I jumped in to join the gushy lovefest, but when I moved my elbows to offer him an embrace, the shaky dining table finally gave up the ghost. With a loud creak, the table tilted hard to one side, sending our wineglasses and plates sliding down the wooden tabletop like they were on a sliding board.

"Oh, no!" I gasped as we all went into action to catch falling food and liquids and fragile plates.

In the end, one plate didn't make it and cherry cola had splashed all over the floor.

The scowl on Mrs. Wayland's face said more than any words.

"Oh gosh, I'm so sorry. I will take care of everything." I apologized repeatedly as the room turned stone silent. "I'll clean up. Evan, go spend time with our guests."

"Thanks, Lena." Evan looked relieved as he stopped trying to soak up dripping liquid with a linen napkin.

Evan, his mother, and the judge moved to the folding chairs in the corners of the living room while I cleaned up the dining room mess and then worked to clean up and clear out the kitchen. Putting everything away proved to be a challenge as I maneuvered around the stacks of shopping bags and boxes, and, well, looked for a place to put everything away.

"Mom and Dad, why did you do this to me?" I closed my eyes and rested my head against a cabinet frame.

I could hear Evan and his godmother chatting about representing Razi in the living room. His mother had stepped outside to take a call on her cell.

And that's when I first heard the noise.

A growing reverberation I could not place caught my attention. I lifted my head off the cabinet and began wading through the bags in the kitchen to figure out the source of the sharpening, buzz-like sound echoing on and off somewhere in the cluttered room. Did I say buzz? I'd never heard a sound like this before. As it got louder, it reminded me of a roaring chainsaw complete with the squeal of a dying animal at the end. The sound kept repeating, getting brasher and louder with each roar and sickly squeal.

"What in the world?"

I frowned at the disturbing noise. Ruffling through the bags for the origin, I noted the sound got more pronounced as I neared Mrs. Wayland's handbag. She'd plopped the leather bag on top of the unfinished raw wood island. I stepped closer.

The noise was indeed coming from her handbag.

"What in the world?" I asked again. A cell phone notification, perhaps? No, she was using her phone outside, I recalled. Plus, I was certain I'd never heard any cell phone sound like the soundtrack of a murder scene.

With slow, delicate fingers, I reached for the zipper pull, hoping to peer inside the cavernous bag, when heavy footsteps thudded into the room.

"Selena, what are you doing?" Mrs. Wayland's voice sizzled and cracked behind me. I jumped as she snatched her handbag, reached in, and silenced whatever the noise was.

I spun around to fully face her, ready to calm her wrath and apologize for attempting to snoop in her personal space.

Wait. Was that fear and not anger in her eyes?

"I'm sorry, Mrs. Wayland. I thought I heard your phone and wanted to get it for you."

"I have my phone, thank you," she retorted while holding up the gold-and-white cell phone she'd been using. She pulled her handbag closer to her and headed for the dining room.

So, what's in your bag? I wanted to ask but my gut told me that question would be dead on arrival. Besides, did I really *want* to know? Just thinking of that noise made me shudder.

"Vanessa—" Mrs. Wayland's voice had returned to its normal composed diction as she called for her friend—"it's getting late. We probably should go before it gets dark."

As Evan helped them with their coats, Mrs. Wayland embraced him with a tight hug and kissed him lightly on the forehead. No hint of our kitchen exchange was in her stance or words. "I know you're still getting settled, so I'll wait to tour the rest of the house."

Her smile was equaled only by Evan's. As he turned away to unlock the door, she looked fiercely at me and held out three fingers.

"Three months," she mouthed, still clutching the handbag strap on her shoulder.

As Judge Grant and Mrs. Wayland headed to Mrs. Wayland's

Benz, their casual chitchat with each other had none of the angst she'd displayed just moments earlier. I tried to make sense of it, but Evan cut through my thoughts with thoughts of his own.

"Where were we?" He kissed my neck and cheeks and lips and tugged at my shirt straps, picking up where he'd left off when we were last alone. Man and wife back from the honeymoon, ready to share their first night at home together.

Let's get this thing started.

6

The Breakdown

Nearly a couple of months had gone by when I began to notice some things I could no longer ignore. Number one: The woman who offered me my new job as a production assistant lied when she said they needed someone to work only forty hours a week. Number two: Betty Crocker had too much time on her hands. Number three: My period was late. Number four: Evan has really black elbows.

First and foremost, the view from News U Need AM's second floor is actually pretty decent. When the sun comes up, you can watch the birds fill up the nearby tree and listen to them sing. When it sets, the sky from that window takes on a pinkish hue reminiscent of the Caribbean postcard I tacked over my desk next to a wallet-sized wedding picture of Evan and me.

Okay, I'm exaggerating. I don't work at the radio station from sunrise to sunset, but it certainly feels like it.

Evan barely seems to notice my schedule. With his new goal of successfully representing Razi at his firm, he's been buried in the case, which has turned out to have more paperwork than loose nails in our deck—and that's saying a lot. Halfway into our second month of marriage, he was coming home close to nine p.m. daily, too tired to do anything but eat the Bamboo Express or Mamma Bella's (depending on who had the better weeknight special) I spooned on our good dishes and watch whatever primetime reality show was on television. Oh, and faithfully perform his marital duties. The man was never too tired for sex.

He was too wiped out to check the leak in the powder room and under the kitchen sink. He had no energy to see why the refrigerator smelled like burnt rubber or to find the home warranty he lost to see if the stove was covered under my parents' limited joke of a policy. He refused to go with me on Saturdays to Walmart to pick out some paint or buy a new window air conditioning unit. He was not up to calling Kunta X with me to go over renovation plans. It had been six weeks, and the only improvement in the house was the yellow shower curtain covered with smiley faces in the hallway bath and the leather armchair he invested in to watch the living room TV.

The slow-going progress of our home improvement project was, in part, how I noticed Evan's black elbows. Most nights, as I stepped carefully down the loose steps and made my way past the lumber that filled my downstairs, all I saw were the knotty-looking black points of his elbows resting on the armchair as he stared mindlessly at the television. The man studied the colored screen like it held answers for his upcoming court case.

He was not getting what was at stake here. I had only a few weeks left before the timer went off on Mrs. Wayland's patience. She'd mercifully avoided coming to the house during this time, satisfied with Evan's twice-a-week visits to her and the good doctor's estate in Bowie, talking incessantly about the big dinner I'm supposed to be hosting to celebrate the completed renovations of the house.

The man had time to drive forty-five minutes each way to visit his mother twice a week but couldn't summon the energy to patch up a watermelon-sized hole in the living room wall or help me figure out how to make repairs myself in the absence of Kunta X returning my calls.

I didn't understand, but I said nothing, other than the occasional "Ooh, Evan," which seemed to get him off me and back to sleep.

Jesus, what am I supposed to do? The thought of resuming regular Bible study attendance almost seemed like cheating. I shouldn't just be trying to get all spiritual when my husband is getting on my nerves. If I had known Evan with his knotty black elbows was going to be getting to me like this, I would have started praying before the man ever proposed. Maybe if I'd had an established routine of regular prayer, perhaps I would have been better able to flow right into a miracle. That's what it was going to take to get this house ready. A true miracle.

I was sitting in church two weeks before Mrs. Wayland's timer was scheduled to ding when I realized I couldn't put off Observation Number Three anymore. I hadn't had a period since we'd gotten married.

The youth choir was up in the loft singing about the whole world being in His hands, and when they got to the part about the itty-bitty babies in His hands, I started crying. I looked at the youngest on the stand, a little girl of about three or four who was jumping up and down, hysterically off beat, her purple robe nearly coming off her, her beaded cornrows clanking and clapping as she twisted her head back and forth. I was getting dizzy just watching her and suddenly became aware of the need to throw up.

I am so not ready to deal with one of those. I don't even know how to braid hair, I've never changed a diaper, and I don't do spit-up. I'd only been a married woman for now a few weeks shy of three months, and having a child was not something I'd put on my calendar for at least another two years.

Maybe five.

I'm crying hard now. Sister Gray sitting behind me waved over an army of ushers and nurses. They rushed to me, telling me to "let it out. God's got it in control, let Him work, sister." These people thought I was overcome with the Spirit, and I was just praying I wouldn't have to sue the pharmaceutical company who promised that one a day would keep the babies away.

Okay, I missed two birth control pills in St. Martin. And a couple more last month. Alright, three. Or ten. But it wasn't all my fault. If Evan had let me come up for air, then maybe I could have grabbed a glass of water to swallow them down. I looked at him now, and he eyed me like I was unhinged for getting full of the Spirit from Sister Zophina's children and grandchildren mumbling off key in the choir stand. One of them—I guessed she was supposed to be the soloist—was screaming a note so high and off, the First Lady, Sister Corrine Knight, hid her face behind a fast-moving handheld fan.

"Yes, Lord," she shouted as the soloist screeched higher.

"Jesus!" I joined her shouts as a sob broke out of my lungs so loud, Evan joined the back-rubbing, tissue-giving circle of women around me. I looked back into his puzzled face, realizing our only discussion of having children was limited to a quick question by Pastor Knight in one of our premarital counseling sessions when he asked if we planned to have any.

"Yes, and we'll bring them up in the nurture and admonition of the Lord," had been Evan's ready response. Obviously pleased with Evan's answer, Pastor Knight moved on to more pressing points of what kind of music we were having at the wedding reception.

And, now, I could be pregnant, about to bring a child into the house that Jack forgot to build, and I'm supposed to be having his mother and company over in a few weeks to celebrate. Does Momma Bella deliver lasagna by the pan?

***

I woke up in the nurses' suite. Sister Phoebe Jackson, the head of the nurses committee, looked obviously pleased she finally had a chance to use the smelling salts she kept at the bottom of her big black purse. I could see Evan looking down at me through a flurry of paper fans. I saw pictures of Weatherbee's Funeral Parlor on floppy cardboard one second, his brown eyes the next. Maybe this was some kind of sign. My life was over. I shut my eyes.

I woke up again in the pastor's study. Apparently, more space was needed for the crowd of gawkers. I'd been moved to the oversized Victorian sofa that lined one wall of the mahogany-paneled room. This time several paramedics blocked my view of Evan. An oxygen mask covered my face as I tried to sit up.

"Evan," I said, my voice barely above a whisper, "I'm okay, but can we cancel the housewarming dinner?"

"Girl, lay down." My mother's voice slapped my ears. "Why do you always have to be so darn dramatic?"

I laid down obediently, closing my eyes as my pressure was checked, an I.V. was started, and someone from the missionary circle asked me if I wanted a peppermint. "Yes," I wanted to shout. My life is tearing apart at the seams, and a red-and-white striped peppermint is exactly what I needed to pull it all back together.

"Selena," a voice as calm as it was soothing spoke right in my ear. I opened my eyes to see Sister Corrine Knight, the pastor's wife, smiling knowingly in my face. She didn't say anything else as she wrapped her fingers around mine and let me cry on her shoulder.

"She'll be alright," I heard her say to someone. "Let me talk to her for a moment." A soft flurry of footsteps scurried out of the room, and I heard the door click closed.

"Oh, Jesus." I could not hold it back again as a new well of tears spilled out. "What am I going to do?"

"You're doing it, Selena. You're doing it right now. You're calling on Jesus. He is your source, your help, and your all. The more you know Him, the more you know that."

I looked at her about to say something when she grabbed my hand again and continued.

"I know you know Him, Selena. I've watched you grow from a little girl like Mia in the choir to the beautiful young woman you are now. I remember the Sunday you gave your life to the Lord and the testimonies you offered both as a teen and now as a young adult ministering to the teens. I know you know Him, that you are saved."

I closed my eyes, letting her words fill me, sensing there was more.

"Selena, it's easy to say God is in control. We come here and clap our hands and recite our favorite verses and shout out that our lives are in His hands, but let me tell you, sweetheart, it's when we start going through the floods and the fires when we see for real God is a bridge and a fire hydrant. Selena, I know you know Him, but I encourage you not to be satisfied with just knowing Jesus as your ticket to heaven. Know Him as your day-to-day source. Pray to Him, listen for Him, be intimate with Him, realize there is no end to knowing Him, and watch Him truly become all you need to face whatever comes your way."

She leaned in closer to me. "And, honey, you've only had Mrs. in front of your name for less than three months. You ain't seen nothing yet."

I wasn't sure whether to feel comforted, understood, relieved, or afraid. Something in her last words unnerved me even more. Did she know something I didn't know? Pastor Knight seemed like a good man. He and Sister Corinne by all appearances seemed to have the whole marriage and family life thing together.

As if reading my mind, she whispered, "It's not always the big beavers that chew on the framework of our lives and marriages. Tiny termites are just as effective at bringing down the house."

The throng of peppermint-carrying, fan-flapping, glass-of-water-offering people filed back into the office. Evan was at the forefront, his arms open, ready to help me to our car. It was time to go home. The IV came out and the paramedics left. I gave one last desperate look back at Sister Corrine. She smiled.

"Why don't you start joining us Tuesday nights for the women's fellowship? I'm about to start a new study on listening to the voice of God."

That sounded pretty heavy, but I nodded anyway, thinking of the time when I was younger and had that whole listening-for-Jesus-to-talk-to-me-through-the-birds episode. I wasn't quite sure how to hear Him then, and though there have been times when I felt His hand guiding my existence, I still wasn't too sure He had something to say about all the major and minor details of *my* life. Half the stuff that went on in my day was either too boring or ridiculous to deal with. I'm sure the King of Kings had other more pressing things on His day planner than teaching me how to fry chicken. Or burp a baby.

As Evan backed out of the parking space and began talking about renting chairs for the housewarming dinner, I knew I had no choice but to hope God really was interested in the minutes of my day.

I closed my eyes, resting my head on the back of the car seat and one hand on my stomach. "Evan—" I cut him off— "you need to know there's a chance that I might be pregnant."

"Really?" His eyes nearly popped out of his head from excitement. "That's wonderful." He slammed the brakes and switched lanes. "Let's go tell my mom."

I bolted upright in my seat. "I didn't say I *was*, only that I *might* be. Don't you think we should wait to find out for sure before telling anyone that—"

It was too late. He was already dialing.

Okay, Jesus. I'm praying, and I'm listening. Even as I thought those words, others came to mind, a verse I'd memorized in Sunday school class years ago. *Do not be anxious about anything, but in every situation, by prayer and petition, with thanksgiving, present your requests to God.* I could still see me with those afro puffs standing up in front of Sister Cheswick (God rest her soul) quoting Philippians 4:6. How did I remember that? Where did that come from?

As Evan continued chatting on the phone and turning toward the Baltimore-Washington Parkway heading to Bowie, I realized I was asking the wrong questions. *I'm praying and petitioning and presenting all my requests to God. What am I not doing?* The verse said to not be anxious about anything, and to pray with *thanksgiving*. Don't worry, be happy. Pretty straightforward, I reasoned.

"Hallelujah." The word sounded forced out of my mouth.

"What was that, Lena?" Evan looked at me, his attention away from the phone.

"Hallelujah," I repeated, the mock enthusiasm in my voice completely missed by him.

"Yes," he shouted back into the phone. "Hallelujah. Praise the Lord. We're having a baby, Mom. And as for me and my house, we will serve the Lord."

"Yep." I could not agree more. "As for me and my...house. Hallelujah."

7

The Parents

My mom used to tell me that behind every cloud there was a silver lining. That Sunday, which my brother CJ nicknamed "Selena's Public Breakdown," started a chain reaction of enough silver to make a showcase at one of Mrs. Wayland's favorite jewelry stores. At least, that's what I believed at first.

I was terrified of taking a pregnancy test, but nobody needed to know that. I wasn't ready for the results, whichever way they went. Evan was on cloud nine telling everyone we were having a baby, and his word seemed to be enough for his family. That's all that mattered. Nobody asked if I'd taken a test or seen a doctor, and I left it at that. All anyone wanted to know was a due date and I gave them one (based on my calculations—how hard is it to add nine months?). Mrs. Wayland believed I was in a "delicate condition" as she put it, and I ran with it. The renovation deadline was extended, and our housewarming celebration was moved to the Waylands' estate, under her direction, at her cost, and with her choice of caterer.

Why would I take any chance at spoiling my good fortune with an actual pregnancy test? My period was still MIA and that never happened to me. What more proof did I need? My life was in a good place. I didn't need the terror of seeing two pink lines to confirm that I was actually going to be someone's mother. My plan was to find and see an OB-GYN *after* Mrs. Wayland hosted our party. Too much was on the line to mess around before then.

Mrs. Wayland was happy to throw another big shindig to invite all her friends and some of mine. True to her fashion, it turned out better than anything I could have put together, with much better presents than I ever imagined. Who knew the difference a dual-headed showerhead could make in a bathroom with no tub? Yeah, there were some random questions about why the party was at her house and not ours, but a quick reply about ongoing renovations stopped those conversations quickly. The project was taking longer than expected but the party must go on, Mrs. Wayland told her friends.

If I'd known my three-month deadline had a nine-month contingency plan written into the negotiations, I would have put my uterus on the table at the beginning of our talks. See, even Evan was cashing in on the deal. With a new purpose to get the house together, he actually started making phone calls to local contractors and electricians as Kunta X still hadn't returned my many messages. Evan expressed renewed commitment to make our house less likely to be declared condemned and more fit for us and a newborn. Without hesitation, men in hard hats and work vans began lining up to give estimates on what promised to be the makeover of the century. Besides the opportunity to have pretty drastic before-and-after pictures for their portfolios, I squeezed out of Evan that his mother had opened a generous line of credit for us to use—well, contingent on our use of a list of contractors she recommended.

I'm glad I know what's going on with my own house.

Now, you would think my parents would be happy to see their old house getting so much attention and having a shot at livability. The way I saw it, they had their chance; they should be happy for me.

Wrong.

Oh, they were happy serious talks about fixing the house were finally happening, but they didn't understand why Mrs. Wayland should get all the say and all the credit. The reckoning began the Monday immediately after our housewarming party at the Waylands'.

***

"Y'all wouldn't have anything to fix if it wasn't for us. Have you forgotten you even have a house because of me and your dad?" my mother mumbled as she blew on a spoonful of beans.

I was having dinner over my parents' apartment while Evan worked another late night.

"Mom, you're right. Because of you and Dad, I have something to fix, as usual. Thank you for your consistency." I knew it wasn't the right words—the right tone—but I hadn't said anything to them about the house since they gave it to Evan and me. She opened the door, and that's what came out. There was a lot more I could have said, but I swallowed it down along with a big gulp of the bean soup. Chunks of smoked ham and onion slid down my throat. "Besides, we left several messages for Kunta X, and he never returned our calls."

"Oh, you know you'll definitely hear from him soon. I'll tell your dad to put some fire under him."

"For real, Ma? You and Dad have been asking him to do things for the past six years. What is possibly going to change now?"

"Kunta X was...caught up with some things, but they're all resolved now. He's really good at what he does. Remember what he did with Grandma Verdine's porch? He's a gifted craftsman once he gets going. Give him a chance. He'll come through." She'd finished her bowl and now munched on a slice of cornbread.

"Mrs. Wayland has already found us some contractors to interview."

My mother pounded a hand on the table. My head tilted back in response.

"Ma, what's wrong?"

"Selena, you don't know what it's like for me and your father when Evan's mother keeps acting like she's delivering you from underneath our shadow. She acts like she's the light in your world, snatching you from the darkness we've supposedly brought you up in. I don't like it. I don't like it at all."

In the yellow glow of the kitchen lamp, the circles and sags under her eyes looked more pronounced. Her red work apron hung on a hook on the back of the pantry door. The apron was slightly stained from her ten-hour stint at the convenience store where she'd been employed for almost a decade. My mother followed my eyes to her apron and then rested her forehead in one palm. A long black mark went across the back of her fingers where a hot dog grill had seared her skin years ago.

"Mom, I..." What was I supposed to say?

She waved the back of her hand at me and pushed out of her chair to stand. "Your father's going to be up in a few hours. He's back to working an extra shift overnight at the warehouse. I need to get some things done for him."

I watched as Mom cleared the table and filled the sink with soapy water. In our silence, plates, glasses, and forks clinked together in the suds, making a song of sorts with a rhythm in each turn of the faucet.

"Why can't CJ help you with some of these chores. Isn't he staying here with you again?" I had to break the silence.

"You know your brother." Enough said.

"You let him get away with too much, Mom."

"If you have a boy, you'll understand." There was a smile in her voice, and I knew the peace was growing back between us, although she'd stirred up another fear I'd been swallowing down every day. She picked up on it immediately.

"So, did you confirm your due date yet?"

"Early to mid-January by my calculations."

"The doctor didn't give you a firm date? That's odd." Her back was still to me as she washed the dishes. *Thank You, Jesus, she can't see my face.* I swallowed hard.

"Yeah, here, let me help you." I grabbed a dishtowel and started drying the dishes she put in the rack.

I hated to be dishonest. I hadn't looked up a doctor yet, though my original plan was to do so that week since the party was over. There was fear at work both ways. On one hand, the idea of actually having a child on the way for me to raise was a terrifying thought. On the other hand, this possible baby had become a savior of sorts. I shuddered at the thought of what could have been had the prospect of being pregnant not come into play at this point in my life. What would I have done about that deadline? Hearing the disdain in my mother's voice confirmed things would have gotten plenty ugly if the Waylands had truly started making demands from my parents.

My mother was quiet again, but I could feel those famous eyes in the back of her head staring me down. I patted my belly, as if the gesture was enough confirmation for both of us to be content with my supposed pregnancy. I knew it wasn't enough. I had to get out of this conversation before it got worse.

Fortunately, I was saved. Kind of.

"I thought I heard my favorite ladies' voices." My father emerged from the bedroom, an unbuttoned navy work shirt hanging from his broad shoulders, revealing a crisp white t-shirt underneath. The belt on his khakis was undone and the scent of Old Spice filled the air. He rubbed his eyes and the graying stubble on his chin before walking toward me with open arms. The creases and wrinkles on his face had deepened over the years, and the skin on his fingers and palms had toughened, but the smile he flashed whenever he saw me proved there was still a part of him that could melt like butter on a stack of blackberry pancakes, his favorite.

"Dad." I returned his embrace. He headed to the fridge after letting me go.

"Clarence, you know you need to get some more sleep. You have to be at your next shift in three hours." My mom followed him and tried to shut the refrigerator door behind him. "And you already ate. It's too late for another snack. We're watching your sugar, remember?"

"Marlene, if you don't let me alone about that sugar. If I want to eat some more apple pie in my own house, I got that right." He grabbed a foil-covered pie pan from the bottom shelf. "Selena, pass me one of those plates from the rack."

"Clarence, don't you see that I'm trying to clean this kitchen?" My mother didn't hide her frustration. "I want to go to bed soon myself, and you're just giving me more work to do. Always gotta clean up after you." She huffed as she shrugged and reached for the clean plate herself and handed it to him.

He grunted in response. "While I'm eating this, why don't you get me a clean shirt ready?"

"What's wrong with the one you have on?" My mother glared at him.

"Button's missing. Just get me a clean one, Marlene, and make sure it's pressed." He sat down at the table and began chomping down the pie.

My mother murmured something indistinguishable and left the room.

"So, Selena," my father talked as he munched, "that was quite a spread your mother-in-law threw for you and Evan yesterday."

"Yes, our housewarming...that wasn't even at our house." I dried another dish and put it away.

"Yeah, the house." My father shifted a little in his seat. "Kunta X will be calling you soon to start the repairs."

"Oh, no need for that. Evan has some plans in the works."

"Evan or his momma?" Dad let out a wheezy laugh.

"Huh? What's that supposed to mean?"

"Lena, come on, now. You've known Evan for what, two, three years now? When have you ever seen him figure anything out for himself? Law school. His Acura. His job at that fancy law firm downtown. Didn't you say his mother pulled some strings to get him all of those things?"

"Dad, that's unfair. His parents are committed to supporting his dreams, and they're in the position to go beyond mere words and can take action with their finances. I understand how they're helping him. That's what our community needs more of, generational wealth that can be handed down to help us all have a step up."

My father clapped, and his wheezy laugh filled the kitchen again. I put down the towel and pan I was drying and grabbed onto the counter edge behind me. My legs shook a little, and my fingers trembled.

"Really? You're laughing at me?"

"Lena, I'm not laughing at you." He settled down after letting out a few more guffaws. "I'm just making a point to you. That brother ain't never had to do nothing for himself is all I'm saying. Every problem he's ever had, his mother's found a way to fix it, including now, from what you're saying, the house that *we* gave you." He suddenly sobered. "And we already gifted a contractor to fix it. We're paying for Kunta X. That was part of our wedding present to you."

My mother reentered the kitchen, catching the tail end of his comments. She leaned against the wall and crossed her arms as they both stared me down.

"Do you have a problem with the man I married, and if so, why are you just telling me?" I kept my voice steady, not wanting to sound disrespectful.

"Easy, easy, Lena. Evan's a cool cat." My father rubbed his chin, drummed the table with his fingertips. "I wouldn't have let you marry him if I thought he meant you harm."

Let me marry him? What was I? Seventeen again? I swallowed hard.

"I'm just saying you've never seen how Evan handles trouble on his own, apart from his momma. You need to be prepared in case he doesn't know how to stand on his own two feet, that's all." He went back to his pie. "Marlene, I need a glass of milk with this."

"Exactly, Selena," my mother piped in. "You need to speak up and not let that woman run your house. She's not the only one who can do things for the two of you. Your father and I can help, too."

"Marlene, did I ask you to explain my words?" My father frowned. "I'm waiting for my milk."

My mother let out a loud *hmpfh* but walked toward the refrigerator anyway. "Pass me one of those glasses, Selena, since your father's legs apparently don't work."

"Woman, I—"

"Okay, okay," I cut them both off, hoping to bring back the peace. "I didn't know the house repairs were so important to you. Mrs. Wayland opened a line of credit at some specialty hardware store, Wood & Beams or something like that, for the contractor we choose to use for supplies. I can tell Evan that's not necessary if you're really willing to help. We'll use Kunta X, and you can pay for everything, not Mrs. Wayland." I immediately regretted my words as soon as they came out. Nothing about my parents' plans or budget were realistic, but what else was I supposed to do?

"Great. Wonderful." My father nodded. "I'll tell Kunta to call you tomorrow. He's giving us a family and friends discount, especially with the baby on the way. Your mom and I will absolutely foot the bill. You can tell Evan and his momma the Tuckers got it from here."

He went back to finishing off his pie. My mother scooted up the crumbs on the table around him with her bare hands.

"Perfect," I heard myself say. I turned toward the sink to finish up the dishes.

Lord, I need a verse, I pleaded with Him as the warm water and suds coated my hands. I waited for another Sunday school memory scripture to come to mind. *Please, Lord, quick.* Only one passage surfaced.

John chapter 11, verse 35.

Jesus wept.

8

The Reset

The next morning, I rose up half an hour earlier before getting ready for work. After last night's dinner at my parents', I knew I was going to need more than the five or so verses I remembered from Sunday school days to figure out what to do next. Weeping along with Jesus was good therapeutic cleansing, but even He had His next God-ordained move in mind when He cried before raising Lazarus from the dead.

This thing was getting serious, I conceded, noting the stack of baby name books and contractor business cards piling up on Evan's nightstand. How was I going to tell him we needed to take a different path for the house? And would the path with Kunta X lead to another dead end?

Being careful not to wake Evan, I slipped a silk robe on over the baby doll–thong combination I'd selected out of my dwindling bridal shower supplies for last night's show-and-tell session. My Bible was still where I'd placed it after the past Sunday's morning service. I grabbed it off my dresser and headed for the only room

I was guaranteed privacy for the next twenty-five minutes: the bathroom.

In the bright yellow cheerfulness of my smiley faced–themed porcelain throne room, I began praying to enter the Throne Room of the Most High.

"Lord, I come to you this morning in the name of Jesus for help. Help me. I don't know where to begin. This house, the baby that might be in me, Evan's mother, my parents, my job—"

Lord Jesus, where do I begin?

Pray with thanksgiving. The words came back to me.

"Okay." I sighed. "I guess I need to begin by saying thank You. Thank You, Jesus, for Your blessings. Thank You for Your love, for even caring about what's going on in my life, for even meeting me here in this bathroom."

I peeked my eyes open, taking in the tens of yellow faces smiling down at me from the plastic shower curtain and the ceramic soap dish. Wasn't there a psych medication that used those same smiley faces years ago? *Stay focused, Selena!* I shut my eyes again, resolved to finish a real prayer of thanksgiving.

"Thank You, Jesus, for giving me a house. It needs work, but it does provide a roof over my head...Well, as long as I'm not standing next to the closet in the middle bedroom where that hole in the ceiling is." I paused before praying again. "Thank You, God, that the hole isn't in the room Evan and I sleep in. And even if it was, thank You for giving us enough money that we could buy a bucket to catch the leaks. Thank You for Evan." With that, I started thinking about all the blessings God had handed to me through the years, both big and small, blessings I had never really thought to thank Him for. There were so many, the thank yous couldn't stop coming. Before long, I realized I couldn't stop at just thanking Him.

"Lord, I *praise* you because You are so good. You forgive me and help me when I don't deserve it. You are wonderful, and I honor You just because You are...God."

As words of praise came out of my mouth, I felt the need to get down on my knees—I mean my head was lying on the freshly-cleaned yellow smiling bath rug. I felt complete awe and amazement for this man Jesus, and I wanted Him to know it. I couldn't quite find the right words to express to Him what I was feeling, so I just stayed there on my knees, quiet, feeling a peace and a calm I hadn't experienced in a long time. The funny thing was I hadn't asked Him for a thing, but I felt content. It was enough just knowing I was in His presence.

True worship. I smiled to myself as my bath rug smiled back. I could have stayed right there, smiling and feeling all happy inside all day, but a loud ring shook me. It was Evan's alarm clock.

That darn clock. He had one of those wind-up metal things that sounded like Jesus was coming back and the angel Gabriel was clanging cymbals to wake up the dead. Anyway, I knew I had about a minute left to get a new verse under my belt for the day, so I quickly sat on the edge of the bathtub and flipped open my Bible.

It was really my grandmother's Bible. Grandma Verdine. I smiled at her memory and took a second to nudge my nose into the binding, catching a whiff of the pebbled leather holding the falling pages together. When Grandma Verdine passed and my mother and her sisters and brothers were sorting through her things, it was the one thing still sitting on her dresser that nobody was picking up, so I did, finding an unexplainable comfort holding what her hands once cradled. I nestled the Bible in my lap and flipped through its thin pages, stopping at verses she'd underlined in fires and floods past. It never occurred to me how much she must have turned to God's Word as a refuge until I noted right then that nearly every page had a handwritten note or highlight on it. I stopped at a verse she'd double underlined:

You make known to me the path of life; you will fill me with joy in your presence, with eternal pleasures at your right hand.

When David wrote those words in Psalm 16:11, he must have had a throne room experience like I'd just had, minus all the yellow smiley faces of course. I reread the verse several times, vowing to add it to my memory bank. The next time I felt frazzled, I would remember to get my joy and peace back by getting in His presence through praise.

I got back on my knees to close out my morning devotion.

"Thank You, Jesus. Amen."

"Lena, are you okay?"

Evan was standing in the doorway, a look of deep concern etched into his smooth features. I hadn't even heard the door open. I'm sure the sight of me bent down on the floor with my head lying on the bathroom rug and my arms stretched over the bathtub was a little alarming.

"I'm fine, baby."

He rushed over to help me up anyway. Of course, I didn't mind his arms wrapping around my barely clothed body. Evan took a hint. I still had a few minutes before I had to get ready for work. Whether he did or not was irrelevant. I told you the man kept sex as an open option.

As I looked into Evan's smiling face and then the many others dotted around the bathroom, it occurred to me this was the first and only completely finished room in the house. I guess God knew I was going to have to have a place to meet Him daily to deal with the rest of my plans—home and otherwise. When I picked out that shower curtain, I never realized it would perfectly tie into my quiet time of praise and worship.

I guess God really does sweat the small details of life.

"Selena," Evan whispered in my ear.

"Yes, baby." My voice was soft like his.

"Before I forget, my mom wants to talk to you today. Something about a mix-up this morning related to the line of credit she opened for our house repairs."

Look at the shower curtain. Just keep your eyes on the shower curtain.

9

The Twist

A light drizzle started as I turned my car off our street on my way to work. By the time I reached Liberty Road, my wipers were in full attack mode. The attack was more on my eardrums than the water streams running off my windshield. The squeaking was soon joined by the ring tone of my cell phone.

"Who's calling me this early?" I started to let it roll into voice mail, but when I saw the number, I knew I had better answer.

"Good morning, Mrs. Wayland." My chirpiness sounded forced as I connected via Bluetooth. Her voice didn't fake anything.

"Selena, I worked hard to secure one of the best interior design teams in the region. You don't know the strings I pulled to get Genevaise Zuzani involved in this project. Genevaise normally doesn't touch anything outside of Potomac these days."

Wait. Huh? Who the heck is Genevaise Zuzani?

I kept my voice calm, steady in response. "Evan and I haven't finalized which contractor we're going with. In fact, I was going to talk to him about that this evening. Thanks though. I know you've been working hard for us, and I appreciate all you've done."

"Selena, I don't think you understand all I've done and all I've had to do to make this work. Genevaise is not a mere contractor, darling. She's an award-winning visionary whose designs have been featured in homes from Hollywood to Manhattan. Evan and I already discussed this opportunity, and he agreed with me that the chance to have Zuzani transform your townhome is too special to pass up."

Again, who the heck is this Zuzani person? And when was this discussion? And why was I not a part of it? I realized I was making a wacky face out the car window when a woman in the red Infiniti next to me made a face back and gave me the finger before speeding off at a green light and cutting into my lane.

"Selena, are you listening? Genevaise was very reluctant to take on your home. The stunt your family pulled just now is completely unacceptable."

"Stunt? Just now?" *What is this woman talking about?*

"Don't play games with me, Selena. You and I both know what this is about. Genevaise informed me one of the contractors working for her company was nearly assaulted by a man at Wood & Beams when they opened at five this morning. A man showed up, claiming to be a friend of the family and argued he'd been given permission to take over the account *I* opened. He identified himself as a Kunta X. Selena, I don't know where this man came from, but let me make it clear to you: He is not to surface again."

Everything in my spirit groaned within me. I'd told my parents about the line of credit. They must have told Kunta X of its existence. So much for my dad saying they'd be footing the entire bill for renovations.

"Mrs. Wayland, I—"

She cut me off before I had a chance to think through an

answer. "Genevaise was irate. Imagine my embarrassment at having to explain your indiscretion of inviting a neighborhood handyman to usurp the plans of her internationally famous design team. You don't know what I went through to keep her from ripping up the contract. I don't think I can convince her not to if you or another one of your 'family friends' pulls another performance like this. Have I made myself clear?"

Contract? My mind raced, trying to absorb what was going on. Maybe Evan knew what was happening, although I don't remember him mentioning any Genevaise Zuzani ever. I'd check with him. I'm sure he wouldn't want his mother telling us what to do with our own house, making contracts and whatnot. The three of us can sit down together and come to an understanding. Easy enough, I lied to myself, imagining my parents being added to the conversation. I pressed the cruise control button on my steering wheel as I turned onto I-695.

"Mrs. Wayland, Evan and I will—" It took me a few seconds to realize she was no longer on the other end. No the woman did not hang up on me a second time. The second time, and as far as I was concerned, the last. Before I could calm myself down to remember her number, my phone was ringing again. It was my father. The red car in front of me braked suddenly, and I had to slam on my own brakes, a scary moment as my tires spun on the slick roadway. My hands shook on the steering wheel.

"Lena, baby, sorry to call you so early, but I had to tell you the good news."

"Good news?" It was too early in the day to feel this miserable. I needed some good news, but I knew this wasn't going to be it. "Dad, did you tell Kunta X about the line of credit at Wood & Beams?"

"Oh, that? Yeah, sweetie. I mentioned to him to use it as a back-up until my money comes through. Everything's going to be alright now. Your dad's got it all under control."

"I thought you said you had good news, Dad." *I thought you said you were going to pay for everything,* I really wanted to say.

"Oh, I do have good news."

He sounded happy. Too happy. Had he been drinking again? And this early? That could only mean one thing. His next sentence confirmed my worse suspicions.

"Kunta X is sitting with me in my truck, and we're on the way to the house. I know we can't see the inside, but he wanted to study the exterior to begin making some notes. The work is about to begin. Wait. He wants to speak to you."

There was some shifting of hands and paper and a loud burp before the familiar raspy voice scratched through the phone line.

"*As-salamu alaykum, shalom,* and what's up?

It's been a while since I've spoken to you, black buttercup.

My sister, I am honored by the presence of your voice on this phone,

And the generous faith you have put in me alone,

To resurrect your home into life divine.

You will not be disappointed with these able hands of mine.

When you see the finished product, you will agree that it is fine.

In the tradition of our ancients, I say a blessing on each room,

And you'll be calling your house a home soon and very soon.

I'm going to go for now, my sister. Stay strong.

It was nice talking to you, but The Poet must say 'So long.'"

"That was deep, brother. That was deep." I heard my father speak as Kunta X ended the call. I hung up and shut off my phone. Cell phones were overrated. Nobody should be that accessible before the workday even begins.

"Jesus!" What else was there to say? Before I could listen for an answer, I slammed the brakes to once again avoid crashing into the red Infiniti in front of me. Well, there went my cruise control. What was I thinking anyway? Rush-hour traffic was already snaking around the inner loop, and in this weather, I ought to be thanking God I wasn't upside down on the side of the highway. As I swerved passed the car, I almost rear-ended the same woman from the stoplight who waved at me with a single finger and was waving again with the same finger. I blew her a kiss and went about my business. I didn't have time for any of this.

***

I guess I should have made time. As I pulled into the parking lot of News U Need AM, the rain slacked up just enough for me to make out a new car in the employee lot. It was a red Infiniti. Could it be? I knew before I even entered the door that the woman who'd been flipping birds throughout my morning commute was in the building. I didn't see her at first, but it didn't take long. She was waiting with my supervisor, Samantha, in my cubicle.

"Selena, you're just in time. I'm leaving to serve as the executive producer for our FM sister station across town. Sorry for the sudden departure. They had an emergency shakeup late last night, and I've been called upon to help immediately. Fortunately, our station manager had a recommendation for a prompt replacement. Please meet Kiona Tandy. She'll be in charge of all production-related tasks starting today. She has some great ideas for injecting more lifestyle and entertainment news into the daily programming, so this will probably revamp into a more exciting job for you, Selena. You're here at a great, transformative moment for the station."

My old boss was all smiles and hope and change, but I felt ready to give a concession speech. I could see the exact moment on Kiona's face when she recognized me. Her handshake, firm and quick, didn't betray the tone in her words.

"Selena, it's nice to meet you, although I believe we've met in passing."

Towering a few inches above me with wavy jet-black hair that tumbled down her back, she was absolutely stunning—with a hint of messy sass. I could tell she was somebody who let her beauty pave the way before her, and in the rare instances when it didn't, her mouth would. Okay, maybe I'm being pre-judgmental, so I'll stop. She uses her fingers to make herself known, specifically the middle ones.

Anyway, I was standing awkwardly in between my outgoing supervisor who worked me like an indentured servant, and my new one who already hated me, wondering what else could go wrong with my morning when I noticed Kiona staring hard at the corkboard over my desk. I'd tacked two pictures on it. One was a candid shot someone captured and emailed to me of Evan and me on our wedding day. I'd printed it out and hung it up. The other was snapped at my rehearsal dinner and featured a gushing me and a smiling Evan standing next to a video still of Razi. The words *Congrats, Evan and Selena* were on a chyron beneath the singer's closed eyes and pursed lips.

"That's *your* wedding picture?" Her eyes were glued on the first picture from my wedding. I joined the gaze, trying to make sense of the surprise in her voice. I was Cinderella in that picture, complete with a fancy dress and pearl tiara. Kiona slowly looked back at me, from my damp, frizzy hair down to my muddy boots. Her jaw locked so tightly, I wished I could find some glass slippers or ruby shoes to click together to disappear. I could not let this woman intimidate me. I stood tall, but she was a full three inches taller than me, and her glare made me forget what I was about to say.

"Yeah, that's me in that photo." I joined her gaze back at the picture. I had to look absolutely goofy staring at the image like I was just seeing it for the first time along with her.

"That's interesting." She leaned in closer and studied the photo for a few more quiet moments. "How long have you been married?"

"A few months."

"And…you know Razi?" She tapped a manicured fingernail onto the other picture.

"My husband is his attorney," I said with all the pride and shine I imagined Mrs. Wayland would express with that statement. No need to mention he was only representing the singer in a small, inconsequential case.

"Very interesting," Kiona mumbled again. "Very interesting indeed." And then she turned away, a slight smirk on her face.

What was that all about?

I was still standing there a few minutes later staring at the corkboard, trying to figure out what was so "interesting" about my pictures when the cramps began.

10

The Heartbreak

I knew a doctor's visit was inevitable, but this was not the picture I'd had in mind.

Ever.

I lay on a padded table in a dim room. A bunch of strangers in white coats talked softly next to a big machine that hummed like one of the motors in Dr. Wayland's antique car collection. I hated the way they murmured, like we were in a funeral home and I was the corpse in the casket that everyone was whispering and tiptoeing around. All I needed was a bouquet of carnations, but Evan handed me an extra sheet.

"Here, wrap this over your legs." He tucked the crisp white linen on top of the other two he'd handed me. I didn't see the point of this impromptu modesty. Everybody in the room had already seen my goods, and they were coming back for more. One of the white coats in the circle broke away from the group and stuck a hand out for me to shake.

Nice. I've been laying here with my legs up in stirrups so you can poke and prod in a place that's barely broken ground, and you just think to introduce yourself? Well, hello to you.

"Hello, Mrs. Wayland. I'm Dr. Nelson, and I'm the lead physician on this shift."

I looked around the room for Madelyn Ernestine Wayland before I comprehended she was talking to me. Dr. Nelson had a look of reserved compassion on her face. I didn't want to hear whatever it was she'd come over to say. With her long blond hair tucked back into a neat ponytail, a lab coat speckled with smiling storks, and a thin notepad she kept flipping through, I knew she meant no harm. Being the bearer of bad news was part of her job. I held my breath as Evan took my hand and squeezed like he was holding me from falling over a cliff.

"I see you were referred to our unit from the ED downstairs." She didn't look at me as she spoke, clearing her throat when she finished.

"Yes. I came here from work this morning after I started cramping and spotting. I'm—I could be pregnant, and I didn't think that was supposed to be happening, unless I'm just getting an extremely late cycle." I held my breath again. Evan reached for his cell phone. *Jesus, please don't let that man call his momma right now.*

"I'm sorry, Mr. Wayland." Dr. Nelson shook her head. "We don't allow cell phone use in this room. It can interfere with the machines and other equipment."

Evan put his phone away and took my hand again.

"As I was saying, Mrs. Wayland..." Dr. Nelson cleared her throat so loudly I wanted to offer her some water. I glanced around the room looking for a cup, a pitcher, a clean fishbowl, anything to keep me from having to sit there and listen to whatever it was she was about to say. Dr. Nelson seemed oblivious to my fidgeting. "You were referred to us by the emergency department. Can you give me the name and number of your obstetrician so I can forward the results of our scans to him or her to discuss with you?"

Now I was the one clearing my throat. Evan's eyes darted around the room, trying to find something to give me. He settled for another sheet.

"Here, Lena." He sat back in his chair all nice and smiley, waiting to hear the name of my doctor alongside Dr. Nelson, who tilted her head at my silence.

"You do know, Mrs. Wayland, that prenatal care is vital to a healthy pregnancy? Don't you have an OB-GYN?"

"I wasn't sure if I needed one just yet. I wasn't sure if I was actually pregnant." It was true, and it was out. And now sitting there next to an ultrasound screen faced away from me and a husband who'd started wearing a fuller beard because he said it made him look more "fatherly," whatever that means, I suddenly realized I wanted a baby. True, I had been riding the whole baby thing to deal with some external, unrelated issues, but I think I had come to accept there might be someone growing in my tummy. I had developed a bond with this evasive stranger who'd rescued me out of a few major close calls. The idea that nobody may have been listening all those times Evan talked to my stomach was heartbreaking.

"Mrs. Wayland," Dr. Nelson continued, "I'm happy to have you establish care here, or I can give you a list of providers for you to choose from. But either way...." Her voice faded as she looked down at her notepad and cleared her throat.

"Can you just tell me what's going on?" I was surprised at how weak my voice sounded.

Dr. Nelson gave me an even weaker smile. "To be honest with you, Mrs. Wayland, we do see a small embryonic sack inside of you, but it's so small, we can't tell if there's anything inside. It's possible that a baby started growing, and for whatever reason, it stopped, and your body is now eliminating the contents. It's also possible that your cycles have been irregular due to your admitted spotty birth control use, and your pregnancy is newer than expected. Your date of conception may be more recent than the dates we're coming up with based on your reported last cycle.

"We can send you for some blood tests and see you back here in two to three days for a rescan. By then, if it's a viable pregnancy, the embryo may have grown enough for us to see a heartbeat. Plus, your hCG levels will have at least doubled if things are going in the right direction for you. I'm sorry, but we just have to wait and see."

What was this about? I groaned inside, determined to keep my smile equal to Evan's. His smile looked as bogus as mine did as all the white coats filed out the room, leaving the two of us alone. He began to peel the layers of sheets off me in silence. I searched for something to say but couldn't think of one word. I knew in my heart we should be trying to talk or hug, or something, but neither of us seemed willing to tip over the pot.

11

The Wait

Baked potatoes. Kirk Franklin. Lawn chairs. Tenth-grade geometry. Yosemite Park.

I scrambled, desperate to cling to any memory or thought that had nothing to do with babies. It seemed like every time I switched channels on TV, there was a baby running unsupervised in green pastures, toothless, and half-naked, selling diapers. Or a mother smiling as she rubbed lotion on her freshly washed bundle of joy, explaining how such-and-such ointment had changed her and her baby's entire life.

Never before had the talk of poopy pants and butt rashes invoked such painful emotions in me. Emotions? No, I felt this physically. Raw. Festering. Pain.

Two days had passed since my visit to the hospital. I was scheduled to have the next sonogram tomorrow afternoon. At Dr. Nelson's suggestion, I'd done nothing but lay in the bed. At my mother's suggestion, I'd done nothing but pray. Or I'd tried to anyway. I never thought I could be so speechless, to Evan, to my mother, to God, to anyone else. I opened my mouth to speak, and all that came out were moans. How could this happen to me?

"That's right, baby, let it out." My mother's voice was barely a whisper. Had I said something?

"It's going to be okay. It's alright to groan and cry a little. For we don't know what we should pray for as we ought, but the Spirit Himself makes intercession for us with groanings and moanings, which cannot be uttered, or something like that. I read it in Romans chapter eight last night."

My mother sat on a folding chair next to my bed. Her eyes were red, but her voice was steady. Wet, crumpled tissues in her hands were soft and smelled of lavender as she wiped them over my eyes and nose. I remembered I was eight and sick with the flu when she started rubbing drops of lotion into the tissues she used to clean my face. It was such a soothing gesture for her to resume that practice, I didn't care that she'd gone through my secret stash of oils and perfumes and other Evan essentials to find the scents I liked most.

"Thanks, Ma." I mouthed the words and tried to refocus my thoughts on curtains, senior prom, ladybugs, and the baby drama on the talk show I just clicked on. Babies. I looked away from the television screen, surprised anew at how painful it was to look in a baby's face right now. All the guests on the episode had popped out babies they didn't want, doing it as quick and easy as a one-night stand. And I might never be a mother. What did I do with that thought?

"Let it out, Selena." Another lavender-scented tissue ran across my face.

Darkness filled the sky when I opened my eyes again. How long had I been sleeping? With the natural sunlight gone and the curtains drawn, the bedroom had taken on a bland white pallor thanks to the one working light bulb on the ceiling fan. Or rather, the ceiling blade.

"I sent your mother home so I could sit here with you. She'll meet us at the hospital tomorrow." Evan, dressed in khakis and a white tank, sat at the edge of the bed, a nervous grin played on his lips. I wondered how long he had been sitting and staring at me.

"Are you…okay?" His smile seemed to teeter between his high cheekbones. I searched his eyes, suddenly wondering what he was feeling. I'd never thought to ask. Had he thought to answer? Maybe we should talk. I sucked in a deep breath, struggling for the right words, the right question.

"How's work?"

Evan stood and stretched before sitting back down and smoothing out invisible wrinkles on our yellow safari-printed comforter, one of many bed linens my parents had included in their "wedding present" to us.

"It's going very well. I got a lot of research done at the office for the case today. You'd be proud of me."

"You went to work?" I suddenly realized I hadn't seen him all day. "I thought you were, well, here, home today, with me. I know it's for Razi, but I'm your wife."

"Selena, you know how much pressure is on me with this case. Your mother said she was going to be here with you, so I—"

"You went to work?" My voice was a hoarse whisper. *I need you here with me,* I wanted to scream, but I didn't have the energy to get the words out.

Before Evan could respond, our bedroom door was swung open. A sterling silver tray piled with fine tableware and linens came in first, followed by a wide bosom flanked with pearls, and finally the drawn-up face of Mrs. Madelyn Ernestine Wayland.

"Selena, you need to eat." There was no greeting or room for argument as she laid the tray, complete with a fresh floral arrangement and breath mint, on the sheets between Evan and me. I didn't miss the lingering threads of recoil weaved in her face as she gave our room a quick look over. This was probably the first time she'd seen the master bedroom. I gulped, looking with new eyes at the zigzag patterned border peeling off the wall and the four-foot-tall wooden giraffe standing in the corner with its face sticking in a fake plant. My mother had originally considered a safari-theme for the bedroom when she and my father lived there. The giraffe was another unfinished project.

Had Mrs. Wayland seen the rest of the upstairs? The thought sickened me.

"I brought over one of your favorites, Evan. I'm assuming Selena will like this as well."

Gotta admit, the woman had that whole Martha Stewart thing down. The way she lifted the silver lids and laid out utensils looked like she had practiced giving fine food to the sick and brokenhearted for years. Rolling steam filled the room with the scent of rosemary and spices.

"Thanks, Mom. I'm going to eat downstairs, if you don't mind. I have a lot more research I need to get done tonight. You don't mind, do you, Lena?" With a wink and before I could answer, he left, leaving me alone with my giraffe, a plate of roasted pork tenderloin with sprigs of tarragon leaves, wild rice, candied carrots, and Mrs. Wayland. Before I could process another thought or emotion, Mrs. Wayland laid a linen napkin on the folding chair next to my bed and sat on it.

"Selena, I know you probably don't feel like eating, but you really need to. Tomorrow is going to be a long day, no matter what that sonogram says. You'll need to take it a lot easier from now on, if that baby is still even in you. All those long hours you work and all those steps you take up and down at your parents' apartment—Evan told me they live on the third floor—it's no surprise you've got yourself in this situation. But I wouldn't worry too much about it if you are miscarrying. You're young..." She patted my arm. "There's plenty more where that came from."

It took all my energy to chew the rice and not spit it out. I didn't have the strength to explain to the woman "this situation" had nothing to do with what I did but what God was going to do. I knew this—was holding on to that fact to salvage what was left of my sanity—but it hurt nonetheless to hear her talk so casually about *this* family member I might not ever meet. My face must have said what my words could not because she was quick to follow up with a too-big-to-be-real smile.

"I'm not trying to sound harsh, Selena. I care about what goes on in that little stomach of yours. Remember, it's not just your child. We're talking about my grandbaby—Evan's child."

I watched as her eyes turned upward and a dreamy expression took over her face. I was certain she was thinking about her other two grandchildren, Tori and Topaz, the twin daughters of Evan's oldest sister Penelope. Those girls had trophies and ribbons from several beauty pageants, a modeling career, an agent, and an acting coach. And they were only turning four in November. Mrs. Wayland had much to do with the blossoming success of her prized granddaughters. I could only imagine her fantasies regarding the firstborn child of her favorite, her son.

But whatever hopes she had running through her head appeared to be short lived as her eyes stopped at the broken ceiling fan and cracked paint above her head. I could see the exact moment when she remembered Evan's possible baby was going to grow up in this house.

"Now, Selena..." The forced niceness in her tone had completely disappeared. "We still need to—" A loud buzz cut her off. I'd heard that sound before. I stopped chewing the tender pork in my mouth, trying to place the memory.

"Selena," Mrs. Wayland said, jumping to her feet, "would you like me to get you some, *ummm*, more to drink?" I'd barely taken a sip of the cranberry ginger ale that had been on the tray, but she grabbed my full glass anyway. As she bent closer to me to pick it up, the buzzing grew louder, and an animal-like squeal joined the chainsaw-sounding noise.

I didn't want or mean to stare at her bosom, but what on earth was she keeping in there? The thought scared me, and from the looks of things, I wasn't the only one shivering in fright. The smile on her face was betrayed by the ice cubes in my glass trembling under her tight grip.

"Mrs. Wayland, I really don't need anything more to drink right now, but thanks for offering. Do you know what that sound—"

"—Well, oh my goodness," she interrupted, nearly shouting. "Is it really ten after? I need to go check that pie I've got baking in the oven." She was out of the room and down the steps before I could remind her our oven sat outside by what was left of the shed.

I pushed the tray away from me, finding some pleasure in the loud clink of silver and glass jangling against each other. As I collapsed back onto the sheets, a pillow pushed onto the floor a stack of baby name books that had been sitting on Evan's nightstand.

I'd gone a full three minutes without thinking anything about babies.

Babies.

Fruit bars. Philadelphia. Aunt Rachel's egg salad. The mute button on the remote control.

My mother says God places every person in your life for a reason. Madelyn Ernestine Wayland, I think I just figured out yours. Your wretched misery distracts me from my own. Where are you when I need you?

Fish sticks. Foot powder. The color green. The color magenta...

12

The Audacity

Evan and I first met at Busboys and Poets in Washington, DC. Not just a restaurant, I'd call the quaint place an experience, a place where souls find respite among books, art, music, and good food—a gathering place that celebrates culture and community. Named after the trades of the Harlem Renaissance poet Langston Hughes, it's the type of sophisticated establishment I imagined intellects and artisans, creatives and free spirits would meet, dine, discuss, and dream.

Maybe that's why Evan first fell for me. He thought I belonged there.

It was my junior year at Bowie, and I was at the restaurant on a mistaken mission. I'd done a service project during spring break with some other students from surrounding HBCUs. Spending the week volunteering at a school in DC, I'd helped tutor third and fourth graders in math. I saw in those sweet children's faces my own, and it hurt. Memories of my childhood, the schools, the teachers I had, the limited resources, and the lowered expectations pulled me into a dark place. By Thursday of that week, I had nearly sunken away, unable to shake away the inexplicable anger and sadness I felt.

One volunteer, Isaiah Graham—we called him Iggy—was a social work student from Howard University. He was average looking—actually, maybe a little less than that. Roly-poly nose, cratered faced, a bit of a square-shaped head over wiry limbs. He felt attainable. With his friendly spirit and pure heart for social justice, he felt desirable. He pulled me aside with a message of hope and positivity based on community action, then invited me to hear a lecture on inequality and disparities in the school system that was scheduled that Friday night at the Busboys and Poets venue.

I thought he was asking me out on a date.

I called Neeka in a frenzy, and she gave me outfit ideas, suggested a new hairstyle, told me to go to the nearest MAC counter for a makeover.

I did all she said.

Then, I showed up to find he'd invited the other seven volunteers to hear the lecture, too. I'd gotten there late, as Neeka had also suggested, as she said the wait would only increase my date's anticipation to see me. Iggy and the others all filled a table, no room for me.

And, he clearly had a girlfriend, a mahogany beauty with sharp eyes and animated hands that moved as she talked next to him.

I found a table in the back, alone, too dressed up to just go back home. The place was packed for the guest lecturer that Iggy had promoted.

Evan came in just as the lecture began and asked to sit next to me. The chair at my small table was the only one not empty.

We jokingly tell others it was love at first sight. For me, it definitely was. Him standing there, asking to sit down, his long lashes, smooth skin, perfectly tapered hairline, trimmed goatee. He was wearing a gray suit, white pinstriped shirt, pale pink necktie, loosened a bit at the collar. A second-year law student at Georgetown, he told me in his introduction. He seemed intent on the speaker as he sat forward in his seat, his thick eyebrows furrowed, elbows on knees, his chin resting on folded hands.

No way he would notice me.

But he did.

"What did you think?" I asked him when the lecturer finished and the applause had died down. A small jazz ensemble took over right after, and the place had roared up with clinking drinks, laughter, and lively discussions.

"Honestly, I don't know. I missed it all. I wasn't paying attention." He looked over at me, his brown eyes piercing mine. "I've spent the last thirty minutes wondering how I would ask for your number."

A saxophonist hit a high note as my soul cartwheeled. "Just ask," I said, trying to remember how to breathe.

He smiled.

We've been together ever since.

***

"Well, there it is. See the wavy lines? That's the heartbeat. Looks like a viable embryo. Based on the measurements, we will need to recalculate the dates of your pregnancy. Looks like it did indeed start a little later than we were thinking. I will caution, though, you're not out of the woods yet due to the spotting you're experiencing, but the heartbeat is a great sign." Dr. Nelson scribbled some notes on her pad as the ultrasound technician continued to prod and press the internal ultrasound wand inside of me. I closed my eyes to focus on good memories to get through the intrusive exam.

"Alright, Mrs. Wayland." The doctor made one more note before looking up at me with a smile. "This is an encouraging finding. You can schedule your next appointment at the front desk." She squeezed my ankle.

And with that, she was gone, and I was officially on the road to motherhood.

"Selena!" Evan gripped both my shoulders and practically slobbered kisses all over my face. "Do you know what this means?"

"Evan, it means we're not out of the woods yet." I sat up on the exam table and struggled to pull up my pants. The instant relief I expected to feel with a good report didn't come. The past three days had been too dark for me to naively believe the birthing-a-baby business had an address on easy street. Too many detours and roadblocks had come up to wreck my innocent view of pregnancy. I'll never look at those sweet little pictures in parenting magazines and maternity catalogs the same way again.

I'm pregnant. Jesus, please don't let this be a dead end.

Evan chitchatted excitedly about baby monitors or teething rings or something or other the entire trek back through the corridor to the main waiting area.

"Mom." His smile said it all.

He and Mrs. Wayland joined in a tearful embrace as my mother quietly exhaled some words of thanksgiving. I guess I should have been relishing the moment, but I was too aware of the other women watching our Hallmark scene in the waiting area of the High-Risk Maternal Fetal Medicine Department of the Baltimore Metropolitan Hospital. One young lady, her hands locked around her well-rounded belly, stared and swallowed hard. Our eyes met for a moment, and I saw the same shock and numbness in her eyes that had been in mine yesterday. I wanted to go embrace her, tell her we'd both make it through okay, no matter what roads we had to travel.

But I guess God had other plans. I say God because I keep reminding myself that every person who comes into your life is there for a reason, as my mother says. I was pulling my purse up on my arm, ready to get going, when the door to the unit was swung open.

My new supervisor, Kiona Tandy.

Now, I've met this girl only once—okay, maybe three times if you count the "finger waves" on the highway—but she stood in the doorway, eyes filled with tears, arms stuffed with balloons, teddy bears, sympathy cards—what looked like the entire condolences section from the hospital gift shop. I'm assuming all that stuff was for me, but her eyes were only on Evan.

"Oh, I'm so sorry to hear about your loss." She collapsed into him, sniffling.

Despite her towering height, she looked small in his arms. Wearing a form-fitting black skirt suit that stopped high enough to show off most of her bare legs, she clutched him tighter, pulling his head close to her neck. I was wondering if Evan could breathe in the cloud of balloons, flowers, and perfume. With her expertly outlined eyes, flawless bronze skin, and loud voice, she'd captured most of the attention in the waiting room.

"Who the—" my mother started behind me, but Mrs. Wayland cut her off.

"Kiona? Is that you? I haven't seen you in ages. How have you been?" Mrs. Wayland was smiling like Bloomingdale's had just revealed its fall line. She grabbed Kiona's hands and studied her up and down. "Look at you. Beautiful as ever. Wait a minute. What are you doing here?" Mrs. Wayland suddenly stopped smiling and glanced quickly at me before taking a couple steps back from the towering beauty.

"I'm Selena's new supervisor at News U Need AM. We hadn't heard anything since her sudden departure the other morning, so I called Evan last night to see how she was doing. He shared with me the terrible news." She shook her head and gave him a sad look. "When he told me she would be here this morning, I knew I had to come offer support. Here, Selena." She quickly thrust her sympathy package in my arms and held me so tight I could smell the pomade holding her almost-to-butt-length hair in place. It felt like a furry boa constrictor had attached itself to my neck.

What in the world was going on? She had Evan's number? How did she even know him? And Mrs. Wayland, too?

"Kiona, I'm okay." My words muffled into her shoulder as I tried to process that Evan knew Kiona. And he had talked to her last night and didn't mention this phone conversation to me. "Kiona, really, I'm okay. The baby's okay. I'm okay. Evan and I and the baby are okay. Kiona?"

It took my mother's not-so-gentle prying to get her off me.

"Oh, you're okay?" Kiona's voice was two octaves higher as she stepped back slowly, her bright pink fingernails digging into a fuzzy teddy bear. "Everything is...okay?" She understood me loud and clear.

I nodded, flashing her the same fake smile she gave me.

"That's wonderful. See, Evan—" She playfully hit his arm— "I told you everything would turn out for the best."

Evan wrapped an arm around me, and I suddenly realized the man had been speechless since Kiona Tandy entered the room. His face was turned away from mine, leaving me to only guess at his expression. My mother's sneer had left nothing to the imagination.

"Well, I guess we need to go now if we're going to try and beat rush hour." I knew I was talking too quickly, moving too quickly, but I didn't know how else to deal with the onset of bubbles bursting somewhere between my chest and my stomach.

"It was good seeing all of you. Congratulations, Selena, Evan." Kiona turned to leave, letting us all have a good look at her full, swaying backside before she sharply turned back around on her heels. "You know, I still do event planning on the side. Remember, Mrs. Wayland? Selena, I would *love* to help you plan your baby shower."

"Not to ruin the surprise, but Selena already has plenty of friends who are planning to take care of that. Friends, people who know her." My mother spoke sweetly, but her stare was nothing short of fierce.

"Well, she can have a shower with her friends—" Kiona didn't miss a beat—"and I'll plan one with the people Evan and I know. Mrs. Wayland, do you remember the birthday party I helped you organize for your youngest daughter at The Velvebon Hall?"

"The Velvebon Hall?" Mrs. Wayland gasped. "Why, that's exactly the place..."

I think the conversation between the two women went on for several minutes before Evan suddenly snapped to attention and grabbed my hand.

"We need to go. I do want to hit the road before rush hour gets too busy like you said."

The sudden seriousness in his tone and the dropped smile from his face disrupted any comfort I gained from the warmth of his hand clutching mine.

I didn't miss the smile Kiona flashed him as we walked out.

Or the hard swallow he gave in response.

13

The Ex

"Okay, so what's the deal with Miss Kiona Tandy? Who is she, and how does she know you?" *And why did you never tell me about her?* All but the last question sped out of me. The thought of even asking the last question left me spent.

We were on our way home, and Evan had said nothing since we'd left the hospital. I thought he'd immediately break into a story that explained how—why—he knew her. But nothing. Not a word from him in fifteen minutes. Rush hour had started early, and traffic on the beltway had slowed to a halt. I figured since we had nothing else better to do, we might as well get this over with.

"Kiona?" Evan looked over at me before drumming his fingers on the steering wheel. "*Hmmm.* She was just an old friend I had before I met you. We were teaching assistants together my senior year at Maryland." The last sentence rushed out.

"Oh, kind of like coworkers." I sat more comfortably in my seat, trying my best not to overreact. "The way *she* was acting, I thought you had something more going on."

"Yeah, well, we were briefly engaged." Evan slammed the brakes as the car in front of us came to another abrupt stop.

Engaged.

He'd said the word so casually, at first I thought I misunderstood him.

"Engaged? I don't recall you mentioning her or that you were previously engaged." I tried to keep my voice as flat and even as his. "You've told me about your old girlfriends Whitney and Celeste, but I don't remember you saying anything about a fiancée."

Okay, maybe I should have let it go, but something wasn't registering. I've never expected Evan to share every detail of his past dating life with me, but the fact that he'd been close to marrying someone else and had kept her a complete secret set off a queasiness in the pit of my stomach. Now that I think about it, my morning—excuse me, all day—sickness, seemed to start right at that moment.

"Kiona Tandy." He shook his head as he spoke her name. "I never mentioned her to you because, well, she was too much drama to even begin to explain. Kiona wasn't good for me." He glanced over at me with a slight smile, although his last sentence sounded more like a question to himself than a stated fact to me.

"When did you call it off?" I wanted to puke and began searching the interior of his car for a bag, a bucket, anything that would protect the black leather interior from my sudden need to vomit. I settled for an empty fast-food foam cup that had been tossed under the seat. I held it just below my lips, waiting.

"We were supposed to get married the Friday I met you, but I met you and that was that." He squeezed my hand and winked, like I was supposed to just leave it alone.

"Wait a minute. You're telling me you had a whole wedding ready and planned the day I met you at Busboys and Poets? What happened? To the wedding, I mean?"

"She didn't show up. She stood me up at the altar, so to speak."

His words ended in a whisper, and I couldn't tell if he was choking up or distracted by the sudden break-up of traffic.

I closed my eyes, remembering the way Kiona had stared at my pictures her first day at the office. Kiona had said nothing about knowing him, not to mention almost being married to my Evan. Something wasn't adding up right. I wasn't sure where to go from there.

"Oh, wow. You must have been devastated. I mean, *you* got stood up at the altar?" I tried to make sense of this new information. My head reeled with images of Evan's mother sitting in an empty reception hall—flowers, candles, gourmet entrées, and linen untouched. An empty bandstand. Ruined plans. *Why hadn't Mrs. Wayland ever bought it up?* "I'm amazed your mom was so happy to see her just now. I would think she would be enraged at Kiona for standing you up like that."

"Mom didn't know about it, the wedding that is. Kiona and I were supposed to meet at the courthouse to get married. She said she wanted a big wedding, but I guess I didn't believe her until she didn't show up. I sat in front of the courthouse for hours after it closed and did some deep thinking, then I took a walk down K Street, saw the sign for the lecture, and ended up going in to distract my mind. And, there you were, and as they say, the rest is history."

He squeezed my hand again and forced another smile. I let go of his fingers and gripped the foam cup tighter. Any second now. I could feel the juices in my stomach collecting for a full release.

"I–I don't understand. You asked for my number just hours after not getting married? You never told me any of this." I didn't know where to begin as I tried to re-live the moment of our first meeting, these novel details changing it all. It was almost impossible to get words out, impossible to imagine.

"Kiona told me she was pregnant, so I proposed immediately. I didn't even have a ring, but I told her I'd get her one. It was a

Monday, I remember. We had agreed to meet at the courthouse to get married on that Friday, but the next time I saw her was the day after I met you. That Saturday. She hadn't even bothered to return any of my calls after standing me up. I went to visit my parents that next day, and there she was, sitting in my parents' living room, showing my mother an engagement ring I'd never seen before. I guess she'd bought the ring herself. She told them a made-up story of how I'd proposed during a picnic on the National Mall. She and my mom were on a website looking at bridesmaids' gowns together."

All I heard was the word *pregnant*. Did Evan have a child somewhere out there? I felt the strength seep from every single muscle in my body. I couldn't even summon my mouth to move.

The car in front of us came to a sudden stop again, and Evan pounded a fist on the horn.

"C'mon, man!" He raised his voice the way my frozen mouth wanted to at that moment. I'd never seen him so animated. When the car came back to life again, his face softened, and he relaxed in his seat.

"But," he continued his story, "like I told Kiona that Saturday, it was too late. I had met you the day before, and it was love at first sight. It was, Selena." He looked over at me, blinking. "I'm not just saying that." He turned his attention back to the road. "When my mother left the room to start calling her friends to tell them of our supposed engagement, I told Kiona it was over between us. I was shocked she hadn't shown up at the courthouse like we'd agreed, and even more disturbed at the ease with which she lied to my family about a fake proposal. That's not the type of woman I wanted to spend the rest of my life with. I knew that afternoon I'd dodged a bullet. Neither she nor I told my mom about the pregnancy. Kiona said she wasn't keeping it once I broke it off with her."

Pain and bitterness shot through his face as I tried to exhale.

"I guess I should have told you all of this." His voice softened.

"It's just that..." He turned to look at me again. "Selena, I beg you, please don't tell my mother. You don't know how much it would hurt me for her to know I'm not the perfect son she thinks I am." He suddenly smiled again, that darn goofy smile that made him look stupid, senile, I allowed myself to admit.

"See, you came into my life just in the nick of time." He had the nerve to grin.

"I was a rebound, an excuse to get back at her." Words finally came.

"Selena, no." He took my hand in his again and kissed it, keeping his eyes on the road. "I married you. You are the woman I want to spend the rest of my life with. That's why I never told you about Kiona. I knew how it would look and sound. I never wanted you to question my commitment to you. But, please—" The worry lines etched back into his chiseled face— "please don't tell my mother any of this. She would be devastated, and I couldn't stand seeing her hurt. Getting Kiona pregnant was a major mistake and an embarrassment for me, but I repented, and God forgave me and brought me to you."

"I don't get it." I tried to sound unaffected. "Guys get girls pregnant every day. And the way your mother so rightfully adores you, I don't see why she would have been so devastated to find out you were marrying your pregnant girlfriend. From what I saw today, your mom really seems to have positive feelings for Kiona."

That was putting it lightly, considering the way the two women greeted each other back in that waiting room at the hospital. I'd seen romance movies with fewer hugs and kisses. I winced, trying to push down a quick pang of jealousy. When Evan first introduced me to his mother the summer before my senior year of college, there was no hint of admiration of me from her. He'd bought me as his date to a fundraiser his mother had organized for his father's medical charity. Mrs. Wayland looked at me like I was a roach crawling on her son.

"It wasn't that simple, Selena. I had a reason for not telling my parents about the wedding or the pregnancy." He paused and bit his lip. I didn't miss the way he glanced at me uneasily before he continued. "Kiona didn't want a quick wedding because she'd already had one. She was married to...to a former friend of mine when...when we got together."

"Wait. Huh?"

He blew out a loud stream of air. "I knew she was married—married to my friend. I knew it was wrong, but...I didn't want to stop. I wanted her. It was stupid of me, shameful. My family met her, spent time with her, never once knowing she was my friend's wife. They'd never met Peyton and didn't know a thing about him. Kiona had just finalized her divorce from him when she told me she was pregnant with my child. That was a Monday, and I thought I'd have it all fixed by Friday at the courthouse. I don't know what I was thinking. I wasn't. It was the craziest week of my life." He shook his head.

A car crash in that moment of rush hour would have been less impactful than what I felt right then. The way my head jerked backward, I was certain I'd given myself whiplash.

Evan seemed oblivious to my trauma. He continued, "It wasn't right. None of it was right. I met you. And *we* were right. I never said anything about this to you because I didn't want you to think any less of me."

Cars whirled past us in slow motion. Time felt suspended. In his sudden silence, all I heard was the loud drumming of my heart. I could feel the cavernous chambers hollowed out by shock, echoing in my ears, each thud on the verge of shattering into tinkling pieces.

My husband, the man I'd married, had left out a significant part of his narrative to me. I struggled to understand how I even fit into his story. The chapters were out of order, pages ripped in half, the beginning of our fairy tale love story rewritten with characters and plot twists I never knew existed.

I'd spent years—grueling, steadfast years—sacrificing potential moments of pleasure to wait for my wedding night, and for what? To give myself to someone who'd clearly, unapologetically valued sex in a different currency than me? What had felt priceless between us now felt like we'd been exchanging cheap, secondhand goods. Bootleg. Knockoff. I wasn't naïve. I knew my husband had experience in the bedroom way before he'd met me, and I had been okay with that. It didn't change what I'd wanted for myself. However, to know he'd devalued the marital bond between another man and his wife, claiming her as his bounty, and then revealing this raw ransack to me so casually... I had to wonder how much he truly treasured the intimacy *we* shared.

I felt cheated, in more ways than one.

"Evan. This is a lot. I don't even know what to say."

"There's really nothing to say at this point, Selena." Evan shook his head. "I broke it off with her the moment I met you. I've had no contact with her until she called to check on you and the baby last night. I was shocked to find out she was your boss. I was shocked to even hear from her. But, she represents my past. You are my present and my future." He reached for my hand again.

My hand lay like a cold, dead fish in his.

As I sat in silence, he studied me, biting his lip.

"Selena, look," he blurted, "my mother never knew Kiona was married, and my old friend Peyton never knew I was the man who took his wife. I met the true love of my life on my first wedding day. That was you. You. And we are together forever with *our* baby on the way. I don't want the mistakes of my past to mess up our future, so let's just leave it all back in the past where it belongs."

He blew out another loud breath of air. "*Whew.* Got it all out." He exhaled again.

He was over in the driver's seat exhaling, and I could barely breathe.

My perfect Evan. Had taken another man's wife. His *friend's* wife. Gotten her pregnant. Almost married her. And never told me.

I tried to think of something to express how I felt in the moment, but words betrayed me. Feelings betrayed me. Numbness started from the tips of my toes and crawled up my legs through my stomach and chest and down my arms and fingers.

"Evan—" My voice was hoarse as snot and saliva pooled in my throat—"I don't know what I'm supposed to do with...this."

"Selena, like I said, it's all in the past." He spoke with finality. "I'm getting everything out now so there's no need to bring it up again. It would kill my mother if she knew the whole story. She thinks Kiona and I broke things up because we took different life tracks. I told her Kiona had to take care of her grandmother in Houston, and we all knew my law career was going to be taking off here. I told Mom it was a mutual, peaceful parting of ways. My parents thought we'd end up back together one day. Well, until I introduced you to them." He paused. I couldn't read his face. "Lena," he continued slowly, "Kiona would never say anything to destroy my mother's image of me, so that leaves it all on you. Promise me, Selena, you will never hurt me by telling Mom. Selena? Please, promise me."

What about hurting me? I wanted to scream, but the mucus in my throat kept my hurt, my tears lodged and locked away.

Simple man, I wanted to yell. *Simple, dirty man.* Instead, *I* became the simpleton and pledged my oath of silence to him.

"Don't worry. Your mother will never find out from me." *That you're a lying homewrecker with more relationship baggage than I could have ever imagined.* I'd always seen Evan as a good man, and at heart, I wanted to believe he was. However, this was some major messiness in which he'd dragged me. I felt sick to my stomach trying to make sense of this hidden part of the man I'd married. "Your secret is safe with me," I mumbled just as the foam cup I'd been holding finally saw some action.

And I meant what I said. I wiped my lips with an old napkin I swiped from the dashboard, the taste of bile pungent in my mouth. I had no plans of telling Mrs. Madelyn Ernestine Wayland her only begotten son had sinned and was hiding a secret as scandalous as they come. Nope, I wouldn't be that fool, that bearer of bad news. I wouldn't tell her—or anyone else for that matter. How would it make me look? Like a rebound for a cheater? I shut my eyes as tears tried to break through.

"Don't worry about Kiona, okay, Lena?" Evan continued. "What she and I had is over—way over."

"But she still had your number," I blurted.

"*She* had my number, not the other way around." He looked at me, eyes blinking in a flurry. "Look, Selena, my only concern right now is you—and our child you are carrying. Now, let's get you home to rest."

He gave me a weak smile as I sat there stunned, numb, dumbfounded, and wondering how I'd missed this whole convoluted history of my husband, this whole shameful secretive side to the man I'd married. What was I supposed to do with this information? How was I supposed to process this? Was there anything else I didn't know about him? I remembered what he'd said the night of our wedding rehearsal, when we stood in the house together for the first time. *"Well, maybe you don't know me, Selena."*

Understatement of the year.

I felt like the ground was slipping from underneath me, swallowing me.

Quicksand.

For the sake of my baby, for the sake of my sanity, I had to survive. I made a conscious decision to block his confession out of my mind, to stay numb to the unidentified feelings that welled within me, to let his words whip over my head and keep going like an ocean wave unbroken by the splintered shipwreck in its wake.

We were both quiet the rest of the way home.

14

The Nerve

Of course, I had no desire to return to work any time soon and face the adulterous ex-fiancée. I considered quitting, but, honestly, I felt the need to keep tabs on this woman who held my husband's darkest secrets. I wanted to study her a bit more, though I wasn't ready to see her just yet. With my new extra delicate condition, nobody was rushing me back. I was still having occasional cramping and spotting, so Dr. Nelson told me to stay off my feet for a little while. A lady in human resources called and said I could take as many days off as necessary. For a couple of days, I had some peace and quiet.

Evan and I tiptoed around each other when he finally came home from work, and we only talked and giggled about safe things: the weather, groceries, the Baltimore Ravens. In those first few days after his big reveal, we didn't once talk about Kiona or even my pregnancy.

Maybe we should have, but we didn't. A sinking feeling was taking over the place in my stomach where butterflies once fluttered at the thought of my husband. No, it was more than a sinking feeling. It was a thousand-pound weight that settled in a deep, dark, quiet place inside me. The weight of my husband's secrets... The pain, the discovery he'd kept so much from me...

In good news, I was even given a reprieve from thinking about the house repairs as nobody—not my parents nor Mrs. Wayland—bought up Kunta X or the other contractors. I didn't even have to worry about getting soy sauce stains on my good dishes as my mother had taken to dropping off pots of soup and casseroles every night, complete with paper plates, bowls, and plastic utensils to take washing dishes off anyone's hands.

For four entire days, I stayed in my bed, doing word search puzzles, watching sappy movies on Lifetime, catching up on old Oprah's Book Club selections.

And then the phone rang one early afternoon.

It was his mother. She wanted us to meet for dinner.

Evan was getting home well past nine most nights now, including weekends, tied up with the case that would make or break his entire legal career, so I couldn't use him as an excuse to avoid her innocent-sounding dinner plans. I tried the only other option: appealing to her grandmotherly pride.

"Thanks, Mrs. Wayland, but I think I need to continue resting for the baby's sake."

"You've had sufficient time to rest. It's dinner I want us to attend, not a parade. I'm sure Evan Jr. has strong genes like his father and will survive you having a nice meal for a change. I'll text you an address and meet you there in an hour."

The line went dead. Did this woman really just hang up on me again? I groaned, knowing I had no choice but to get ready and to get going. I had no desire to get into a confrontation with her because who knew what would come out of my mouth. Evan's secrets hung over my head like a hot, wet, wool blanket.

She's already decided on the gender and name of my child. I groaned again at the thought as I pulled myself from my bed. I took a quick shower and went through a heap of wrinkled clothes I'd flung in a basket from the dryer two weeks before. I settled on a black skirt and a plum blouse. Simple, elegant, and more cheery-looking than I felt. When I got into my car, I turned on a local gospel station, hoping the tunes would uplift my spirit. Within seconds, I turned it off.

When I entered the restaurant exactly sixty minutes later, her greeting was straight and to the point. "Sit down, Selena. Enough is enough. It is time to get back to business."

She'd made reservations at The Pink Teapot, an upscale restaurant in downtown Baltimore where the food and décor were "appropriately cultured" as Mrs. Wayland put it. Cultured by whose standards was my question. To me, hot wings and fries sure beat sesame seed–crusted chicken breast and feta cheese and spinach on toasted crackers any day.

That's what Mrs. Wayland ordered for me, insisting I open my mind and expand my palette and that spinach was necessary for a strong, healthy baby to grow. I can only imagine what else she would have asked the waiter to bring me had she known of the pinto beans and biscuits dinner my mother dropped off the night before.

Sitting across from her at the pink-and-silver-striped table, I could see where Evan got most of his features. The long, narrow nose that flared out subtly at the base. The high cheekbones. The eyes that looked like they had been traced and cut around almonds. He was her twin in all his features. The only gene I could see Evan inherited from his father was the one marked color. Both he and Dr. Harold Wayland shared a similar rich hue of dark hazelnut, though Evan's skin looked warmer under his jet-black curly hair and long eyelashes. What was left of the doctor's hair was bright silver, and his eyebrows were too bushy to detect any warmth underneath them. Dr. Wayland seemed to have all the persona and presence of a nondescript bookend. His money and career status held things up and together, but he never quite seemed to be the star attraction. Mrs. Wayland took up the whole shelf.

"We'll have the white wine I tasted earlier." Mrs. Wayland directed the waiter. I quickly held out a hand.

"Sprite's fine for me."

She glared at me for a second before her face softened. "Of course. We don't want anything to harm our little baby."

She kept a smile on her face until the waiter walked away.

"So, Selena, during this recent break you've had, have you picked out a color from the samples I emailed you for your first-floor window treatments? I think any of them would go nicely with the ideas of Genevaise, but she is particularly fond of the metallic silver."

She must have seen my face drop because she quickly added, "Remember Genevaise Zuzani, the interior designer? She is the one who helped redecorate my bedroom. I remembered how much you praised our master suite when I showed you the pictures after our renovation, so I'm certain you'll love her decorating philosophy."

I watched as her smile at the approaching waiter returned. She thanked him for her wineglass and took a long sip. I shifted in my seat feeling bubbles starting to form yet again in my stomach.

"I haven't really been checking my emails, and to be honest, I'm not familiar with Genevaise." My voice was a mere mumble.

"I really had to pull some strings to get Genevaise Zuzani and her team to agree to do this project. She was quite stubborn at first. As I told you before, her firm usually focuses only on estate-sized projects, but after I assured her you'd be willing to go along with her ideas of an eclectic modern theme, she became quite excited."

"Mrs. Wayland, I appreciate your hard work in helping me—"

"Oh, and I really have tried to keep you at the center of this project. I wanted your house to incorporate the lifestyle Evan knows without making you feel too uncomfortable in your own home. Genevaise agreed."

"How nice, but I—"

"Her ideas were inspired by your urban upbringing and the view of the public housing projects Evan told her you once had as a youth. She said seeing the metallic dressers your parents left in your bedroom sealed the vision in her mind."

"Mrs. Wayland, I'm sure that Genevaise is a— Wait. Did you just say that woman was in my bedroom?" The bubbles in my stomach were coming to a head.

"Of course. Evan took a long lunch break just before your little incident to give her a complete tour of the house. Any good visionary designer must know what she is working with."

I didn't know the man had lunch breaks, to hear him talk of his long days. And he sure enough hadn't spent one of those long lunch breaks with me. Before I could fix the look on my face, Mrs. Wayland broke in with more.

"Don't worry, Selena. You'll feel right at home when it's all done. Wait until you see the sketches. Every room in the house, including the nursery, will incorporate a tasteful blend of steel, concrete, and exposed brick. Genevaise is calling it 'cityscape revised,' and it is ingenious work. There's already preliminary talk of your home being featured in next year's prestigious *House and Studio* magazine's 'Best Of' edition. Isn't that exciting?" She took another sip of wine.

"Excuse me, Mrs. Wayland. I need to go throw up."

Okay, maybe I shouldn't have said those exact words, and I definitely shouldn't have been as loud, but with the way I felt, there was no pretty way for me to get away from that table. Mrs. Wayland sat there wide-eyed and shocked as I all but pushed the approaching waiter out of the way to get to the restroom in time.

It turned out to be a false alarm, but I stayed locked up in the marble stall for ten minutes, nonetheless.

I guess that wasn't long enough because when I finally did emerge from the safety of the bathroom, someone else had joined our quaint dinner party.

Kiona Tandy.

She sat there at the table, hands all daintily clasped to the right of the extra place setting a waiter had laid out for her. When I got to my seat, both she and Mrs. Wayland were giggling at a story involving Kiona's Pomeranian puppy.

"Oh, there you are." Mrs. Wayland acknowledged me, but her smile was fixated on Kiona whose own fake smile was fixed like steel darts aimed at me. Mrs. Wayland seemed oblivious to the hate. "I had Kiona join us today because she had some great ideas for your baby shower. I know this may be a little beyond your usual tastes, but I think you should hear her out."

"Uh, my baby shower?"

"Hi, Selena. I'm so glad you and the baby are doing better." Kiona stood and hugged me, smacking air kisses on both my cheeks. I wanted to cringe at her phoniness but instead gave her the same plastic smile back. No need for World War III just yet. I needed to explore her intentions. We both sat down before she continued.

"I don't want this to be awkward, so let's just get this out on the table." Her smile looked as real as a three-dollar bill and was worth less than that. "Yes, Evan and I were briefly engaged, as I'm sure you know by now. We broke it off amicably when my Meemaw grew ill in Texas and I knew I wouldn't be able to fully give Evan the attention he deserved. I had to go care for her, and Evan had to continue working toward his law degree in DC, his moral obligation to live out our ancestors' wildest dreams. We respectfully sacrificed our relationship to pursue what was right and noble, knowing and believing that if we were meant to be, the universe would reunite us at the right time."

"Self-sacrifice is the ultimate demonstration of love," Mrs. Wayland gushed.

The way my stomach turned.

"Love is one thing. Soulmates are another, and Evan found that with you, Selena. The stars did not align for Evan and me to be together, and I fully respect that. We weren't meant to be. I'm just honored to be in your universe, and I'll do whatever I can to help you both continue to shine."

She gingerly took a sip from her wineglass as Mrs. Wayland clasped her hands together and beamed. "What a beautiful story of emotional maturity. I'm so glad we can all be adults here." She directed the last words to me, a stern threat unmistakable in her tone, as if she expected me to push the table away, pull out my earrings, and pop that phony piece of lying trash right in the mouth.

Was that too vivid?

"What a...story." I demurely picked up my own glass. What was I supposed to do? Expose the truth right then and there? As if Madelyn would believe the horrible tale of her son over the saintly saga Kiona—who clearly didn't think Evan would have told me what really happened—presented.

Kiona dug in her bag, took out a small binder, and laid it on the table. "Like I said, I'm excited for the two of you, and I would love to plan your baby shower. Evan told me how much you like bubbles, so I came up with an exciting plan."

"Bubbles?" *What? And had she spoken with Evan again?* "What are you talking—"

"So, look." She spoke right over me. "I have a friend who owns a lodge in the Poconos, and she's agreed to let us rent it out for an entire weekend of festivities early-February, three weeks before your due date. It will be the height of ski season, which Evan should love, but don't worry. I know you'll be in no condition to ski. There will be plenty of other things for you to do. I've developed a pampering itinerary just for you. *Oooh*, I'm so excited," she squealed. She reached for my hand and squeezed like we were best girlfriends. "Madelyn knows how much I love planning events."

I didn't miss the first-name basis between the two of them. Here I was married to the man, and I nowhere near felt comfortable calling Evan's mother "Madelyn."

"And you are so good at planning events, too," Mrs. Wayland gushed. "Kiona, tell us more."

"Okay, the bubbles." Kiona flipped through the binder and reviewed some jotted notes. "I know you're wondering how bubbles tie into a ski lodge at the Poconos. That's the thing. You know how they have those champagne glass whirlpool tubs in some of the hotels up there? Well, we're going to have a champagne glass theme for your baby with a six-foot-tall ice sculpture as a centerpiece in the rental. Everything will be sparkling and bubbly. We'll call the weekend 'A Toast to Baby.' We'll have some sparkling cider for you, but all the guests will get their own vintage bottle of champagne as a favor, and I had this wonderful dish with a foam sauce in London last summer that would be the perfect entrée for the main dinner. Like I said, it will be a weekend of activities. I bought along copies of the proposed schedule for both of you to take with you. I can't wait."

She sat back in her chair, and Mrs. Wayland practically looked like she wanted to kiss her, the way she beamed and *oohed* and *ahhed* at the typed proposal.

"Oh, this is perfect, Kiona. I always loved your creativity and your ability to come up with original themes. Isn't this wonderful, Selena?"

"Well," I searched for something positive to say, but the idea of Evan skiing down slopes next to Kiona dressed like a sexy snow bunny while I lapped up plates of English foam in bulky maternity clothes was not my idea of a good time. "Thanks for your, creativity, but I think the Poconos might be a little far for my family and friends to come all the way for a baby shower. Plus, both my parents tend to work weekends, and truthfully, a lot of my closest friends might not be able to afford such a lavish retreat—and, to be honest, we don't really know each other like that for you to throw me a shower."

I ignored the growing displeasure on Mrs. Wayland's face. There was no fight in me. None. Wasn't sure if it was because the idea of Evan didn't excite me at the moment or because the thought of Evan and Kiona's entanglement had left me numb. I could use some Neeka muster right then, but I was too embarrassed over it all to even confide in my best friend.

"Oh, but we're getting so close, Selena," Kiona said, pouting, "and, honestly, planning events is my passion. This would be so fun for me. With the terrible stress of your pregnancy, this is the least I can do for you and Evan. Listen, I knew you would be worried about your friends not being able to make it. That's why I want to reiterate your family and friends are probably already planning what they want for you. This weekend will be just for Evan and Madelyn's closest friends. There are people you probably haven't met I know who would love to come. Madelyn, you remember Diane and Lisa, don't you? I was thinking..."

Her voice reminded me of a swarm of bees, a long, pain-filled drone. All I could think of at that point was how I was losing what little control I had over my own life. My husband, my home, and now even the baby growing in my uterus all seemed to be claimed by forces just out of my reach. I wanted to scream, but the waiter was spooning some sauce onto my plate, explaining some French process of cooking that was done to season the chicken. Nah, this probably wasn't the best time to scream, at least not out loud.

I wanted to tell Miss Hot Pants and The Mother to butt out of my life, leave me alone, but all I could see was the expression on Evan's face. *"Please don't tell my mother. It would hurt me for her to know.*" It was like walking on eggshells around Mrs. Wayland. How do you not peeve someone off who already hates you so that the person you are trying to love doesn't turn on you too?

I put a smile on my face as they continued talking about my baby shower. Inside, I tried to remember my smiley face morning devotional. I wanted to disappear into another dimension, feel God's presence through praise. Instead, I felt my cell phone vibrate in my pants pocket. It was my mother. Something told me to let it roll over to voice mail, but I needed an escape and picked it up anyway.

"Hi, Lena." My mother's voice sounded tired but cheery. "I'm outside your front door with a spaghetti casserole. I've been knocking for a while now, but I don't see your car out here. Are you home?"

"Uh—" I glanced over at Mrs. Wayland, who I could tell was eyeing me carefully although Kiona was still chattering away. Mrs. Wayland wore her curiosity like a shade of neon orange lipstick—nothing subtle about it. "Yeah, I'm actually out right now. At dinner. Sorry. I should have called to tell you. Thanks though. I can swing by later and pick it up for tomorrow night."

"Oh. Who are you out with?" my mother inquired. "I didn't realize you were feeling so well. I really would have preferred taking you out to eat tonight myself. I've had a taste for Denny's lately."

"Yeah, well, I'm feeling a little better, although I probably will be going home to rest again soon. Maybe we can do that another night, okay?"

I didn't miss Mrs. Wayland's arched eyebrow rising another degree at my last question into the receiver.

"Okay, Selena. I'll let you go. Don't worry about coming by. I'm heading for bed as soon as I get home. I'll bring over the casserole tomorrow morning on my way out to work."

"Alright. See you then." Mrs. Wayland was making me uncomfortable the way she stared at me talking on the phone. I wanted to end the call, but I wanted my mother, too.

"Oh, and Selena, Kunta X will be by on Saturday to start the work on the house. I know we put you through a lot with this, and—" She hesitated, bracing herself for words she rarely uttered to me— "and I'm sorry. Thanks for letting us take care of this for you. You don't know how much it means. I love you, Lena. Get off your feet now. Good night."

I wanted to smile. I wanted to cry. I wanted Mrs. Wayland to *not* ask me who I was talking to. I knew if she knew it was my mother, the conversation would turn back to the house and only God knows what else. The hormones were raging through me like fire. I could feel tears forming to try to break the flames.

"Was that Evan?" The Mother asked me over the rim of her wineglass. Kiona, her fork in mid-air, looked like she was holding her breath waiting for me to answer.

"No, *uh*, a friend." I quickly let the crusted chicken slide down my throat. It wasn't a lie. My mother has always been a friend to me.

"Oh, the one with the afro who always wears those humongous hoop earrings? What's her name, Neeka?" Mrs. Wayland asked.

I could hear the complete disdain in her voice, see the curl of disgust in her lip as she said my best friend's name.

"I'd love to meet your friend," Kiona cooed. "In fact, we *should* meet to ensure our shower plans don't overlap."

"No, that wasn't... Yes, that was... I mean—"

"Either it was Neeka or it wasn't. It's not a difficult question, Selena. Unless you have friends we don't know about."

We? Who is we?

"Ladies, can I get you dessert? Our chocolate truffles were featured in last month's *Food and Wine*."

Saved by the waiter.

As we politely turned him down and reached for our coats, I didn't miss the unmistakable glare in Mrs. Wayland's eyes. What I saw in those moments as she paid the bill and ushered us out of The

Pink Teapot was more than annoyance. It was disgust. Even Kiona could see it. I could tell by the mischievous smile that oozed onto her face.

I allowed myself to accept then that whatever were Kiona's plans and interests for Evan, for my baby shower, and for her friendship with Mrs. Wayland, my good was not her intention.

Jesus, you're going to have to fight for me, I prayed to myself as I walked to my car. Mrs. Wayland and Kiona whispered and giggled by Mrs. Wayland's Benz while I pulled off.

I was only a few months into this whole marriage thing, and already I felt like I was in the fight of my life. As the old folks say, "Pray for me, saints."

15

The Pop

I took the long way home trying to absorb all that had just happened, trying to figure out next steps. Before I realized it, I was back at Cylburn Arboretum, the place where Evan and I married. An expansive garden and green space, it also had an old mansion, walking trails, and inviting benches on its grounds. I parked my car in the lot and listened to the silence, enjoying a rare moment of space and solitude in this part of Baltimore City. I listened as I walked over crunchy gravel and then I nestled on a bench near a small colorful patch of blooms where numerous butterflies flitted.

A woman sat on another bench opposite me, a child of around a year old in her charge. The woman looked like she was in her mid-forties, maybe even fifty—streaks of gray ran through her auburn hair. The youngster toddled with uneven steps around the bushes and flowers, squealing and clapping as butterflies danced around her head. I watched as the woman took out some bubble solution and began blowing them, adding to the child's delight. The woman grinned at me as she saw me smiling at the young girl's joy. Simple pleasure.

The squeals turned into tears when the bubbles popped before the child could catch them. The woman blew more bubbles, and the girl's cheers began anew.

"You have a beautiful granddaughter." I offered a genuine smile, admiring the little redhead's mop of curls and chubby, cherubic cheeks.

"Oh, she's actually my daughter."

"Oh, I'm sorry." I wanted to kick myself for the stated assumption.

"Don't worry about it." The woman waved her hand with a genuine smile. "Happens all the time. People see these strands of gray hair on my head and naturally think I'm either the nanny or the grandma. Nope, Isabella was my late-life surprise."

"Oh, wow. Your first?"

"Yup. Was minding my business in life, and she came along."

"A surprise blessing, I see."

"A blessing, yes, but not going to lie when I say it's been a bit chaotic."

"Don't scare me like that. I'm expecting my first in February. I have enough chaos already with the people in my life." I swallowed hard, hoping this new person growing inside of me wouldn't add to the fray.

The woman smiled as she took a moment to dig up a sippy cup and hand it to the toddler.

"Well, I've come to learn it's not about the chaos around you. It's really how you see yourself in it."

I nodded like I understood, but I guess she called my bluff because she kept talking to explain.

"Are we like these bubbles that float around in the wind until they pop? Or are we woman enough to stand on our own two feet, able to withstand the wind, no matter which way it comes or how hard it blows?"

I watched as she took another breath and blew through the bubble wand. A new flurry of translucent bubbles burst into the space between us. The woman's daughter reached for as many as she could, this time purposely popping them with her pointer finger. Her laughs continued, no tears.

"I hear you, but how do you even begin to stand when the wind is a hurricane?"

"I guess it depends on what you're standing on and how securely you're attached to the ground below you." She shrugged.

I shrugged, too.

I didn't know if there was some deep lesson to take with me as I finished watching the girl and her mom enjoy the late afternoon sun. I didn't feel strong enough to stand—yet. It was comfortable on the bench, watching the butterflies, eyeing the bubbles meandering through the air. I didn't know from where all the bubbles had come that were popping off in my life or even why they were there. What I did know is that the winds of chaos seemed to be just starting. A strong breeze that rustled the leaves and scattered fallen flower petals on the ground told me there was still more gusts to come.

***

Evan was sitting at the kitchen table when I came home, law books, papers, and writing pads a sea surrounding him.

"We need to talk." I plopped into the chair next to him and tried to lay my head on his shoulder.

"Not right now, Lena." He shook me off and buried his head back into his work.

"Yes, right now." I pushed my head deeper into his arm and grabbed the hand he was writing with. "Please, we need to talk."

"Wh–What are you doing, Lena? You messed me up. Wernowski likes us to write out our notes in long hand with no errors before we type them up. Makes us catch errors in our arguments or teach patience or some other Mr. Miyagi trick. Now, I've got to start over!" He crumpled the yellow lined paper into a ball and added it to a pile of other balls I'd just noticed on the floor.

"Are you going to leave all that trash there? We have a trashcan, you know, right in the space where the oven you haven't put in should be."

"Oven? What? Lena, look, I don't have time for petty stuff right now. I've got to finish working on this case."

"Petty stuff?" I glared. "Oh, us having a place to cook food and a roof with no holes and a toilet that doesn't leak with each flush is petty stuff? I guess where you come from sitting in a dry room that doesn't smell like mildew and eating home-cooked meals are luxuries."

"Home-cooked meals? Are you kidding me? You don't even know how to boil an egg. Since when did you start caring about a working oven?"

Oh. No. He. Didn't.

There have been two times in my life so far when I have had to pray to God Almighty to keep me from slapping someone in the face. For real. The first time was when I was in the sixth grade and a girl named Tyreena Baker spit on my new shoes.

The second time was staring me in the eyeball at that moment. I had never imagined I would feel for Evan what I felt right then. How on earth could this pretty man with the hands and arms that made me swoon, with the goofy smile and luscious lips and the charm and intelligence that would be on any woman's wish list, make me feel nothing but pure rage? I didn't even know where to begin, but I knew it had to end when I realized I had two of the wineglasses Mrs. Wayland picked for our registry in my hands ready to throw across our joke of a kitchen.

"Lena, what are you doing? My mother got us those glasses. Hold on, baby. Okay, you win, let's talk," Evan yelled.

He had been yelling for some time, but it wasn't until his voice reached this new high octave that I registered what he was saying.

A dark calmness took over me. "When I said I needed to talk to you, you pushed me away. When I said something about the oven, you belittled me. But now, all of a sudden, you're interested in hearing me out. Why is that?"

I wanted him to say something, anything else about his mother.

I was ready for the confrontation.

Instead: "You have glasses in your hands, Lena, baby. I don't want you to hurt yourself—or me for that matter. I know you're mad, but do you really want to cut up this pretty face?" He was actually smiling as he rubbed his smooth cheekbones. Smiling like there was no reason for me to feel like slapping him silly.

"Aw, we've had our first fight." Evan carefully took the glasses out of my hands and drew me into a tight embrace. I felt stiff, suffocated in his arms and wondered if he noticed. Apparently, he did not.

"We've officially had our first argument as a married couple. Got it out the way. I didn't mean to talk about your cooking. I know you're trying. Guess I should be trying a little more, too. We're partners in this, and that means for meals, also. I've just been so stressed over this case. It's the first one they're letting me lead, and it's my one chance to show Wernowski and Associates they picked the right man for the job. I don't get the sense I was their first choice, so I've got to really prove to them I can do this, that I belong there." He let go of me and exhaled before settling back into his seat and picking up his pen again. "Whew, I'm glad we got that out and it's done. I love you, Lena." And then he fell silent, writing again.

Did he really think that was it? That this was over? Was I missing something, or did we just *not* talk about everything that was collapsing in my world and in our home, emotionally and literally?

"What is it?" He finally paused to look up at me where I stood with my arms crossed and my foot tapping the floor.

"You actually think this is just about the oven?" I couldn't believe this Georgetown-trained attorney had a brain that was so dysfunctional.

"Oh." He looked back down and resumed scribbling as he inattentively mumbled, "Don't worry, Selena. The toilet and the roof will be fixed soon, too, okay?"

"That's just it, Evan. *Who* is going to be doing all this fixing? Do I have any say as to what happens in my own house? Are you going to be doing all this work, or are you reserving all your energy to have private lunch breaks with your mother's designer in our bedroom?"

With that, he stared at me with a confused, maybe even slightly hurt look on his face.

"Selena, I don't know what you're trying to say, but you need to calm down and be rational. Of course you have complete say about what happens in our house. As far as Genevaise Zuzani is concerned, she is a sixty-three-year-old woman with the deepest voice I've ever heard who doesn't go anywhere without her design team entourage. That lunch break I spent with her was because she showed up at my job with her assistants Xander, Yuri, and Moonlight, and her cat Phillipe wanting me to choose between Industrial Gray and Silver Spectacle paint chips.

"I had to bring her—all of them, including the cat—here, to our bedroom, to avoid further embarrassment at such a conservative law firm as Wernowski and Associates. Do you understand now why I have to work double hard on this case? I can't have the people at the firm thinking I'm a joke, and that scene surely didn't help. I didn't tell you all of this because I've been consumed with this case, and honestly, I forgot. But since we're talking about it now, if you don't want Genevaise working on our house, just tell me."

"I don't want her working on our house. Kunta X will be starting this week." There, it was out.

"Okay." Evan sighed, his attention back to his legal pad. "I'll let my mother know."

That was it? You mean that was all it took? If that was the case, I had to add something else: "Kiona said you told her I like bubbles. What was that about?"

"What?" He looked up at me like I'd said something insane. Maybe I had. Bubbles were the theme of the day for me, it seemed. "Selena, really? I'm trying to work, and you're talking about bubbles."

"I just want to know what you told her about me. About us. And why."

"For real, Selena, I have no idea what you're talking about." He tapped his pen on his notepad. Seeing I hadn't moved or even uncrossed my arms, he added, "Maybe I told her you gave me bubbles when we first met. I don't know."

"All these conversations you're having with Kiona have to stop. I don't want you talking to her without telling me about it."

"Kiona is a non-issue, but okay, don't worry. I have nothing else to say to her." He went back to writing.

"And I don't want her throwing me a baby shower."

"Wha—" He looked up for a second but then went back to scribbling. "Okay, if that's what you want. Get some rest, baby girl. It's been a rough night."

I stood tapping and huffing a few minutes more, unconvinced that all my concerns had really been addressed, but when he said nothing else, I retreated to our bed.

As I closed my eyes and then reopened them due to a new onslaught of nausea, I knew that the queasiness I felt was caused from more than my pregnancy. In the pit of my stomach, I knew all was not over—even if Evan thought it was. If the bubbles were indeed the theme of my day, I felt like something in me—in my marriage—had just popped. We'd just said a lot of things to each other, but really nothing at all.

    Forget trying to stand against the wind. I had to find a way to keep all the wayward bubbles of my life and marriage from floating out of my reach and bursting out of my control.

16

The Friend

Take delight in the LORD, and he will give you the desires of your heart. Commit your way to the LORD; trust in him and he will do this: He will make your righteous reward shine like the dawn, your vindication like the noonday sun.

Psalm 37:4–6 was double underlined and highlighted green in my grandmother's old leather Bible. Scores of bright smiley faces stared down at me as usual from the shower curtain hanging near my head. I appreciated the cheeriness, and I kept this space meticulous.

In the throes of first trimester morning sickness and the confusion that had become my life, the bathroom was now a permanent fixture in my morning routine. It was here that I met the Most High in prayer and Bible study for worship and direction, with my knees on the floor—and my head somewhere near the toilet. My grandmother's Bible lay open on the yellow floor rug, the only solid foundation I had in a world that was quickly spinning out of my control. I was nauseous and tired. And still irritated.

Very irritated.

Only a day or two had passed since our "first fight," as Evan so excitedly called it, and very little had been said between us other than the mumbled nonsense he gave me when I asked when he would break the news of our change in house renovation plans to his mother.

"Don't worry about it, Selena. I'll take care of everything" was his response when I told him I didn't understand what he'd mumbled.

I wanted to feel reassured. I wanted a good cry. And a hug. Maybe my anxious and annoyed feelings weren't feelings at all, but pure hormones, as the pregnancy website I had bookmarked online said. Regardless, I still wanted a hug. Instead, I got a phone call. I raced from my throne room to answer.

"Selena, where have you been?" It was my homegirl, Neeka. "I've been trying to call your cell, your work, your house, and not getting an answer. Your mother told me the baby is okay, thank God. Is everything else alright? Do you need me to set your mother-in-law straight?"

With that, I began sobbing into the phone.

"That's it! What's the woman's address?" Neeka demanded.

"No, no, Neeka. It's not Mrs. Wayland. It's not *just* Mrs. Wayland. It's everything. Everything and everybody is getting on my nerves right now. This house, Evan, his ex—I mean, my new boss."

There was no way I was going to even begin to tell Neeka about Kiona. That would pretty much guarantee I would see both of them on the evening news that night, I was sure of it.

"I'm sorry," I continued. "Don't think I've been avoiding you. I haven't been back to work yet, my cell phone has been mostly off, and I just haven't even felt like looking for the cordless phone here when it rings. Don't take it personally."

"Girl, you and that landline. I don't even know why you bother with it, but, listen, don't apologize. I know the deal. Just tell me why you're crying. Everything *is* fine with the baby, right? I need to know you're okay."

For whatever anybody could say about Neeka—and believe me, there have been many things said—I knew my girl would always have my back more than anyone else in this world. Anyone, that is, except maybe my mother.

Okay, and Evan.

Maybe.

That's a weak maybe, I'm realizing more each day.

"Don't worry about me, Neeka. The baby, as far as I know, is fine. Although truthfully, I think I'm going to stay scared until I'm holding little Boo-Bear in my arms."

That was the first time I had openly expressed my pregnancy fears and also the first time I had said out loud the little nickname I had given the baby growing inside me.

"But like I said, don't worry about me. I'm fine. Just hormonally off, if anything, you know?"

"Okay. Just checking. If there's anything I can help with, including a trip out to the Wayland Estate, please let me know, girl. On another note, I've got some exciting news to brighten your day."

I knew that tone. "What's his name?"

"Seriously, Selena, I know I've come to you over the years with one boy after another, but this time, I've found a man. Not just any man, but the man I know I'm going to marry."

"Marry? This is serious. I don't think I've ever heard that word come out of your mouth. Who is this lucky someone? And I hope you've known him longer than twenty-four hours."

"Give me some credit, Selena. I wouldn't be throwing out the 'm' word for the first time ever after only twenty-four hours. It's been forty-eight."

We both let out a good laugh, and I realized how much I had

missed the sound and feel of glee. Only Neeka could do this for me, considering how bad the last few days had been.

"Okay, so tell me about your future husband." I tried to picture what kind of man would be able to finally pin down Neeka.

"Remember that restaurant you were telling me about in Roland Park where Evan took you for brunch on your last birthday, the one with the crab-and-shrimp omelets?"

I smiled at the memory then remembered Evan's black elbows and ex-fiancée. "Yeah. What about it?"

I was there Wednesday for brunch when this fine brother in a suit was seated alone at the table next to me. Well, he asked to borrow the saltshaker from my table, and we didn't stop talking until the restaurant closed at three. We spent the rest of the day talking on the phone, then yesterday, we spent most of the day at the Inner Harbor on one of those cheesy boat cruises I used to joke about. It was actually a lot of fun. We talked, danced, laughed, and enjoyed the all-you-can-eat crab buffet.

Evan and I had met in a restaurant. I ignored the shot of pain that pierced me.

"*Ummm*, that's a lot of free time for a Thursday. Does this brother have a job?"

"Girl, he owns an investment company. I Googled him, of course, and discovered he was featured in *Baltimore* magazine as one of the top fifty eligible bachelors in the area. But that's beside the point. Selena, this man makes me feel special and beautiful, and we haven't even kissed yet. And to be honest with you, I'm in no rush. The mere pleasure of his company has been fulfilling. He actually seems to be genuinely interested in what I have to say."

"So, basically, he has a few screws loose in the head." I couldn't resist.

"Selena, I'm going to get you. But seriously, I want the four of us to go out—you, Evan, me, and him. Sunday afternoon. I'll text you the deets. As quiet as it's kept, I value your opinion. You got a good man for yourself, and I need you to feel this one out for me. I really think he could be The One. I wasn't even looking for him, so I want to make sure I'm not overlooking something major. On the plus side, he's got a thing for Jesus like you do."

"Well, take it slow, Neeka. I'm happy for you, but let's see what his issues are first before we start picking out wedding gowns." After just learning about Evan's skeletons—and this following a few years of dating him—I was a little suspicious of males in general. "What's his name anyway?"

"Peyton. Peyton Anderson."

Peyton. Peyton. Why does that name sound familiar? I wanted to summon a face, a memory, but nothing came. Pregnancy brain in action, I guessed.

"Well, Peyton it is. I'll get Evan on board, and we'll go out soon, I promise. Believe me, I really *want* to meet the man who's got you off your game, girl." We both laughed as we ended the call.

So, my girl Neeka might be ready to settle down. "God, You're showing me right now anything is possible." I shook my head as I bolted back to the bathroom to finish my morning business.

I broke the news about Neeka and her new man to Evan when he finally came home at 10:30 that night.

"That's great, Selena. I'm happy for her," he murmured to me without looking up from his law books. "We can meet Neeka and Peter Sunday evening for dinner. That's fine."

"Not Peter. His name is... Pierre? Pierre Abbottson? Something like that. I can't remember his name."

"Yeah, sure. That's fine," he mumbled.

"And Evan?" I had to know. "Did you talk to your mom about the house?"

"Yeah, sure. Don't worry, Selena. Everything's taken care of. Now, if you want me to go out on Sunday, you have to let me finish working here." He planted a big wet kiss on my arm before turning back to his work.

"Finish your work soon, babe. I'll be upstairs waiting." I blew a kiss and headed upstairs. Two hours later, I was still waiting. I gave up and fell into an uneasy sleep.

17

The Poet

Well, I guess Evan really did talk to The Mother because bright and early Saturday morning, I was awakened by a familiar, alcohol-infused voice.

"*Knock, knock.* Hello. It's a quarter to eight.
I have arrived, my young sister, to demonstrate,
The skill of my hands and the sweat of my brow,
To transform your house into a home that will wow.
Your abode at the moment is busted and broken.
It will be whole soon. The Poet has spoken."

Kunta X was all smiles, smoke, and liquor when I opened the door for him. He wore a paint-stained one-piece carpenter's suit that had a screwdriver and hammer in one pocket and a forty in another.

He must have followed my eyes because he quickly added:
"Don't be alarmed. Have no fear.
The rest of my tools are in my truck, my dear."
The rest of his tools, I was soon to discover,
Were three more forties, a drill, and a picture of his dead mother.

Good gracious, it's contagious!
Now I can't seem to get out of my mind,
The voice, the smell, the way the man rhymed.

Anyway, I wish I could say I was comforted to see my residential disaster zone at the beginning stages of help, but how would any person in their right mind feel if the man hired to do the helping was pouring a libation of malt liquor to his dead mother in the dried-up flower patch in front of one's house? Kunta X offered a sonnet about how calling on the ancestors for their blessing, wisdom, and help was the only proper way to begin repairing a home.

All I know is that in the name of Jesus, I better not see some spirits walking through my hallways. With all the mess and broken appliances and leaks and holes going on in my house, the last thing I needed added to the mix was dead people.

Kunta X, like my Grandma Verdine, came from that generation of black folk who would talk about seeing deceased relatives knocking on their windows and standing at the foot of their bed like it was perfectly fine, normal, and nothing to fear. I don't mean no harm, but if I ever saw my aunt Olivine or my uncle Joe—and they were my favorites—staring at me as I'm trying to drift off to sleep, I'm liable to start cussing. I'm still traumatized to this day from my great-grandfather's last words to me as I cried at his hospital bed when I was thirteen years old.

"Don't worry, Selena, I'll come back and visit you."

Oh. Heck. No. Don't need the visit. A browse through the family photo album will do me just fine, ya know?

Anyway, as I silently pleaded the blood of Jesus over my home, my husband, my baby, and myself, Evan finally decided to get out of bed. He stopped in the doorway of the kitchen where I was watching Kunta X fool around with a measuring tape and write notes on the back of a candy bar wrapper.

"Good morning, Evan." I forced a smile as I tried to read his face. "This is Kunta X, my father's good friend and handyman extraordinaire." Hey, doesn't the Bible say speak those things that aren't as if they are, or something like that? You can't blame a sister for trying. "He's going to be helping us with the house."

"Greetings, young warrior, young African chief.
The Elder is here to help dispose of your grief.
The burdens of this house are no longer yours.
I am here to repair, to rebuild, and restore.
Unfortunately, I did not foresee
How heavy, how intense this burden would be.
There is much to consider. I must ponder this mess.
The Poet must think. The Poet must rest."

And with that introduction, Kunta X collapsed into one of the kitchen chairs, pushed a stack of Evan's law books and papers off another seat, and put up his feet. He opened a small flask of malt liquor, threw back his head, and guzzled down the brew with a loud burp.

Quivering, I turned to face Evan who had never left his post in the doorway. His eyes were wide, his mouth agape, his feet frozen.

"I can call my mother right now," I whispered. "I am sure she'll understand our decision to get our own contractor." And even if she didn't, I was prepared for the showdown with my parents. Enough was enough. "Evan, what do you think?"

"Man..." He finally spoke his first words of the day. "That's a deep brother right there. So, tell me, Mr. The Poet—" Evan scrambled to an empty seat at the table, knocking over the last pile of his books in the way.

"Just call me X." Kunta X crossed his propped-up feet.

"X. Cool. Like Malcolm." Evan nodded slowly. "Tell me, X, do these rhymes just come to you while you're talking, or do you have pre-planned phrases in your head?"

"Youngblood, the power of the spoken word

Must be felt, not just heard."

"Deep. That's so deep. You remind me of a sociology professor I had back in undergrad. Wow."

I left the kitchen to lie down. And when I returned two hours later to fix a quick lunch, The Poet and The Fool were still sitting there, engrossed in a lively conversation about crickets and the moon.

In fact, they talked the rest of the day. And when Kunta X returned the next morning, Evan settled back into dialogue with him after only two window beams had been measured.

"Selena," my mother chirped into the phone Sunday afternoon, "thanks again for letting Kunta X do the work at the house. I'm not even mad that you missed church this morning. I'm sure you had a lot to go over with him. You'll never know how much it means to me and your dad that you're letting us take care of this instead of your mother-in-law. I know the house is going to look great once it's all done."

"Yeah. Thank you, Mom."

Really, what was I supposed to say?

18

The Uh-Oh

By Sunday night, I was ready to go out and meet Neeka and her new man. Even Evan had finally pried himself out of his seat next to Kunta X to prepare for our double date. I had already decided Baby Boo-Bear and I were well enough to return to work Monday morning, and a night out with a good friend was just the thing I needed before D-day.

Kiona Tandy was waiting at News U Need AM, I knew.

But I didn't have to think about that right now. I was dressed to impress in a cute little black number I knew wouldn't get much more play once the maternity clothes became a necessity. Evan looked good himself when he emerged from the bathroom, a light cloud of seductive-smelling cologne following him. He noticed the way I stared at him and gave a delicious smile. Was this the hormones at work in me? I felt like ripping the clothes off the man like a four-year-old with a Christmas present.

I caressed his hand as we entered the downtown jazz establishment that had been a favorite of Neeka's for as long as I could remember. My affection must have been an extra confidence booster for an already confident man, I noted, as Evan seemed to walk like he owned the world. That's why I was taken aback at the sudden change in his gait as the maître d' walked us to the table where Neeka and her date were waiting. Evan slowed down so fast I felt like I was nearly dragging him the last ten feet to the table.

"Oh, my goodness. Girl, look at you." Neeka was all smiles as she quickly stood and gave me a hug and a quick peck on my cheek. "You are glowing. I'm so glad you and my godbaby are fine. Hey Evan, are you going to help my girl with her coat and chair or what?"

I looked over at my husband who stood frozen in place with what looked like a deer-caught-in-headlights expression.

"Evan, are you okay?" I asked. Something truly wasn't right.

"I know what it is."

I followed the tenor voice to the man standing behind Neeka. Now, she had told me he was a successful businessman and a good listener, but girlfriend neglected to tell me he was also the second sexiest man in Baltimore (behind my Evan, of course). With eyes dark as chocolate, caramel skin smooth and bright, and a smile that would make you forget your momma's name, I had to keep myself from staring and drooling. The focus was on Evan, I reminded myself, and why he had suddenly become paralyzed and speechless.

"I know exactly what it is. Evan's never seen me with my dreads. How have you been, man?" Neeka's date shook his golden mane and reached out to Evan for a fist bump. Evan came back to earth, threw on a smile, and returned the greeting.

"Okay, so I take it you two already know each other?" Neeka beamed as we all went for our seats.

"Yeah, me and Evan go way back," her date continued.

Evan let out a giggle that sounded somewhere between a snort and a pig squeal as he flashed a grin and nearly tripped into his chair. What the heck was wrong with him?

"Good. Well, Selena, meet Peyton Anderson." Neeka waved her arms like she was revealing a prize on a gameshow.

Only this was a game I wasn't ready for and already knew I was on the losing side.

Peyton. The name registered. *My mother never knew Kiona was married, and my old friend Peyton never knew I was the man who took his wife...* Evan's confession from days earlier.

And now it was my turn to become dizzy, sick, and dumbfounded. "Uh, well, uh, nice to meet you, Peyton. Yes, Peyton. I've heard so much...I mean, good things really...about you. Let me sit down." I was so disoriented as Evan pulled out a seat for me, I almost ended up on the floor.

Neeka looked at both Evan and me like we were unstable. Even Peyton had an expression of concern.

Get it together, Selena, I told myself. I didn't want to embarrass or offend my best friend at such a pivotal moment in her life. But Neeka was in too good of a mood to let our obvious awkwardness ruin the evening.

"You two truly were made for each other." She laughed.

I didn't miss the warm exchange of glances between her and Peyton, and I knew then this man wasn't leaving any of our lives any time soon.

Evan and I ate in near silence as Neeka and Peyton talked to each other about almost everything—from their childhoods to the present moment. Nothing was said about exes, fiancées, adultery, or other misfortunes.

We finished the evening watching the two share a large ice cream sundae. Evan and I said we were both too full to eat dessert, but I knew the real reason neither of us could stomach another bite.

I had to admit, I'd never seen Neeka look as alive and at peace as she did that night.

And I'd never seen Evan look so terrified.

19

The Heck?!

I hated that Evan's past was a weight on my present. I hated feeling like I had to walk on eggshells around my best friend's newfound happiness for a transgression I didn't commit or even have a part of. I hated that I couldn't come up with words to even tell Evan how I felt, or that he may not even listen if I had the words.

And, most of all, I hated that Kiona Tandy was my new boss.

Evan and I simply didn't talk about it or talk about her. That's what he wanted. And I hadn't been able to sort out my feelings or response to his request.

"Welcome back, Mrs. Wayland." The words were kind, but the tone sounded more like a snarling growl coming from between Kiona's barely opened yet somehow still smiling lips. "I had your team take on extra shares of work in your absence, so it's only fair now that you handle the overflow waiting on your desk."

And that was how my Monday morning began.

The day would only get worse, I soon discovered as I noted first the chilly reception I received from the few coworkers I had befriended in my short time at the radio station. Then I saw the "overflow" on my desk. Well, let's just say Niagara Falls has less of an overflow than what Kiona had waiting for me.

I thought my former boss had it in for me. I was wrong. Compared to the demands Kiona typed up in a memo tacked next to my pictures, my life before her was peaches and cream. I couldn't make sense of this woman. One moment she was playing nice wanting to plan my baby shower (not happening), and the next moment she seemed intent on making my life a living hell. The common denominator in her choice of actions was who was around. If Mrs. Wayland or Evan weren't there, I was left to fend against her controlled fury. I spent all of Monday morning, afternoon, and a good part of the evening, typing, making numerous phone calls, preparing reports, reading reports, scrubbing floors, washing windows, dusting... Okay, maybe I'm exaggerating a little, but I'm not lying when I say I didn't have time for a single break, lunch or otherwise, in the ten hours and seventeen minutes I clocked that Monday of my return.

Kiona was still at her desk when I left. I could hear her trying out various tones and inflections as she repeated the line, "This is Kiona Tandy with the entertainment tea. Here, have a slurp, but be careful. It's hot."

I rolled my eyes as I gathered my things, wondering if I should remind her that even if her entertainment segment was approved by the parent company, she'd still be the producer and not the radio personality. The hosts on the station were long timers who weren't going to stop blabbing and lecturing on serious news and politics anytime soon. And the programmers would rather play binaural beats and infomercials all night over tabloid fodder and celebrity gossip.

And her wishful tagline was stupid.

I wanted to say all these things, but I kept my mouth shut.

Our eyes met in a mutual glare as the elevator doors closed with me inside.

Not going to lie, the thought of quitting was ever present. If I left, though, how could I keep what felt like a necessary eye on the woman who clearly wanted my man? Bringing up Kiona felt like a taboo topic with Evan, and I didn't want to break the peace. I didn't want to know what he thought about me working with her because, well, what would it mean if he even had an opinion about it?

That said, I was going to win this battle.

Little did I know there was a bigger war waiting for me at my home.

***

When I got to my house at quarter after seven, I was both surprised and relieved to see Evan sitting in the living room, a wide grin on his handsome face.

"You're home early." I pecked him on the cheek. Not wanting to mess up his obviously good mood, I ran my fingers through his jet-black curly hair and nestled beside him.

"Hey, Lena." He sounded excited. A legal pad lay on his lap, a pen rested between his fingers.

"You seem happy. How's the case coming?" I massaged his temples as he closed his eyes and gleefully dug his head into my shoulder.

"It's over. All done."

"Really?" I sat up as a wave of relief washed over me. I felt like our home life could finally resume.

"Yup. The trial was over at 10:30 this morning. I've been home ever since."

"Really?" I relaxed back next to him, glad to see him so happy. "So how does it feel to be finished with the first really big case of your career?"

"Exhilarating."

He looked so excited I momentarily forgot the burdens of my

day. "And, more importantly, how does it feel to be on the road to becoming a world-renowned entertainment lawyer?"

"Couldn't tell you, Lena."

"I know the feeling must be overwhelming. It's going to take some time, I'm sure, but you're officially on the path to your dreams. How amazing." I had never felt prouder of him.

"No, I mean, I don't know the feeling. I didn't win today." He was still smiling—beaming, really.

"Okay...what?"

"I lost the case, Selena. I mean, I really lost. It was terrible. It was supposed to be an easy, open and shut formality, so minor the press didn't even bother to pick it up. So minor Razi didn't even have to be there himself. That's how bottom shelf this issue was. I totally crashed and burned.

"The judge said he'd never seen such a... How'd he put it? 'A monstrous failure of legal preparation.' Before he gave his ruling, he questioned my intellect, my understanding of the judiciary system, and my common sense right there in front of the entire courtroom. Right in front of Razi's manager. I'm so glad Razi *wasn't* there. But you know who else wasn't there? The plaintiff. The guy suing Razi for copyright infringement didn't even come. He just had his attorney show up with a vinyl briefcase, wearing a cheap orange suit. It's like the plaintiff didn't even think he would win, didn't even try, but I blew it."

A smile surprisingly still filled his face as he continued. "Selena, I lost the defining case of my career to a stack of old, wrinkled papers in the hands of a lawyer who looked like a pimp from a 1970s Blaxploitation movie. I mean, brown fedora, huge gold pinky ring, and all. At least, Razi wasn't there in person to watch me flop his case, but Wernowski himself of Wernowski and Associates *was* there to witness the whole thing."

What? "Oh, Evan. This is a lot. I'm sorry. I'm really, truly sorry."

Did I mention he was still smiling? I was sorry and also beyond confused.

"Don't be sorry, Selena. Really, it's okay." His pearly whites radiated.

"Is your job... I mean, you didn't get, well, you weren't—"

"Fired? Oh yes, I was most definitely fired." Evan nodded, his head bobbing up and down like it was on a short-stringed yo-yo. "Wernowski chewed me out in front of Razi's manager to save the face of the firm. He chewed and spat me out with such anger, Razi's manager felt sorry for me. He pitied me. Pulled me aside before he left and gave me his card with his personal cell number. He said their team may consider giving me another chance to represent Razi down the road again once I have more experience and to reach out once I do. Well, he said this probably out of respect for my mother. He's always happy to help her with her charity events, so I guess I'm officially one of my mom's charities for him to help."

"Oh, Evan, I'm so sorry." I was stunned really.

"And speaking of charity, I'm going to go ahead and volunteer for that pro bono law clinic downtown that helps creatives. That will keep my law skills active while I pursue what's next for me."

"Oh, that's good, I mean, I guess. Razi's manager kind of still likes you *and* you are already mapping out a plan for what's next. You're going to be okay. We're going to be okay. No, not just okay. We'll be good." I tried to relax, but something in Evan's beaming eyes and too-happy smile kept me from easing back in my seat. "Like the Bible says, everything works together for good." A verse from one of my early morning quiet time sessions kept repeating itself in my mind and found its way on my lips, more for my comfort than his, I admitted to myself.

"You are exactly right, Selena," Evan boomed a little too loudly. "Everything does work out for good. The loss today opened my eyes to my real destiny, and for the first time in my life, I can't wait for tomorrow to come so I can begin my new career."

"New career? Wait. You're a lawyer. You passed the bar. You had a bad day and may need to reset for a moment, but you still have a career. What do you mean by a 'new career?'"

"Selena, you're going to love this." He giggled. I looked again at the papers in his hands and noticed for the first time the rectangular black box at his feet. "

"What am I going to love? What are you talking about? And what is all this stuff?" Squiggly black lines and dots filled the pages he held. I reached for the black box, not realizing it was open. Wooden black pieces with silver buttons fell out and rolled onto our scrap of a carpet.

"Wait, Selena." His smile dropped. "Be careful with that. That clarinet is made from grenadilla wood and cost twenty-five hundred dollars."

"Clarinet? Twenty-five hundred dollars? Evan? What is going on?"

"I was going to wait to tell you about it once I finished my first song, but what the heck?" His goofy grin came back as he stood and gave a playful bow. "Introducing... Evan-Essence, the Clarinetist. Like the word *evanescence*? Get it?"

"What?"

"I'm not just any old kind of clarinetist, either, Lena. I'm going to talk to X about touring the open mic poetry circuit and letting me play my smooth notes behind him. I figure once I get my name out there, other poets will want to use me as their backup, too, and before you know it, I'll be so big, I'll have a record deal. My music itself will be the poetry. Maybe X and I will even open for Razi one day. Can you see it?" His eyes looked distant, as if he was imagining a cheering crowd.

"Uh, Evan, I didn't even know you could play the clarinet." Okay, really, where was I supposed to begin?

"I was first chair in fourth grade. My band teacher, Ms. DiPasquale, gave me a silver star for my scales, and she even let me play a song I made up at the spring concert that year. It was called 'Above the Solar Sun.'" He said this with the pride of an award-winning maestro. "I admit, Selena, I didn't remember a single thing about playing, but I found some YouTube videos of this man who gives all these tutorials and clarinet lessons online, and it all came back to me. Listen to this, Lena."

He had that woodwind put together and was screeching out what sounded like a cross between fingernails across a blackboard and a subway train scraping along metal tracks, all before I could go online to look up a local psychiatrist.

Surely the man needed to be medicated. Or maybe I did. Maybe I was the one viewing the world through insane eyes. Have a broken house? Have a baby on the way? Great. Sign up for volunteer work and start taking kazoo lessons. Life falling apart? Wonderful. Use your law degree to join a marching band.

"Okay, Evan, we really need to talk." Had I really married a fool? Or was this some type of psychotic break I was witnessing? What signs had I missed? I wanted to throw up and could feel the bubbles stirring in my stomach.

Bubbles.

"Selena—" Evan had the nerve to still be smiling—"that night we first met was magical. Remember the band playing after the lecture, that saxophonist? The stimulating conversation around us? The art? The soul? Somewhere I've gone off track trying to be all Johnnie Cochran when really I think I'm supposed to be more John Coltrane. I need to reclaim myself. For us." His eyes were wild. Mine couldn't blink.

"When I left the courthouse today, I prayed for a sign on how to begin again. I came home, thinking about going solo with my law career, which led me to thinking about actual musical solos, and, then, I turned on the TV. *SpongeBob SquarePants* was on, and would you believe it? Squidward was playing his clarinet. I know he's just a grumpy animated octopus, but it showed me how anything or anyone can be used to bring a message of purpose to this world."

"What the—"

"Don't you see, Selena?" He interrupted and clapped like a thunderbolt had shot through him. "I prayed for a sign, and I got it. And when I went to the music store, this clarinet was the featured sale item. Confirmation. I know it sounds bizarre, but can't you see how it all lines up? I don't want you to worry about a thing. This is a new and different original act. I'm going to practice and perfect it and make this work and then get out there on stages and places like where we met. I promise I won't be on the road longer than a week at a time so I can spend as much time as possible with you and the baby."

And then he picked the clarinet up again and began what sounded like a cat mating call.

"Evan!" I snatched it out of his hands and leaped to my feet. "Have you lost your mind? I mean, really, have you gone insane?"

"Selena, I—"

I stuck the reed in my mouth and blew as loud and as hard as I could. I didn't even want to hear his voice.

"What the devil is going on in here?" A smooth alto woman's voice came from behind me. Mrs. Madelyn Ernestine Wayland. *Is that a key in her hand?*

"I was about to knock at your door, but when I heard what sounded like a flock of geese honking in here, I let myself in with the key Evan gave me. I didn't think you would hear me over that awful noise. Selena, whatever are you doing?" She was looking at *me* like I was unsound.

"Yes, let me tell you exactly what I'm doing, Mrs. Wayland. Your lovely son—"

"Oh, Mom—" Evan cut me off — "I'm so glad you're here. I have exciting news. I left the law firm today to pursue a full-time music career. Why aim to represent singers and artists when I can just be one? Selena was just showing her support for me. I'm so grateful and thankful for her belief in my dreams. Hasn't God blessed me with a wonderful wife?"

"*What?*" both Mrs. Wayland and I shrieked together.

"Evan, surely you didn't leave your wonderful, well-paying, and esteemed position to follow an outlandish fantasy? This was your idea, wasn't it, Selena?" Mrs. Wayland hissed my name and glared at me with pure hate and anger.

"Oh no, Evan." My eyes were only on him, not ready to even begin addressing the venom his mother was spewing at me. "No, sir. Don't you even try to pin this foolishness on me." I couldn't believe my ears. "This is all *your* doing. You were fired and I am truly sorry about that, but you can't play a single musical note. I would never encourage you to do something as ridiculous as the plan *you* just came up with."

"Fired?" The brown of Mrs. Wayland's face drained into an ashen gray. She thrust a hand onto the wall as if to keep her balance.

"I don't call it a firing. I call it a life reframing," Evan's jaw clenched. "And don't be so modest, Selena." He looked at me with a supplicating smile before turning back to his mother. "Mom, my beautiful, supportive wife came up with the whole idea. She wants me to pursue my true heart's desire. You don't know how much it means to me that Selena has my back." There was pleading in his eyes when he looked back at me.

But this situation called for no mercy. I crossed my arms and turned to stand next to his mother and face him alongside her. Mrs. Wayland was silent as she stared at me and then back at his hurt face. And then:

"Oh honey, Evan, I don't know what happened, but if this is really something you want to do, how can I not support your dreams? I believe you have whatever it takes to be successful in whatever you do. If this fails," she said, turning to glare at me, "then we'll all know whose fault it is, won't we, Selena? I hope, young lady, you know what you're doing getting my son to leave his job."

"Evan was fired." I crossed my arms and then uncrossed them seeing a searing pain shoot across his face.

Mrs. Wayland shook her head as if was impossible for the words *fired* and *Evan* to exist in the same sentence. "My husband and I have sacrificed so much to get Evan to where he is, but if he wants my support with this new dream you've got him chasing, how can I not support him? First, the house, and now...this." Her voice trailed off.

I realized then we would always be on opposite sides of the battle line. The only reason she was going along was because Evan said I supported him. And she wasn't going to be outdone by his wife whom she clearly disdained.

"Evan, you know I will stand behind *you* one hundred percent. I–I have to go home now." She choked up, and I saw genuine sorrow and heartbreak in her eyes as she turned to leave.

As the door closed behind her, Evan tried to pull me into an embrace. "Thanks, Selena, for going along. It would hurt my mother's heart if she knew how bad I failed in court today. Thank you, baby. I—"

"What about my heart? And what about our baby? You know we have a child on the way, and diapers aren't free. Do you really think this is the time to be playing around with a clarinet? I'm all for you wanting to chase some dreams on the side and do volunteer work, but my job alone isn't going to hold us up. You lost your *good* job today, and you want to watch clarinet videos on YouTube as a next step? Have you lost your freaking mind?" I pushed his arms off me, glared into his face, and silently asked Jesus to keep my lips from speaking evil.

He looked confused and then he smiled again. "It's all going to work out. I promise."

"So, you're going to call Wernowski tomorrow, tell him you were ill today and not at your best, which is obviously true, and see if he'll let you back with a mentor or something, right? You can tell them Razi's manager hasn't given up on you." My voice was slow and steady. "Or, you can call your godmother and see if she has any connections at another firm. Evan, which one of these plans are you going to pursue?"

His smile turned into an ice-cold grimace. "I told you my plan." He turned his back to me and began screeching into the clarinet again, snapping a finger every now and then.

All I could do was storm up the steps, slam the bedroom door behind me, curl up in the bed, cry, and listen to what surely sounded like the migraine-inducing soundtrack of my life.

20

The Debut

"Welcome to The Lerato Lounge. My name is Brother Sango, and I want to welcome you to our home here," a white man in a black dashiki and a tiger-print turban shouted from the small platform acting as a stage. "*Lerato* is an African name that means 'love,' and that's exactly what we do here on Fridays' open mic nights. We love on each other and on the acts that grace our stage." Brother Sango inhaled from a hand-rolled cigarette and tucked a blond strand of hair back under his turban before continuing. "Hit it, Rasheed."

A man with the longest, thickest dreadlocks I'd ever seen began beating a pair of bongos, his head swaying to a beat only he seemed to make sense of. The compact room of small tables and barstools around me was filled with people of all shades of brown, some visibly high or drunk, most laughing or chatting loudly, all seemingly ignoring the little white man with the big animal-print turban hopping around on the stage. A doorway on the side of the room opened from time to time, and a thick veil of herbal smoke and incense escaped with every door swing.

I was so confused.

In the dim, hazy light of the basement club, I wasn't sure if I felt any safer than I had waiting in the trash-filled alley for a sumo wrestler–sized bouncer to let Evan and me in.

"Selena, thank you so much for coming. You'll never know what this means to me." The Fool was sitting next to me, licking his chapped lips and wetting the reed of his clarinet in his mouth.

"You'll never know what this means to *me*," I murmured back as I clutched my handbag closer to me. I knew I looked out of place, naïve, scared.

I was.

"Father, forgive me, for I have sinned." I felt like praying, wondering how far I was supposed to take this supportive wife business. The only reason I came was because Evan told me his mother was also coming.

I guess the war went two ways.

Oh, where was Sister Corrine Knight, the pastor's wife, when I needed her? I remembered her words to me that fateful Sunday of my breakdown. *"And honey, you've only had Mrs. in front of your name for less than three months. You ain't seen nothing yet."* Oh, how right she was, I shook my head at the thought of my newlywed innocence. I had no idea marrying someone truly meant marrying their meltdowns as well. I made a mental note to catch up on the video blog she kept on the church's website, on a tab for the women's ministry. Maybe I could find some direction, 'cause, baby, this wasn't it.

Evan and I had become one—one unit of measurement, one stamped package. We were bound on the same path forever, plunging forward to the same destination. For better or for worse. And we hadn't even made it to our first anniversary. What was waiting at the fifth year? The tenth? The twenty-seventh?

I fought to hold back visions of Evan and me gray-haired with canes, living in a rainforest, scraping larvae off a tree for sustenance, dancing in the music of the wind while Kunta X recited some bad poem about morning dew, monkeys, and the circle of life.

"You will not have to fight this battle. Take up your positions; stand firm and see the deliverance the Lord will give you ..." A verse from 2 Chronicles chapter twenty I had read that morning in my "throne room" quiet time cut through my thoughts. Sitting next to my smiley faced shower curtain, I had opened right up to the story of King Jehoshaphat's victorious battle against three armies. Truly, I felt like I was fighting three armies: Evan, Mrs. Wayland, and Kiona the scheming ex-fiancée. King Jehoshaphat sent singers out before his warriors. Was I supposed to start singing behind my simple husband's bad notes? Drown out his performance with my questionable alto voice?

No, Dummy.

Okay, Jesus didn't really call me a dummy, but I felt like he was leading me to sing a song of praise to Him for how he was going to show up in the craziness that had become my life. So, I sung a quiet song—in my head of course. Whatever Evan was about to do on that stage was guaranteed to be enough torture for the drugged-out crowd surrounding us. My feeble vocals would only put them over the edge. And that probably wouldn't be a good thing.

Brother Sango picked up the microphone again. "To start out the night, we're going to have a dance by Glitter Greg." He left the platform with an exaggerated bow.

A slightly enthused applause came from the crowd as a barefoot, muscular, bronze-skinned man wearing a bright yellow t-shirt and denim cut-off shorts slid leisurely onto the stage. I waited for the music to begin, but there was none, save for a few random rolls of the bongos from Rasheed who stood to the side. Glitter Greg slowly removed tubes of glitter glue from his shirtsleeve and color by color streaked the glittery goo onto his face, arms, and legs. The crowd *ooh*ed and *ahh*ed in wonder and glee with each new stroke. Was I missing something?

Evan leaned into me with a solemn look on his face.

Praise Jesus, I thought. *My husband must finally be seeing the error of his way and coming back to his senses.*

This was not a place for sane people. It was definitely not a place for a Georgetown-trained lawyer with a baby on the way to start a new music career playing an instrument he had just picked up after a near twenty-year hiatus. His last public performance had been a spring concert in fourth grade.

I wondered how Glitter Greg's movements would have interpreted "Above the Solar Sun," Evan's fourth grade masterpiece.

Lord Jesus.

Everything in me was collapsing.

"X told me this was a deep place. He wasn't kidding, Selena. He should be here any minute now. I feel so, so... Don't you feel this vibe, baby?"

So much for sanity.

I thought of his parents grappling to accept this new reality of their esteemed lawyer son. Then again, Dr. Wayland seemed too distant to care, at least not more than what the bottom-line cost of this "adventure," as he termed it, would be for him. He seemed to believe this was a passing phase and Evan would be back in the courthouse before any real damage was done to his professional reputation. Mrs. Wayland on the other hand? Man, I tried to imagine what Mrs. Wayland's reaction would be whenever she made it past the bouncer standing at the alleyway door.

I didn't have to imagine long. The side room door—the door that led to the room with the distinctly scented smoke and incense aromas—swung open, and a white-suited and white-gloved gentlewoman appeared, red peeking through her otherwise brown face. Mrs. Wayland had come in the wrong way, and whatever sights and sounds that accompanied that marijuana den she'd just walked through had the woman glaring right at me. I watched as she maneuvered through the maze of tables and stools until she reached our table. Her eyes never left mine.

"Mom! You made it. Thanks for coming." Evan seemed oblivious to his mother's horror. She seemed oblivious to him, staring only at me. Murder was in her eyes.

"Selena—" she started but then froze as her eyes suddenly caught notice of Glitter Greg on stage. By now, his entire face, arms, and legs were a mass of blue, green, red, orange, and purple shimmering goop. Her red face turned a deeper shade of crimson as Evan pulled up a stool for her. She nearly fell onto it.

"All that money we spent at Georgetown," she murmured over and over.

I felt sorry for her. I felt her pain. It was my own. I almost reached out for her hand. Almost. And then another voice took over:

"Oh, Evan, this is wonderful. Are you ready? Are you nervous?"

Kiona Tandy.

Where had this heifer come from? Now it was my turn to glare. I turned to face her tall, statuesque frame and watched her extend her slender manicured hands onto Evan's shoulder for a gentle massage.

Oh. No. She. Didn't. Where is Neeka Mack when you need her? I imagined what my best friend would have said—done—if she had witnessed Kiona's blatant flirtatious gesture. But then again, if Neeka knew about Kiona, then her new prospect, Peyton, would surely find out Evan was the evil man who stole his dear ex-wife. And Lord knows, I don't think I could handle a drop more of drama right now. Forget how Evan would feel. And Mrs. Wayland for that matter.

I'm with child, you know. There's only but so much drama a pregnant woman can take.

How did my life get so complicated? I looked back up at the

stage where Glitter Greg stood momentarily frozen with his eyes glued to the ceiling.

Where had I gone wrong in life?

"Evan, I'm so proud of you, reaching for your dreams. Let me know any way I can help, especially with Selena's delicate condition. We don't want her to overextend herself." Kiona flashed me a phony smile. I wanted to smack it right off her face. She took a seat next to Mrs. Wayland.

Why, oh why couldn't I be as strong and as vocal as my girl Neeka? This beauty wanted *my* man. I needed to stand up to her, tell her off, or something. Was prayer really enough for this situation? I wondered. I looked over at Evan who was grinning at Glitter Greg on the stage like the Alvin Ailey dancers were performing their signature *Revelations* suite.

Did *I* even want this man?

Mrs. Wayland's evolution of color had turned from light brown to bright crimson to ghostly pale. Real talk: I didn't even know black people could turn so many shades. Meanwhile, up on the stage, Glitter Greg had pulled out banners and streamers with all manner of butterflies, fish, and football helmets painted on them. Instead of twirling them gracefully through the air, he threw them across the stage in anger, spitting on them, grunting, and tearing them apart in a frenzy that reminded me of a fight Neeka had once gotten into with a girl name Vaszsharina Pope when we were fourteen.

"Deep, my brother. Deep. Let's give Glitter Greg a hand." Brother Sango was back on stage, and the crowd of drunks and addicts and Evan stood to a rousing ovation. Glitter Greg was too busy stomping in rage on the streamers to take notice of the applause. Two men had to come out of the "smoke room" to carry him off the stage.

"And now, for our next act of the evening." Brother Sango looked over the hazy room with glazed eyes. "Please welcome to the stage our own Master Poet, Kunta X, and his new protégé, Evan-Essence the Clarinetist." The crowd resumed its chatter and laughter. Evan scanned the room for the missing Kunta X then sprung to his feet.

"Oh well, I guess it's just me for now. I'll start, and X should be here soon."

"Go get 'em, Tackle," Kiona cooed and clapped like a maniac. I narrowed my eyes at the nickname and wondered at the history behind it.

Evan leaped onto the stage and moistened the clarinet's reed a few times before grabbing the microphone. "Hey, y'all." Nobody was listening but me, Kiona, and a horrified Mrs. Wayland. "Thank you for having me tonight. I'm so honored to be here," Evan continued, fingering the instrument. Even Brother Sango paid him no attention. Instead, he was engaged in a hearty conversation with a group of people sitting at a table near the front of the room.

"Anyways," Evan said, smiling, "doesn't look like X is here yet, so I'm just going to go with the flow…and let the vibes flow from my clarinet." And then he put that reed in his mouth and honked.

Now, I don't know what made me think a miracle would happen and the screeches and squeals I'd been hearing all week would suddenly turn into a melodious composition just because he was standing on stage, but there my husband, Evan, was, standing in the spotlight, sweating profusely and playing notes that sounded like a *National Geographic* special on dying wildcats.

I was completely embarrassed for him and frightened for me and my baby's future, but I had to admit, it's hard not to find some level of respect for somebody so willing to put it all out on the table like that. What if I pursued my secret dreams like him? What if I pursued Jesus's life purpose for me, whatever it was, like that? What if I was willing to look like a complete and absolute fool for His glory and my good?

Mrs. Wayland looked like she was having a seizure in her seat.

Kiona beamed and clapped along. The crowd continued to ignore him. And he kept on squealing injured dolphin calls.

Just as I was wondering how long my ears and pride were going to be tormented, Kiona jumped to her feet and ran onto the stage. Evan paused for a second but then kept right on playing. She grabbed the microphone, closed her eyes, took a deep breath and began talking in a deep, husky whisper.

"My soul...is a garden of...lettuce leaves," she breathed into the microphone, "flapping in the fresh air, rolling in the soil, chewed by the...bunnies." She took another deep breath and held the microphone tighter. "I am a free...scarecrow, liberated on...on the path to Oz." She swung her hips and moaned loud enough for the vibrations through the speakers to get under my skin.

Evan stopped playing. The room silenced. All eyes were on her. And then Evan put that clarinet back in his mouth and blew like Kiona needed that squeaky mess to breathe out her next line. The crowd roared to life, clapping and cheering even louder than they had for Glitter Greg.

I'd had enough.

I grabbed my purse and marched to the door, pushing the bouncer out of my way to get out of that zany place with its zany people and my zany husband and his zany ex. It wasn't until I was halfway down the dark alleyway that I realized Mrs. Wayland had followed me out. She was running out of breath trying to catch up with me. When she did, I didn't hold back.

"Now look, I had nothing to—"

She cut me off, collapsing her heavy frame into my bony shoulder with a loud wail. "Selena, I can't handle this. You've got to make this stop. You've got to talk some sense into him," she wept.

I realized I was holding her up as her body shook and shivered with tears. If any up-to-no-good passersby were planning to attack us in that trash-filled dark alley, they probably were too frightened from the unhuman noises coming from Mrs. Wayland's throat and the steely expression that had settled on my face.

"Don't worry, Mrs. Wayland. I'll put a stop to this."

In retrospect, maybe I should have jumped on that stage and started singing along with Evan that night. Maybe things wouldn't have gotten as bad as they were about to get. But I didn't. I didn't even sing songs of praise to Jesus for his salvation and victory. Instead, I uttered these words to Mrs. Wayland: "Don't worry. We'll work together and put an end to this—fast."

Mrs. Wayland suddenly straightened up, and I could tell she had become aware of where she was and what she was doing. From the look on her face and the way she smoothed down her clothes, I couldn't tell which alarmed her more: that she was standing in a filthy alley in her expensive pearls and white gloves and white suit, or that that she had just hugged and was about to conspire with her daughter-in-law.

"Well, then..." Her lips inched into a devious smile. "I think I have a plan, but you're going to have to play along for this to work."

That should have been my first clue. The woman wanted to be—no, *had* to be—in control no matter what. But, as desperate as she was, I think I was even more so.

"Anything you want, Mrs. Wayland." My voice was expressionless, my soul fatigued. "I need my Evan back."

Mrs. Wayland frowned at my last statement, but then she sighed, shrugged, and smiled again. "I've had enough for tonight. Are you going to be home tomorrow at noon?"

As we walked to her car and I listened to her explain the need for an intervention, I realized even then I had in some way taken my eyes off Jesus and made a deal with the devil. Happily ever after was rewritten for me and Evan right then during those brief moments outside The Lerato Lounge.

21

The Plan

Turns out we weren't the only ones with plans. The next day, I learned two things.

First of all, Mrs. Wayland and I had left the lounge too soon the night before. Apparently, Kunta X had been there all along, passed out drunk and high on the floor in a darkened corner of the smoke room. When he heard the rousing applause for Evan-Essence and Miss Kee-Kee, as Brother Sango dubbed them, he emerged from the den and went immediately to work introducing himself as their road manager.

"From my legal eye, this is a good start for a contract." Evan held up a napkin to me that had a few lines scribbled on it in blue ink. "I'm going to type this up and have X and Kiona sign it."

This he said to me as I tried to swallow down my late breakfast of cold hash browns and some rubbery ham steak I'd warmed in the microwave. Had the man been drinking last night? Or was there really such a thing as a contact high?

There was a pause and pleading in his eyes as he looked at me, biting his lip. "Look, Selena, I'll cut to the chase: I know you're probably concerned about me going on the road with Kiona because of our past history and all, but really, there's nothing to fear. You are the only woman I love, and I'm glad I get to share my life with you. However, if you don't want her to join me and X on the road, just say it, and I'll call the whole thing off."

"It."

"Huh?"

"You said, 'just say it, and you'll call the whole thing off.' Well, I'm saying 'it.'"

I knew this probably wasn't the best time for a smart aleck response, but I needed my dingbat of a husband to hear me loud and clear. With all that had transpired over the past week, I was convinced he had some slowness going on in that brain of his. "I don't know how you're missing it, but the woman is all over you. I don't trust her, and I don't want you hanging out anywhere near or with her."

"Oh, Selena!" His hopefulness turned into anger. "Why are you acting like this? You have no reason to be jealous. I don't want Kiona, and she doesn't want me. She's a dreamer, that's all, just like I am, wanting to bring peace and hope and all that's good and pure in the world through the arts. That's all she's about. I would think you'd appreciate that about her. Please put aside whatever you think you're seeing and realize how great an opportunity this is for me to start living out my dream, for us, for our family. I promise you, Kiona is not after me. For anything, she's trying to be your friend. The woman's throwing you a baby shower."

"Baby shower? I thought we talked about this already?" My calm words betrayed the scream that shot through my innards. "I thought I told you I don't want her throwing me anything. And when did this conversation occur? And how did she know to show up at the lounge? I thought you said you wouldn't be talking to her."

"Yeah, well, we've only talked about the shower, which is for you, by the way. She's doing all this planning for you. It's supposed to be a surprise. And besides, she said the deposit for the lodge in the Poconos was nonrefundable. But that's beside the point. We were talking about my dream here, and you're trying to change the subject. As far as my and Kiona's act is concerned, didn't you see the way those people loved us last night?"

"Evan, those people were high." Was he really that clueless? "Taking Kiona on the road with you is only half of the problem. Ain't nobody going to pay to hear that noise. Kiona's poetry is stupid, and Evan, you can't even play the clarinet. I'm sorry to break the news to you, but music is not your thing. What you are doing is absolutely ridiculous. You need to go back to your day job—quickly."

His anger deepened. "So that's how it is, huh?" Evan narrowed his eyes. "I really thought you were supporting my dreams all this time. It hurts to know when I'm really trying to put my heart out there, my wife doesn't have my back."

"When did I ever say I agreed with this madness? Evan, even your mother walked out."

"I know. She called me this morning to tell me how she followed you out to talk some sense into you and then went home immediately because you upset her too much. She's very disappointed with the way you behaved."

"Now, that's a big fat lie. That is not what she said to me. Even she wants this to stop."

And that's when I realized the second thing. My deal with the devil apparently had fine print I hadn't read. I should have known then Mrs. Wayland hadn't revealed to me all the details—or motives —of her scheme.

Evan glared at me. "You just called our act stupid. You just called my dream ridiculous. And now you just called my mother a liar." He stormed to the front door and opened it before turning to scowl at me.

"Selena, when I married you, I didn't realize how many issues you had. You are a jealous and bitter woman. I'm going to pray for you." With a slam, he walked out.

I swung the door back open and marched behind him as he kept his back to me and hightailed it to his car.

"I have issues?" I screamed after him. "I have issues? Did you really just say *I* have issues?"

A neighbor, a little old lady with a fresh press and curl and a four-prong cane looked up at me as she grabbed a grocery bag from her car, parked two spaces over from Evan. She shook her head and headed to her door. Embarrassed at her frown, I stopped in my tracks and silently watched as Evan revved up his car, backed up, and sped away.

"Running that pretty man away," I heard the lady mumble as her keys jingled and she entered her townhome.

I stood alone in the midday Saturday sun for a few moments. With nothing else to do, I went back into the house.

22

The Actual Plan

I sat on a folding chair in the living room in a state somewhere between hot tears and nausea. I couldn't believe how my life was ripping apart at the seams. I felt helpless, confused, and uncertain how to stop it. Afraid for my future. Afraid for my marriage. And my baby.

I thought of calling Neeka, but all I could think about was the hurt on Evan's face and the pain and fear in my heart. All I could hear were his angry, misled accusations. I felt completely misunderstood by him, preyed on by Kiona, and betrayed by his mother. I thought of calling my parents but could only imagine what both my mother and father would say if I told them all that had happened. I'd shared nothing about Evan's new career path with them. My father would have a field day.

I didn't have the energy to dial the phone or explain the drama to anyone who knew and loved me. I was pregnant with my first child and less than halfway through the first year of my marriage.

This was supposed to be the happiest time of my life. Never before had I felt so alone and depressed.

I plodded to the kitchen to grab a pint of Ben and Jerry's ice cream. And a bag of salt and vinegar potato chips. Okay, and some leftover shrimp egg rolls and a bowl of Cap'n Crunch. In the midst of my pregnancy craving binge fest, I heard a knock at the door. I looked at the clock on the microwave. It was eleven forty-five. Mrs. Wayland said she would be coming over today to go over how we would have an intervention with Evan, Dr. Phil style.

For once I was glad she was coming. I had a few words for her. I couldn't wait to get started with our scheduled noon "intervention." The knock sounded again, and I marched right to the door, one hand clenched to my hip.

"Mrs. Wayland—" I shouted as I swung the door open, but nobody was there. I looked to the right, then the left. Nobody.

And then a meow.

I looked down. An obviously expensive, purebred white cat with long fur and a tan beret was perched on my steps.

"Oh, she *is* home." A voice came from around the bend of our end-of-group townhouse. A voice and then a face. A petite white man wearing a black shirt, black jeans, and black cowboy boots appeared. Around his neck and from both wrists hung a mix of silver and gold chains with what looked like symbols and charms from every religion known to man. They jingled as he bounced up the short stairway to my door.

"We are all coming," he said. "We were just discussing landscaping ideas for the side of the house."

"We? I'm sorry, who are you?" But even as I spoke, two other men and a very tall woman came from around the corner and joined the first man on the porch.

"Yah, this must be her." One of the others, a finely chiseled blond-haired, blue-eyed man with a thick European accent of some sort beamed at me.

"Okay." I was trying to make sense of this group on my porch. "What? Who?"

"Oh, yes." The tall, graying brunette, dressed in a stylish orange sweater dress with several strands of beaded jewelry to match, had picked up the cat and was stroking its long fur as she greeted me. "You must be Selena. You *are* a cute little thing, oh, yes. I am Genevaise Zuzani. It is a pleasure to finally meet you."

Evan was right. She really truly did have the deepest voice I'd ever heard on a woman. Some of the bass singers in the men's choir at my church had nothing on her.

Genevaise grabbed my hand for one single firm shake then extended her cat's paw. I narrowed my eyes, but she smiled, her coral lipstick and peach eye shadow flawless on her tanned skin.

"And this is Phillipe. Oh yes, dear, go ahead, shake his paw. He won't bite. Please, if you don't shake, he will be offended." I saw slight irritation form on her face as she tightened her colored lips, waiting for me to shake her cat's paw.

Speechless, disoriented, and now embarrassed to admit it, I went ahead and did it. I swear the cat rolled its eyes at me as I pumped his little paw up and down. Genevaise smiled again, pleased and ready to introduce me to the rest of her entourage.

"And here you have the best design team assembled in the world, as far as I am concerned. This is Rev. Dr. Matthew Ainsworth, though he prefers we simply call him Moonlight." She pointed to the petite man in cowboy boots. "He is our international expert on divine interior design. He will use deep meditation and the time-honored principles of several ancient practices to help achieve optimal vibrational balance in your home. He will require a lot of silence and space to do his work, oh yes, but I know you will be ecstatic at the results. He is a master at what he does."

"Genevaise is too generous with her words." The man known as Moonlight gave a demure smile, bowed his head, and enveloped my hand with both of his in a warm shake, his charms and jewelry jingling with each move.

Um....

"And this—" she gestured to the hulky blond "—is Yuri. I found him carving a chair out of a tree stump in a small village in Eastern Europe. He oversees furniture and fixture design, and he will also supervise the construction crew who are on their way. Yuri is more than a craftsman. He is an artist. His carved creations are sculptures. When he finishes, your home will look like a gallery people would pay to come see."

Yuri stepped close to me, took my hand, and pulled it to his lips, never once breaking eye contact.

"I love black women." His whisper was almost a growl.

The third man, a thin, gingersnap-colored black man with a red Mohawk and silver sunglasses crossed his arms. "And I am Xander." His accent was clearly British. "I will be picking the colors and textiles for this project and believe me—" he slid his sunglasses to the tip of his nose— "this *is* a project." This he said while looking me up and down. He didn't extend a hand to shake. I crossed my arms as well.

"Oh, yes." Genevaise Zuzani continued to stroke Phillipe. "Xander Jauq'sahn is our color and sewing expert. He used to work in a hair salon in London but found his life calling creating custom linens."

"Once you know how to color and sew in a weave, you can color and sew just about anything." Xander snorted, his upturned nose directed at me.

I felt like I was in a daze as the designers pressed past me into the ruins of my living room and begin studying the holes and cracks and missing pieces.

"Oh, yes." Genevaise frowned as she sat Phillipe on the floor. He immediately began circling me with his tail raised. Genevaise didn't seem to notice. "It is just as I remember. Sad. Yuri, pass me the sketches again. Moonlight, are you ready to get started with your exercises? Oh, I see you have already started. Wonderful."

All eyes turned to Moonlight who was lying on his back on my kitchen floor. His eyes were closed, and his arms were stretched out on either side of him.

Finally, I snapped back to my senses. "Look, Genevaise, everyone, it's very nice to meet you. However, I'm sorry. I think there has been a major misunderstanding. Mrs. Wayland—"

"Hush, dear." Genevaise spoke sharply. "Moonlight needs silence for his work."

"That's very nice, but Mrs. Wayland—"

"*Shhh.*" This time Xander chimed in. Yuri blew me a kiss.

"Look..." My patience was waning. "Y'all need to—"

"Oh good. They're here." Genevaise clapped her hands as a white van pulled up in front of my house and several men in hardhats got out. They carried buckets, sledgehammers, and plastic bags and marched in like they lived here. Before I could get a word in, the knotty pine walls of my living room were coming down, and a heavy mallet had crashed through the drywall in my dining room.

Stunned at the chaos that had suddenly taken over my house, I wondered what the commotion would do to Moonlight's concentration, but he looked like he was in a zone. He had gotten up from the floor and was now hopping from one foot to the other and chanting in a language I didn't understand.

"He spent a year filming monks in several Asian countries and then six months camping next to a reservation in Montana to make observations for his dissertation," Genevaise whispered with much excitement. "He often resorts to secret ancient rituals that he's perfected with Western philosophy when the quest for spiritual equilibrium in a project is more complex than usual."

"What the—"

"Oh good." Genevaise silenced me with an abruptly raised hand. "He's almost done. Selena, do you mind if I boil some water in your microwave before they shut off the electricity? Phillipe needs his afternoon catnip tea. Don't worry, I bought my own bottled water." She beamed at her beloved cat.

"Okay, okay, enough. *Stop!*" My scream seemed to shake the whole house. Everybody froze, even Moonlight, who struggled to keep his balance on one foot. All eyes were on me. "I don't know what is going on here, but I didn't give anybody permission to start tearing up my house."

"Oh, honey, it's already tore up," Xander said.

I looked away from him and continued. "Please fix whatever you just did and leave. Mrs. Wayland—"

"Is right here, darling. Hello, Genevaise. It's great to see you and your team again. Please carry on." It was twelve o'clock on the dot. She'd timed her entrance perfectly.

Madelyn Ernestine Wayland stood in my doorway beaming. Her best friend and Evan's godmother, The Honorable Judge Vanessa Grant, stood beside her. Mrs. Wayland had her backup. I wished in that moment I had called Neeka. She would have backed me up and backed over everyone in that room.

"Selena." Mrs. Wayland came over to give me a hug. I almost pushed her to the ground. She wrapped her arms around me anyway. "I knew you would object, but this is the only way. I told you yesterday you would have to play along in this plan to get Evan back to his senses. You remember our little deal, right?"

"There is no longer any deal between us. And even if there was one, my house was not in the negotiations."

"But it's always been. See, I believe this house is a huge part of the problem. All these broken things in here—the leaks, the holes, this old dirty carpet. Who knows what type of mold and bacteria is floating in this air?"

At that, I realized some of the workmen had masks over their mouth and noses. A mallet was being used to destroy the block of raw wood that had been my kitchen island. Splinters and sawdust joined whatever else, real or imagined, floated in my house's air.

She continued to talk to me, her voice like that of a pre-K teacher gently talking to one of her charges. "I think something in the air here has temporarily deactivated Evan's mind. That's why we're going to get this house fixed up so he can think clearly again."

I pouted like I was a preschooler. "But we're already getting the house fixed." My heart sunk on so many levels as soon as I said those words. Mrs. Wayland said exactly what I thought to myself.

"By whom? What's his name? Evan told me. Kunta X?"

"Yes. And he's going to do a great job," I replied with such earnest conviction, I questioned my own sanity.

I was trapped. Mrs. Wayland knew it. The Judge, who had been standing behind her nodding at me in pity, knew it. Shoot, even I knew it. And they knew I knew it.

Kunta X wasn't fixing anything. Even if he wasn't about to "go on the road" with Evan-Essence and Miss Kee-Kee, nothing he could do would come close to the skilled work of this professional team of contractors. And, although I hated the "Cityscape Revised" design theme drawn on Genevaise's sketches, I knew I did not have the money to hire another home improvement team, especially with Evan quitting his well-paying position. Plus, we had a baby on the way. We had to have a livable space for a newborn.

Mrs. Wayland saw the defeat on my face and smiled. "I haven't had the pleasure of meeting this Kunta X, but if his plans for this house are anything like the so-called plans he has with my son, I cannot stand idly by. Selena, I'm going to get this house fixed for you, and everything will be okay."

"You told me you were coming over today for an intervention."

"Selena, this *is* the intervention."

I glared at her, praying to God I wouldn't let such a destructive force as hate take root in my heart, but I ain't gonna lie: In those moments, Jesus and love and grace and forgiveness were not at the forefront of my mind.

"They are shutting off my water, my electricity. They're tearing down my walls. How are Evan and I supposed to live like this?"

"Oh, you're not going to live like this, dear." This time Judge Grant spoke up. "You can stay with your mother-in-law. There's plenty of room at her house in Bowie."

"That's right, Selena. I think once Evan is back in an acceptable dwelling and eating appropriate, healthy food and not the carry-out junk you've been ordering and the bean casseroles your mother's been bringing here, he will come back to his senses, and you will have your Evan back." She struggled to get out that last sentence.

I didn't see any of this coming. The woman was pure evil. "But we can't move to Bowie," I stammered.

I scrambled for an excuse that didn't involve me cursing her out. I was really trying to stay a Christian. I needed Jesus on my side. "Bowie's an hour away from our jobs. That's too much of a commute."

"Evan doesn't have a job, remember? You somehow got him to quit. And I'm sure we can work out some type of telecommuting arrangement with Kiona. She has been more than helpful to you and Evan despite your obvious ingratitude."

"First of all, Evan didn't quit. He lied to you. He was *fired*. And there is no way I'm going to begin to believe Kiona has my best interest at heart. You can believe that lie if you want to. And speaking of lies, why did you tell Evan that you were trying to calm me down last night? Maybe you forgot, but I wasn't the one shaking and sobbing in the alley."

"Oh, you poor child. You don't know the first thing about men and marriage." Mrs. Wayland clucked her tongue. "How can we ever get Evan to come around if he feels like all the women he loves are against him? He needs to believe his mother is on his side. Trust me, this is the best way. You stay on your side of the fence, and I'll pretend to stay on his. Just see it like I'm playing the devil's advocate. Kiona is just being the sweetheart that she is. She's trying to rescue him gently. I would tell you to try to emulate her, but I recognize attaining that type of class might be too high a goal for you."

"Maddie," The Judge whispered, patting the monster on her arm as if to say that was enough.

I decided to ignore the Kiona remark and the blatant insult, but her other comment, I couldn't let slide. "You, the devil's advocate. That's one way of putting it." She narrowed her eyes at the insult, but I was not moved. "Mrs. Wayland, I hate to mess up your plans, but Evan and I are not going anywhere. We will stay in this house during the entire renovation project."

"That's what you say now, Selena, but it's going to be mighty drafty when all the windows are out and the roof is gone."

"Oh, you don't know my childhood, Mrs. Wayland. I know how to survive many things." Why did I say that? I wanted to kick myself. Too much information.

"Fine then, suit yourself. But Evan never had to suffer like you and your family, and he won't start now. I know my son. He'll be back in his old bedroom the moment he sees the work being done here. At heart, I believe he knows he's too good for the low standards you and your family offer him. I was hoping he would come to that realization before a baby came, but it's too late now. Don't worry, Selena, for my grandchild's sake, I'll play nice with you. Maybe one day you might even become close enough to being a respectable lady with a respectable house that is worthy of my son. Until then, Evan is coming back home to me. Come on, Vanessa. Let's finish shopping."

A kick to the gut. A karate chop to the teeth. A punch in the nostrils. Her words felt like physical weapons, and I stood stunned. No one—absolutely, no one ever—had talked to me the way this woman thought she could. I was speechless.

The Judge gave me a steely smile. Whatever sympathy I thought was there, I'd clearly imagined. The two turned to leave. Tears blinded my eyes and choked up my throat. I was beyond a place of response.

"One more thing, Selena," Mrs. Wayland snarled, "if you ever call my son a liar again, I will see to it he never believes another word you say to him."

And with that, they were gone.

The construction crew and design team had been busy chatting and working during this whole exchange. As Mrs. Wayland's Benz pulled away, I groaned in my spirit, wishing I'd fought and clawed a way to get in the last word. But Xander somehow managed to pull that off.

"*Umph.* She told you."

23

The Women's Ministry

"...and Lord, you know us intimately. Our thoughts, our dreams, our desires. Our strengths and shortcomings. Please help us, Lord. Fix our hearts, fix our lives. Please fix everything that is concerning us right now. Please love through us and let us always be aware of your tender loving care and concern over us. Thank you for this time. You are welcome in our meeting tonight. Speak a word to our weary souls so that we may be women who glorify You. In Your name we pray. Amen."

I opened my eyes along with the other ten or so women sitting in a circle around Sister Corrine Knight, the pastor's wife, in the basement of the church. The AC was on high blast, and the metal chair was cold on my behind, but Sister Corinne's engaging smile and encouraging prayer made the room feel warm.

I knew most of the women sitting with me, and truthfully, I felt very much out of place. I was the youngest one there and probably the only one who was not a regular attendee of the twice monthly women's Bible study. A good number of the women present were considered church mothers, women who had retired long before I was even born, with great-grandchildren and dead husbands to their names. Sister Bertine Brown, the organist, was there, as well as her gossiping cousin Fran Delaney. I was convinced Fran only came to the women's meetings to get the latest scoop so she could have something to talk about when she got on the phone with half of Baltimore later. I made a mental note not to divulge too much of my business. I didn't want any word of my problems getting back to my mother.

My mother.

Most of my life, I had always gone back to my mother when I found myself in a quandary. When I was eight years old and Tameka Ringgold had all the children in my third-grade class chanting "Porkie Pie Pigeonhead, Selena Tucker should be dead," my mother went up to the school and told the whole class off, including the teacher for not stopping the cruelty.

When I was in high school and came home crying because Stephon Rogers asked Neeka to the prom instead of me, my mother got her co-worker's son, a strikingly handsome star basketball player from another school district, to take me. She even let him drive me there in the new Lincoln Navigator some college recruiter out west "loaned" him. (I even forgave the fact that she and my father drove behind us, waited in the parking lot of Martin's Banquet Hall, then followed us home. My mother still says they didn't do that, but my father's 1981 rusted Chevy Citation with the license plate BIG POP is unique to the East Coast, as was the outdated blond Jheri curl my mother wore at the time.)

And when I was a college freshman and had a roommate who kept leaving her moldy dishes and dirty drawers on *my* bed, Ma was the one talking to the resident assistant demanding I get a single room. All I did was stand behind her with my arms crossed, my lips pursed, and my head cocked to one side as she gave the quivering RA an ultimatum.

I guess what I'm trying to say is that I'm a grown, married woman now, with a baby on the way, and I can't keep running to my momma to fix things for me.

Sister Corinne is saying that's what Jesus is for, among other things. I know that inherently—been knowing it. But I guess the problems I'd been facing up to this point in my life didn't have the same weight and meaning as the war I felt like I was in now. I was fighting for my marriage and my sanity. And our finances as well, I realized. I was fighting for the future my child would be born into and the present Evan and I had to share.

I was about to be a mother myself, and I wanted to come through this victoriously. I wanted my mother to know she had raised a strong warrior, even if I didn't feel like one at the moment—a warrior with her own voice who could demand respect and get it, a warrior with her own two feet who could stand when necessary and her own two knees who could pray as mandatory.

A part of me really just wanted to go to my mother's apartment, squeeze into her lap, let out a good cry, and wait for her to tell me what to do. But I wasn't going to go down like that. There was no way I was going to tell her Evan and I had spent the last few nights at a hotel per my insistence while our home was being transformed into some kind of urban art gallery of steel and concrete. There was no way I was going to tell her Kunta X was still coming to the house, but not to make repairs. He and Evan spent days and evenings in the basement, writing rhymes and screeching on that darn clarinet. The noise blended right in with the drills and hammering going on in the rest of the house, I'm sure.

I refused to listen to any of that foolishness in our hotel.

Evan said nothing else to me about Kiona, though I knew she was still very much a part of Evan's act. She contributed her poems during their rehearsals via cell phone. That should tell you something about the quality of her poetry. Any poem that cn b typed n2 a txt mssg with shorthand and emojis is not a poem at all, as far as I'm concerned. It's a travesty. It's an embarrassment to Shakespeare, Langston Hughes, Nikki Giovanni—heck, I bet Dr. Seuss is probably rolling in his grave right about now.

Yes, I was checking his phone, text messages and all.

Evan said very little to me, period. And that was fine with me.

Kiona had changed her tone toward me at work—smiling every time she saw me, giving me fewer assignments to complete.

It looked all well and good, but I knew not to trust her. And I'm not being paranoid.

If Evan, Mrs. Wayland, and Kiona wanted a fight, then that's what they would get. If they wanted to be dirty with it, they'd better know I was prepared to be dirtier.

"Again, we would like to welcome Sister Selena Wayland."

When I heard my name, I tried to get my mind back on Jesus and focus on the godly discussion.

Sister Corinne continued, "Not only is Selena a newcomer to our study tonight, but she is also a newlywed."

"*Hmmm.*" Fran Delaney, the organist's gossipy cousin, studied me with a squinted eye, her hands folded over her wide belly.

"And," Sister Corinne said, beaming at me, "from what I've heard, God is blessing this new union with a new bundle of joy. When are you due, Selena?"

"Late February."

"Didn't you just get married the end of April?" Fran frowned. "*Hmmm.* May, June, July, August..." She counted quietly a few more moments on her fingers. "I guess those months add up right. 'Course if that baby miraculously shows up as an eight-pound preemie, and it ain't been nine months of marriage, some other questions might be rightfully raised." Her frown deepened.

"We were married when the baby was conceived, if that's what you're wondering." *Not that it's any of your business*, I wanted to add.

"Oh, I didn't say you weren't, Sister Wayland. It's just that these young girls today have different ideas than when I was comin' up. When I was your age, for example, wasn't no such phrase as *baby daddy*."

"You got that right, Francis," Fran's cousin Bertine piped in. "We just called *your* 'baby daddy' Thomas. Or was it Richard? Or Carlos? Did you ever figure out which one was your son's father?"

"Bertine, now you know—"

"Alright, ladies," Sister Corinne gently interjected. "Let's save that discussion for another time. What's important is that we lift each other up in love and prayer, and if accountability for purity and integrity is ever needed for one of our sisters, we must offer it with a spirit of gentleness and humility. Nobody is immune to mess ups. Any one of us can get sidetracked from God's perfect plan for our lives. But His grace is big enough to forgive and restore us all. I talk about many of these topics on my vlog. Watch and share. Now, let's get back on task and start our discussion of tonight's Bible verse. Mother Torres, glad you could make it out this evening. Would you mind reading Proverbs chapter fourteen, verse one, to us?"

"Sure." Mother Gina Torres, the president emeritus of the senior usher board, adjusted her glasses and began to read out of a worn Bible. "The wise woman builds her house, but with her own hands the foolish one tears hers down."

Without thinking, I laughed out loud. All eyes turned to me. Even Sister Corinne flashed me a side eye.

"I'm sorry." I immediately regretted my outburst. "I wasn't laughing at the verse. It's just that my house is in such a state of shambles that somebody could probably pull the whole thing down with their bare hands. When Mother Torres read that verse, I got this vivid picture in my head of my home collapsing with one slight tug, and it made me laugh, that's all."

"*Hmmm.*" Fran crossed her hands over her belly again and leaned all the way back in her seat. "So, you say your home is in shambles? My Lord. Ain't you only been married for a few months? What's going on inside that house of yours? Your husband ain't doing right?" She leaned forward. "Or is it you?"

"Francis—"

"It's okay, Sister Bertine." This time I interjected. "I didn't explain myself correctly. I was talking about my actual house, my townhouse, that is. It needs a lot of renovation and I could use some wisdom on how to fix it up real good." That was all I was going to say about that.

The First Lady rejoined the discussion. "You know, Selena, you bring up an interesting correlation. You are talking about the wisdom needed to build a literal house. This verse starts there and expands into what Sister Fran is talking about: building a home."

Fran smiled, obviously pleased she had in some way enriched the dialogue. Sister Corinne continued: "As women, we know how we want our homes to be for our families and ourselves. A wise woman invests the time and energy required to make her dwelling a safe and welcome place. She layers bricks of love with a mortar of patience. There are windows for transparency to keep communication lines open and to let sunlight in, and curtains to shield and protect loved ones from the prying eyes of outsiders who mean to do harm.

"She knows when a remodeling project is necessary to tear down a wall and open up space. She furnishes her home and paints it with her own individual style and taste. And most importantly—I guess I should have said this first—she builds on a solid foundation.

"Like the parable Jesus gives in Matthew 7:24–27, a wise woman will build on a rock, not on top of sand. And no greater rock is there than Jesus." Sister Corinne smiled deeper. "As far as getting wisdom to know what to do about specific homebuilding projects, the Bible tells us reverencing the Lord is the beginning of wisdom and that God promises to give wisdom liberally to all who ask.

"There are so many scriptures that define and describe what wisdom looks like, what it is. Wisdom is personified as a woman in many verses in the Book of Proverbs. Read chapter two and the first six verses of chapter nine for our next meeting. I think you'll find these verses enlightening." She spoke to everyone, but she winked at me.

For some reason, that wink bothered me. Did she know how bad things were going in my marriage? Had something I'd said given away the complete and utter devastation of my failing house and home? Lord knows, I needed some good old-fashioned wisdom to know what to do and what to say to help get things right, to feel better about my marriage, to feel better about myself.

I had made Christ the foundation of my life, I was certain. I just didn't know how to build from there, it seemed.

Fran still studied me from her seat, the corners of her mouth turned down, her arms crossed. Every few moments, she ran her tongue across her teeth and pulled at the hairs on her chin. Her eyes never broke away from my face.

Did I look as bad as I felt?

I scribbled down the Proverbs verses Sister Corinne had offered, but I knew already I wouldn't be joining the women's bimonthly Bible study again anytime soon. I felt too exposed, and I didn't trust Fran Delaney.

24

The Blackmail

After the closing prayer was given and the lemon pound cake and punch had been served, I nearly ran to my car, deliberately avoiding conversation with anyone. As I turned out of the church parking lot, my cell phone rang.

Neeka.

"Hey, girl. Where you been?" She sounded happier than usual.

"Nowhere you haven't."

It was our old greeting, our same shared laugh. It felt good to have a loyal co-conspirator to talk to again.

Oh, we had a good time on the phone. Neeka and I laughed and carried on like the good old days, giggling and talking about everything and nothing in particular, so much so that I realized after I hung up that nothing of significance had really been shared between us. I said nothing about my current dilemmas and problems, and I knew nothing more of what was going on in her life, other than her views on the latest episode of a show we both watched and the best way to deal with static cling on a short skirt.

On one hand, it had felt good to escape, albeit the escape was only for thirty minutes or so. But for those minutes of laughter-filled conversation with Neeka, I didn't have to think about Evan, Kunta X, and that silly clarinet. I didn't have to consider how many nights Evan and I would be able to afford at the hotel now that we were down to one income and trying to get ready for a baby. I didn't have to freak out trying to imagine what my bedroom was going to look like with metal beams and concrete walls. I didn't have to worry about Madelyn Ernestine Wayland's plans or Kiona Tandy's malicious desires.

The lack of substance in our phone conversation made me wonder how much time Neeka and I had wasted over the years avoiding real issues. How often had we gone on and on about songs and movies and makeup to the point that one or the other of us had hung up the phone feeling no better than when we first said hello? How many opportunities had I missed to share my feelings, my faith, or even my failures with my best friend? Or for that matter, considering how much I didn't tell her during that phone call, how much of her life and fears and opinions had I missed?

What was I talking about? I don't think I'd ever missed a single one of Neeka's opinions. But she's missed mine.

A lot of people have missed mine.

I realized then I'd spent a lot of my life hiding, and not just behind my mother. I wanted to believe I was getting better at being authentic, but I also knew I wasn't going back to the women's Bible study. I'm not sure what that says about me, but I know that's not a good show of progress. I shook my head at my own sorry self. Then again, aside from Sister Corrine Knight's warmth, I hadn't felt very welcome.

It had been a nice temporary escape talking on the phone with Neeka, but on the other hand, I had been so far removed from my reality during our phone call I'd forgotten the problem that came with our proposed plans for an upcoming weekend.

Just before we hung up, Neeka invited Evan and me to go out on another double date with her and her friend. "It's serious between us, Selena, and I want you along every step of the way." I had been so thrilled to hear Neeka's excitement that I agreed wholeheartedly to meeting up with her in a few Saturdays for a twilight cruise aboard the Bay Queen at the Inner Harbor— completely forgetting her serious friend was none other than Kiona Tandy's ex-husband.

I was back at our hotel room, standing in the shower. Or should I say hiding in the shower, as I'd been letting the hot, steamy water run down my back for the past forty minutes. It was late, I had work tomorrow, and Evan was actually there and not in the basement of our house composing sonnets. I could hear his snores coming from the full-sized bed on the other side of the bathroom wall.

The fact that he could sleep so peacefully while I tossed and turned all night infuriated me.

As I finally cut the water off, all I could think about was the last double date with Neeka and her man. Both Evan and I acted uncomfortably awkward upon meeting and sitting at the table with the unsuspecting Peyton Anderson. I could tell our clumsiness irritated Neeka on what she was hoping to be a monumental night. That date truly had been a milestone in her personal life. By having Evan and me there with her, she was announcing to the world she was ready to settle down and had finally found the man who made her want to leave all other men behind. And he seemed like a good catch—a quality, intelligent, hardworking man who accepted her fully, faults and all.

I thought I had that once.

I tried not to feel envious.

Marriage seemed like it had changed everything about and between Evan and me. Nobody had warned me it could get this bad.

The Bible presents marriage as this perfect divine plan making one out of two, so I guess there's a purpose in my union with Evan that honors God. I wanted to know what that purpose was and how to get and maintain marital bliss. Perhaps the secret to success beyond the altar was written somewhere in those sacred pages. Sister Corrine Knight could probably direct me to a few passages, but not if it meant I had to sit anywhere near Fran Delaney again.

I looked in the mirror and waited for my reflection to fight its way through the steam. My stomach was finally beginning to show off my baby bump in real fashion—the baby Evan and I created in our early months together as husband and wife.

Kiona carried his baby once. While she was still married to Peyton, as Evan tells it.

The thought depressed me. And I couldn't tell Neeka a thing about her.

And what depressed me even more were the eggshells I felt like I was being forced to walk on around one of the few people who I knew genuinely cared for me.

Neeka and I hadn't talked about much during our phone conversation, but for those last seconds at the end of our call when she invited us on the double date, I could hear in her voice the sheer excitement of true love found.

Peyton Anderson wasn't going away any time soon, and I knew the truth was going to have to come out. Because both Evan and I professed to be followers of Christ, sin can only stay in the darkness but for so long. Neeka and Peyton were going to have to find out what Evan and Kiona did, come hell or high water.

I thought of Mrs. Wayland and knew both hell *and* high water were coming, as well as volcanoes, hurricanes, and tsunamis, too. I shuddered at the thought and looked back in the mirror.

The steam had cleared, and my reflection had finally come fully through. All I saw was my round belly. It looked like somebody had stuffed a mini football under my skin. The sight invigorated me as I imagined my baby hiding just below the surface. My baby—a person who not too long ago felt like a distant enigma, and now there's no denying his or her presence. The joy I felt looking at my growing stomach sent butterflies tickling through my abdomen.

Wait...

Those butterflies... I'd been feeling them on and off for a while... Could it be?

A rush of tears flooded my face as I finally recognized my baby's first kicks. Wow. A real life was inside of me. I was going to be a mommy. I, Selena Diane Tucker Wayland, was going to be somebody's mother.

"Hey. You okay in there?"

I never noticed that the snoring in the adjacent room had stopped.

"I'm okay, Evan." Tears took over my voice, and he shook the door.

"Selena, what's wrong? Are you okay? What are you doing?"

"Everything's fine." I opened the door to let him in, and he stared at my stomach also.

"Wow. You look like you've gotten bigger since last week. So beautiful." He looked at my face. "Why were you crying? What's wrong?"

He cared that I'd been crying.

A new deluge of tears shook through me at the thought that my husband still cared about me. My sobs alarmed Evan even more.

"Look, Selena, I'm sorry about what I said to you the other day. You're pregnant, and I was being unfair. I know those hormones have you feeling wacky and are keeping you from thinking straight, so I forgive you for being jealous and bitter...and unsupportive of me and Kiona's dream. I know you can't help it right now."

Him and Kiona's *dream.*

I wanted to smack him.

Right on the cheek and hard enough to echo through the entire bathroom. And probably through the room, out the door, and down the hallway too.

Seconds earlier, I had been in a state of elation, excited, joyous beyond belief over the baby growing and kicking in my belly. Now, I felt like pure violence.

Anybody want to see and hear and know my authentic self? Well, watch out. Everybody's about to get a taste of just how alive and kicking *I* am.

"Just so you know, Evan," I told him as he blinked all innocently before me, "we have a double date with Neeka and *Peyton Anderson* a few Saturdays from now. Neeka's reserved tickets for us to go on a dinner cruise at the Harbor, and I assured her we'd be there. And I'm assuring *you* I'm going to tell both of them your dirty little Kiona secret."

I watched his face drain of color and then darken. "What's wrong with you? You know you can't do that, Selena. Why would you do that? Are you trying to destroy all of our lives?"

"You mean like how you and your mother are destroying mine? Oh, what is your poor mother going to think when she finds out her sweet little baby boy is a liar *and* a cheater? She's so busy trying to make sure you have the perfect house to live in, what's she going to do when I tell her how you're a homewrecker? Oh, and she thinks Kiona is such the perfect lady. I can't wait to see her face when she finds out she was *married* to another man when you two hooked up."

Fear and anger filled Evan's eyes. "You really wouldn't hurt me like that, would you? You're really going to say something? Don't do this to me, Selena. I don't know if I could ever forgive you if you do."

"Listen, there's an easy way to keep me quiet. Just come with me on that dinner cruise, act like you've got some sense when you see Neeka and Peyton, and maybe, *maybe*, I'll reconsider spilling your secrets." I narrowed my eyes. "Oh, and also, this Evan-Essence and

Miss Kee-Kee dream, it stops, you know. Wake up. It's done. Are you getting me?"

Evan shook his head slowly. "So, now you're going to blackmail me to get what you want. It's all about you, no consideration of me. That's evil, Selena."

Was it, though? I was just trying to be my authentic self. I had a choice to make.

If—no, rather *when*—Peyton finds out his dear old college buddy was the man who broke up his marriage, he's going to be enraged at Evan, and in turn Neeka will be upset that I knew and didn't tell her if I wait too long to do so. And if—no, *when*—Mrs. Wayland finds out the secret Evan has been hiding from her, she'll be angry at him for not being perfect, he'll be angry at me for exposing his imperfection, and Kiona...well, she'll just look like who she really is.

Was this really blackmailing my husband to get him to comply to my wishes? I shook off the thought. My life was too complicated. There's only so much drama a pregnant woman should have to deal with. I had been dealt a winning hand, and, if I played my cards right, I could take down the whole house.

The wise woman builds her house, but with her own hands the foolish one tears hers down.

Of course, I wasn't looking for a Bible verse to flash across my mind, but the scripture from the night's earlier meeting flashed through my mind anyway, blinking neon lights and all.

I had a choice to make. What were my options?

"That's it, huh?" Evan stood right outside the bathroom entrance. "You're really going to blackmail me—my dreams, everything I'm trying to do—just to get your way?"

"So, it's a date with Neeka and Peyton. Yay!" I slammed the bathroom door in his face.

I could almost hear in my mind the dying sizzle and pop of a flashing neon "Caution" sign.

I was the one who yanked the plug.

25

The Vlog

It was the morning rush hour, it was raining, and my windshield wipers were moving faster than my car, but I still felt on top of the world. Momentum was in my favor, and I felt unstoppable. After a night spent on the far opposite sides of the bed, Evan had been quiet as I chatted nonstop about baby names and gift registries. It was a one-sided conversation, but I didn't care.

For the first time in weeks, I didn't have to hear anything about Kunta X's latest rhyming revelation, or Kiona's idea for stage lighting, or Mrs. Wayland's suggestions on crib mobiles based on her research on brain development. For once, I had the final say in all those issues, and Evan knew it. He had no ground to stand on. If he even looked like he wanted to say something about his clarinet, all I had to do was say a sentence with the name *Peyton Anderson* in it, and Evan would keep his mouth shut. I was in the driver's seat, and he was the hostage, bound up with rope, sitting in the back with a blindfold on. His sullen mood hadn't bothered me one bit during our shared continental breakfast in the hotel lobby before I'd left for work. I'd drunk my hot chocolate, gulped down three cherry Danishes, some green grapes, and showed him a picture of the sage-and-brown stroller I wanted our baby to have, all with a smile and exuberance like nothing had shifted between us.

Okay, maybe I was bothered a little, I admitted to myself as I parked my car in front of the radio station. It was nice to finally have some control over things, but I kinda sorta missed feeling like Evan and I were on the same team. I missed feeling like we were partners together and not power brokers struggling to negotiate who would call the shots in our marriage.

I missed our friendship.

When I walked down the aisle that perfect day in April, I was expecting companionship to be waiting on the other side of the altar, not conflict.

And certainly not the need to resort to blackmail.

Oh, well. I did not ask for this scenario. How else was I supposed to deal with a situation I didn't see coming?

I settled into the workday, willing myself to focus only on the meetings, the paperwork, the phone calls I needed to complete. When Evan popped in my mind or Kiona smirked as she passed my cubicle, I tried to feel good about my power play but, honestly, it wasn't sitting right in my soul. By the time I got to lunch, I felt ready to scream.

Too queasy to eat, I stayed at my desk thinking I'd distract myself with some random YouTube videos—something to make me laugh or at least distract me enough from the discomfort and turmoil that nagged me. I was planning to search for funny animal videos or newsreel bloopers, but a recommended video caught my eye.

What is First Lady doing in my recommendations?

The sight of the pastor's wife, Sister Corinne Knight, smiling from a still frame felt like a sign from the Holy One. I knew immediately it was one of her video blogs, or *Victory Vlogs*, as she termed the videos she posted on the church's website. But I'd never watched one, so how had it even popped up as a recommendation? I felt uneasy, like God had a direct message for me. I groaned and pressed play...

"My ladies, I'm so glad you joined me today." Sister Corinne smiled from a large, cushy chair in the pastor's study. She wore a pale pink t-shirt with the words *Goodness and Mercy* encrusted in rhinestones across the top. Her silver-streaked hair was pulled to the side in a long twist-out ponytail. Rose-and-white- eyeglasses framed her oval face, a soft contrast against her pecan brown skin.

"I have a sweet and short message for you that I hope brings some encouragement," she continued. "As many of you know, my precious granddaughter, Zoe, is the light of my life. She's an eight-year-old ball of beautiful energy. Well, I had her over my house this weekend, and to my surprise and disappointment, I discovered my favorite bottle of Chanel shattered on my bathroom floor, after she was supposedly taking a bubble bath in there. I guess Zoe thought I would not notice the broken glass or the overwhelming scent that she tried to cover up by spraying Febreeze *and* Lysol. Yes, ladies, the headache you just imagined from the clashing overdose of odors was my reality.

"Well, my Zoe was in tears when I talked to her about it. She thought I would send her back home and was afraid I wouldn't buy her a birthday present this year. Oh, I hugged my little darling and told her I would forgive her, but she would need to help me clean up the mess and air out my home. She was so happy at my extending forgiveness, she smothered me with kisses and went back to her happy, giggling self.

"Imagine my surprise, then, when just a few hours later, I heard her screaming at a friend who broke her Barbie doll. Oh, the yells I heard and how the slam of my front door shook my house when she literally pushed our crying little neighbor out onto the porch.

"You know, the whole thing reminded me of the parable Jesus shared in Matthew 18. You know the one, in verses twenty-three to thirty-five, of the servant who was forgiven his massive debt by his master who then went on to treat very harshly a fellow servant who owed him mere chump change in comparison.

"My ladies, how often are we like my sweet Zoe or that angry servant—happy to embrace mercy from God but unwilling to extend it to others? Here's my point, ladies: We can be right, or we can be righteous. Was my granddaughter right about being upset over her broken Barbie? Of course. Was the servant right for being angry about money he was owed? I'd say yes—and I bet a bunch of you are shaking your head right now, thinking of that man or friend or relative who owes you something. This new way of thinking about forgiveness is not about focusing on right or wrong, but rather focusing on the comparison of God's extended grace to us and how He's made us righteous despite what we've done against Him.

"Now, before you think I'm advocating that you should let people walk all over you or you should gloss over being wronged, consider the context of this parable. It comes right after Jesus shared how to address sin. Don't get it wrong. Sin and faults and wrong-doing are absolutely to be addressed and done so directly and head-on. Sometimes that addressing is done privately, and other times in a public forum. Read the chapter.

"What I do want you to focus on is forgiveness and justice go together before a righteous God who is willing to forgive us as we forgive each other. Isn't it interesting that Jesus teaches on forgiveness in the context of settling accounts? When we forgive others, we give permission for God to do the final accounting. I don't know about you, my ladies, but I wouldn't want to be the one left on the judgment books of God. So, with that in mind, I ask you one last time, are you seeking to be right or righteous? Yes, this is a hard one.

I'm trying to absorb it all myself. Until next time, selah." She ended with a chuckle and her hand reaching for the camera to shut it off.

Right or righteous? I rolled my eyes, sucked my teeth, and prayed for mercy and help all at the same time. What did any of this mean for me, anyway? Was I supposed to simply carry around my husband's secrets and let his mother and ex-fiancé have their way all over my life? Was that the message? Couldn't be it. Didn't sit right with me.

Perhaps I needed to meditate on it a bit more. Perhaps the message would make more sense when it needed to. I didn't see how it applied to me at all at the moment. I shrugged my shoulders and went forward with my search for funny cat videos, determined to force myself back into a good mood.

I mean, when it came to my marriage and Evan, I had the upper hand. When you have a good hand you play it, right?

26

The Bomb

My forced good mood and high hopes extended into the evening as I picked up with Evan where I had left off that morning. He was quiet over our dinner of cheese steak subs and fries as I pointed out cribs and changing tables to consider for our registry. His black clarinet case lay locked and lonely next to the hotel room's nightstand. I kept my eyes off it and off him, too. His sad puppy look was seriously threatening to mess up my hopeful disposition. I'd fought for and deserved this good space.

And then the bomb.

I was clearing off the little table where we had shared our greasy meal. An old episode of *Good Times* played on the television, and Evan was stretched out on the floral spread, his eyes glued to the ceiling. I was talking about a comforter—a pale green Noah's Ark themed baby comforter to be exact—when Evan finally broke his silence.

"Selena," he said, rolling over to his side and placing his head on his elbow, "we need to talk."

"We don't have to get that one if you don't like it, Evan. I thought the green would be a nice neutral color since we're going to wait to find out the gender, and the animals going two by two would go nicely with the pastel animal water fountain my mom found at a yard sale. Did you like the panda bear blanket better?" See, my mind really was only on baby business.

"No, the blanket you picked is fine. That's not what I want to talk about—"

"Well, we meet with Neeka and Peyton Anderson Saturday, and—"

"No, Selena, this is not about Peyton or Kiona or X or none of that. Listen."

"I'm listening, Evan." Actually, I was glad he cut me off at the mention of Peyton's name. Even I'd grown weary of my juvenile antics.

He sat up on the side of the bed, sighed, and stared off into space. Several seconds went by before he spoke again. By the time he opened up his mouth, my heart felt like it was beating in my throat. I knew whatever he had to say was going to be bad.

"Selena, I called my job today and spoke with Wernowski himself." He studied a moving black thread on the floor. At least I hoped it was a black thread. *Lord, how long are we going to have to stay in this hotel again?*

"Listen to me, Selena." Evan continued, "I can't get my job back. And too many of the quality law firms in this area heard about my disaster at court. It was awful. I panicked. My nerves got the best of me, and I forgot everything I had prepared. After all these years of straight A's and honors and placing first in debate team competitions, when it came time to perform on my own in a real court setting, I failed. My law career is over."

"*Awww,* Evan." I walked over to him and wrapped my arms around him, laying his head on my pregnant belly. The baby fluttered. "Your career isn't over. I'm sure you aren't the first attorney to get a bad case of nerves during his or her first real case. I bet every lawyer, new or not, has at least one bad day."

"No, Selena, it was worse than a bad day. I didn't even tell you about the song and rap I did when words failed me."

"The...huh?"

"Anyway, what I'm trying to say is that my clarinet, that's all I've got for now. I'm going to make it work—without Kiona, don't worry. She doesn't have to be part of my act. But until I make it big, we need to really watch how we're spending our money. The house is nowhere near ready, Lena. As you know, Genevaise and her team have completely demolished everything to start building from scratch. She told me today it's going to be a few months before it's in move-in condition."

"Okay, so..."

"So, we aren't going to be able to keep spending money on this hotel room." Evan took a deep breath and blurted out his next words. "Selena, we're going to have to move in with my parents."

I think I actually heard the *kaboom* echoing in my ears. At least I felt it. An instant migraine took over.

"I am not staying with your mother."

"Come on, now. Don't be like this. What other options do we have?"

"I am not staying with your mother. I—we—we can stay with my parents. That way I'll be closer to work."

"Your parents have a one-bedroom apartment and a loveseat for a sofa that your brother is usually on. Just where would we be sleeping? My mother has four extra bedrooms and five extra baths. What's your problem, Selena?"

What was I supposed to say? *I can't stand your mother? She hates* me? You don't know that every time you turn your back, she's giving me the evil eye and hurling horrible insults at me?

"Why don't we find an apartment with a short-term lease?" I wished then we had never terminated the lease on the studio apartment we were originally going to rent after our wedding.

This was all my parents' fault, a part of me suddenly raged. If they hadn't given us that messed-up house we wouldn't be in this predicament now. The thought sickened me. I loved my parents dearly, and I knew they loved me, but they had to have known gifting a money pit would only bring problems—to me *and* my marriage. Isn't that what happened to them?

"And furnish an apartment with what, Selena?" Evan asked. "And pay with what? If we stay with my mom and dad, we can stay rent-free. We'll be able to save up for the baby better. And you know my parents' home has all the fixings—home theatre, exercise room, the updated spa bathroom in the guest suite. It will be just like we're at a resort. Think of it as a few months' vacation."

The man was crazier than I thought if he thought I was going to be relaxed, restored, and refreshed under his mother's watchful eye daily. *Every day with Mrs. Wayland.*

There was no way that was going to happen.

"What about my job, Evan? That's a long commute, and I don't want to look for a new employer in the middle of my pregnancy. I can't *not* work as both of us can't be unemployed. Somebody's got to be making money to do all this saving you're taking about." My eyes pierced his. I couldn't believe the best career path he could come up with for himself involved a clarinet he hadn't played since grade school. He fingered the case as I glared.

"I'm sure you can work out some kind of telecommuting schedule with Kiona. You know my mom has extra office space in her house. Imagine that, you can work from home, and I might be able to convert part of my father's garage into a studio."

His eyes drifted off into la-la land. In the silence that followed, I halfway watched the TV as JJ and Thelma bickered back and forth. Bursts of laughter and *Dy-no-mite* punctuated my racing thoughts.

I couldn't believe Evan was sitting there daydreaming about tooting the day away as I would be sitting under his mother's watchful, judgmental, scheming eye *morning, noon, and night*. Was he for real?

I looked deep in his drifting eyes. There was still innocence in them, I believed. Innocence, but delirium, too. Especially if he thought I was going to be spending both my workday and my home life with his mother. His eyes came back into focus just as mine went awry.

"It's just for a short while, Selena. We can stay there until our house is done, and then it will be just the three of us. The end of February will be here before you know it, and we'll be settled back in our own *new* space way before then, ready to raise and enjoy our baby. Please, Selena. I don't want to argue with you tonight. I'm tired."

I didn't feel like arguing either. I didn't have the energy anymore.

"Okay, Evan. Whatever." I cut off the lights and collapsed on the bed beside him. He immediately pulled me close. Flickering shadows from the television filled the silent space between us. I could smell the hotel shampoo in his hair and feel the prickly skin of his unshaven cheek rubbing against my neck. Tears I didn't feel like explaining to him spilled out of my eyes.

All I wanted was a sane husband and a livable house of my own. All I could see was months of torture and then years of living in a house decorated with steel and concrete.

The episode of *Good Times* that had been playing on the TV went off, and I could hear the studio audience giving its final applause.

Where was my happily ever after?

27

The Buzz

I was able to get Evan to squeeze a few more weeks at the hotel due to a collection of coupons and specials, but there was no denying or delaying the inevitable.

We had to move in with his parents.

Now, here I was, sitting in the Waylands' kitchen at the breakfast bar, a homemade strawberry-banana smoothie in hand. We'd only been here one night, and already all my clothes had been sorted and arranged by color and style, exactly one centimeter apart in the generously sized walk-in closet in the guest suite.

Not by me of course.

You would think I'd be at peace this Saturday morning having just utilized the oversized rain shower in the earth-toned slate-and-marble guest bath. You'd think I'd be enjoying the view of the surrounding golf course from the guest suite's screened-in balcony where fresh coffee and fruit and plush white slippers sat waiting for us.

For Evan, really. I'm just a benefactor to the luxurious perks by marriage.

And you'd really think I'd be enjoying this kitchen with its white-and-black granite countertops, stainless-steel appliances, custom-finished cabinetry, and fully stocked built-in refrigerator, especially considering I'd left a home where the kitchen sink sat in multiple pieces in the backyard.

You'd think.

But instead I was sitting at this breakfast bar, trying my best to ingest a freshly made fruit smoothie as I looked over a detailed press kit featuring Evan-Essence and Miss Kee-Kee.

The electronic press kit had been discussed weeks ago, I was told, long before I'd forced Evan to cut Kiona from his "act." However, the designer—one of Kiona's friends—had just delivered the final version.

I stared at it now on Evan's iPad, which he'd left on the counter. I could not take my eyes off the central image.

There was a jungle for a background with all manner of wildlife, waterfalls, and creepy-looking eyes peeking through the leaves. Both Kiona and my Evan were forefront and wearing animal-print attire. I should say *barely* wearing because all Evan had on was an open vest that showed off his muscular arms and chest as he knelt in a loincloth with that clarinet perched between his lips. A nearly sheer leopard-print scrap of material struggled to contain Kiona's voluptuous curves. She held a half-eaten apple and posed looked like she was dancing under the moonlit tropical sky, one arm arched over a hip. The two of them were locked in an eerie gaze with each other.

Oh, and arms—I assumed they belonged to Kunta X based on the gold ankh bracelet on his wrist—hovered around the canopy of lush trees, extending over the entire photo in an elongated circle, like he was the god of this backward Garden of Evil. I mean Eden.

The words *First Bite: The Official Initial Tour of Evan-Essence and Miss*

Kee-Kee were typed below the image. There were bios and fact sheets inside the portfolio, but I couldn't get past the photo.

Evan's eyes. The way he is looked at that snake of a woman. I knew that look.

"I thought you said you were going to put an end to this."

Mrs. Wayland's hiss slapped my ears from behind. Although it was only eight o'clock on a Saturday morning, she was fully dressed in a pale green suit, matching heels, elaborate beaded jewelry, and fully made-up face. A near-empty glass pitcher of freshly squeezed orange juice sloshed in one of her manicured hands, and she balanced a tray of half-eaten breakfast delicacies her husband had munched on in the other.

I rarely saw the man. He was like a blip on the Wayland radar that stayed on screen long enough to fund the whole contraption, but out of range enough to be left alone. I knew from just the brief hours I'd already spent under her roof that the good doctor was locked away in his private study in the east wing of the house and probably would only surface for the night's formal dinner, unless he received a page or phone call that required his presence elsewhere.

Mrs. Wayland and I had been cordial to each other since Evan and I pulled up with our humble bags and belongings the day before. But then again, she and I hadn't been alone with each other until now.

"This press kit concept was created weeks ago but won't be put in use. At least that's what I've been told." I shrugged and stared again at the photo. My stomach turned anew.

"Selena, I'm not talking about the press kit. I'm talking about the clarinet honks screeching from my garage. I have been holding up my end of our agreement, but there's only so much I can do, pretending I'm on his side. You assured me you would help put an end to this musical maestro madness." She glared at me from under perfectly outlined and arched eyebrows as she slammed the breakfast tray onto a counter near the sink.

"I'm working on it." My voice was hoarse as both our eyes settled on the image of Evan and *"Miss Kee Kee."*

"Evan told me he was pushing Kiona out of the act." Mrs. Wayland's words felt measured. "I'm assuming that was your urging. However, remember, Kiona is doing her part to help him come back to his senses with this. You need to keep your eyes on the big picture and goal here. The more they work together, the more she'll be able to help ease him back to sanity." She glared again at the photo. "Madness," she hissed, giving me another accusatory glare before turning to leave the kitchen.

"That's what Kiona told you, huh?" I mumbled and shook my head to myself, too exhausted to fight.

Caught between a rock and a hard place. The phrase my mother often used applied to my current condition. My mother was furious about our move and the total takeover of our home by the Waylands. I heard my mother's anger in the pans she banged around her kitchen on the few trips I made to their apartment. I listened to her rage as she scraped plates and rattled dishes when I sat in silence in their home. We didn't talk much it seemed these days, and my visits had grown fewer. The topics we needed to talk about held too much emotion—for both of us. I was pregnant and tired, and she was just tired. We left a lot alone.

Evan and I were to meet Neeka and Peyton later on that evening. I should be excited to have a reprieve and meet with my best friend on a twilight cruise at the Inner Harbor, but a part of me dreaded the whole event.

I took another sip of my fruit smoothie, distressed, stressed, depressed, oppressed.

Where was Jesus in all this?

I admit, I hadn't had one of my in-depth Bible study sessions in a while. Actually, I can't remember the last time I really said more than a last-minute phrase or two to the Almighty. This probably would be a good time to pray. Mrs. Wayland had disappeared into the laundry room to toss into the washer the apron and dishtowels she had used during her breakfast preparations. They could have easily had a housekeeper to manage such tasks, but Mrs. Wayland seemed to prefer reminding everyone of the continued sacrifices she made and consummate skills she had to maintain a perfect house all by herself. She'd wash and fuss over teeny tiny loads just to prove her point or seek adulation for her meticulousness. I knew when she finished with the laundering, she would be returning to the kitchen to first complain and then tend to the small tub of dirty dishes.

I guess I could help, seeing as how we were staying there rent-free.

Rent-free, my behind. I felt as though I was paying with my mental health.

I really didn't want to be in the kitchen when Mrs. Wayland returned. I finished my smoothie and placed the glass in the sink.

Okay, I rinsed it out before I left. I owed that much, I guess.

Twenty minutes later, after washing, drying, and putting away my glass, the plates and teacups on Mr. Wayland's breakfast tray, and the other dirty dishes in the sink—and wiping down all the counters, cabinetry, and the hardwood floor—I was wandering the halls again, thinking I needed to just go ahead and get back into conversation with God. I wished I had a map of Mrs. Wayland's house to find that den I saw in the basement when she'd given me a quick tour last night. It was small, big enough to fit only a chair and a bookcase, but the French doors that enclosed the space made the room feel both luxurious and private, I remembered thinking. I headed down to the lower level and its maze of rooms to find and claim it. I had just found the corridor where I thought the room was when I heard a peculiar sound.

A buzzing noise.

I'd heard that sound before. The day we returned from our honeymoon, when Mrs. Wayland and the judge came over for dinner, I had heard that buzz coming from her purse. And then I had heard it again on one of the nights during my miscarriage scare, when Mrs. Wayland served me dinner in my room. Both times, she had looked as alarmed as I had looked confused.

The noise was coming from what I remembered to be her craft room to the left of the little den.

Yes, curiosity got the best of me. I looked both ways down the hall, making sure I was alone in the long, luxuriously carpeted basement's central corridor.

Nobody.

With a hesitant hand, I turned the crystal knob to enter the ornate room where Mrs. Wayland crafted centerpieces and unique arrangements for her events, as well as personal projects for her friends' homes and her own. She'd said what the room was during the tour, but the door had been closed and I hadn't seen the inside.

The door squealed open with barely a push. I looked back behind me to see if anyone had heard the door's surprising protest, but other than a loud laugh coming from Evan in the media room, nobody seemed to notice I was snooping through my mother-in-law's private sanctuary and creative space. I turned back to study the craft room, leaning forward to try to identify the source of the sound.

The buzzing had grown louder with the open door, but the view in front of me momentarily distracted me from my fact-finding mission. My mouth was agape as I took in the shades of pale pink, lemon yellow, seafoam green, and the rest of the rainbow of pastel colors that lined the walls in the form of fabrics, ribbons, and ledges filled with paint bottles, strands of beads, and more. The room was a crafter's fantasyland, meticulously organized with white shelves, dressers, a sewing cabinet, and a large worktable that ran nearly the entire length of the room. A linen dress form stood in the corner nearest the doorway wearing a silver feather boa and a rhinestone-studded fedora. A crystal chandelier dangled and glittered in the center of the room.

"Okay, Mrs. Wayland, I see you. Nice." It was impossible not to admire her space, not only for its exquisite décor, but even more for the intricate workmanship it displayed. Floral arrangements, custom-decorated candle holders, jeweled favor boxes—all projects in various stages of completion—lined her worktable.

The soft, delicate sophistication of the room made the buzzing noise that much more disconcerting. The grating sound still reminded me of a chainsaw, and the animal-like squeal that punctuated it seemed to even make the little one inside of me jump.

I followed the sound to the opposite end of her room. There, a floor-to-ceiling bookshelf, complete with an antique rolling ladder, took up the entire wall. On the floor in front of the bookshelf sat Mrs. Wayland's purse. I recalled how I'd been close to unzipping it the first time I'd heard the noise coming from it, the day Evan and I had returned from our honeymoon. This time I was determined I would succeed with my quest for an explanation for the bizarre noise.

Except the sound suddenly stopped and something else grabbed my attention.

A massive scrapbook lay open on one of the bookcase shelves.

Okay, so first let me admit that I got on the first step of the rolling ladder and gave a gentle push to glide to the next section. Felt like something you'd see in a movie, and I wanted the experience. That's how I discovered the book, next section over, on a shelf eye-level from my perch on the first rung of the ladder. Pictures, mementos, and artifacts from Mrs. Wayland's life cluttered its pages. Awards, candid snapshots, certificates, and family photos from her childhood up to the present day filled the leather-bound book. Spelling bees in grade school, synchronized swimming and ice-skating in middle school, equestrian competitions and volleyball championships in high school and college. I stared at a thin, youthful Madelyn who seemed to judge me with her sharp eyes and smug smile even from the yellowed clippings and glossy pictures.

The awards and accolades continued into her adult years with the pictures moving beyond her posing with her solemn-faced parents and socialite friends to major public figures in politics and the arts. A picture at the Kennedy Center standing in a shimmering ball gown next to Razi. A snapshot of her standing next to the mayor of DC at a groundbreaking for a new cultural arts center in the Adams Morgan neighborhood. I already knew these highlights of her life. I flipped back to her younger years.

There were multiple pages dedicated to every year of her life starting with baby photo contests she'd won. Every year of her life had pages upon pages of highlights.

Every year except year sixteen.

Only a single page existed for that year, and only one thing was featured on the single page: a dried rose. Its petals were blood red with decaying brown on the edges. Its stem was wrapped in a torn piece of candy wrapping; off-white, thin tissue wrapping like that found in a box of chocolates. Looked like some handwriting was on the crinkled paper. I squinted to see the words: *We were young when we first met. I was Romeo to your Juliet. You stole my heart, I stole your mind. Two thieves who had to serve time, Sentenced to live—* The words stopped abruptly where the paper was torn.

Hmmm.... Let me find out Mrs. Wayland had some young love, some boo thang back in her day. I didn't know whether to smile or cringe at the possibility.

Funny, there was nothing else from that year – no awards or recognitions, no newspaper clippings; nothing but a dead rose and lines from an unfinished poem on a torn piece of chocolate candy wrapping.

Wait a minute.

Chocolate candy wrapping.

I'd just seen something similar on another page, I was certain.

The year Evan was born.

I turned to the page and noted what looked like another piece of the same torn wrapper. It was taped under Evan's newborn photo. Another line of the poem was written on it ... *Forever a part*.... That's all that was there, the torn edges leaving the remainder of the poem a mystery. A single dried blood red rose petal – probably from the same rose from her sixteenth year – lay just beside the broken line of poetry and Evan's photo.

Were Dr. Wayland and Mrs. Wayland star-crossed teenaged lovers? I could not recall Evan ever sharing his parents' relationship origin story. Now, I was intrigued. Were the two romantics at heart? Flipping through the album, I'd noted numerous pictures of them together at artsy events – well, mostly foundations for them, anyway. There were also photos of them at art gallery openings, dance performances, and even a book release party for a former national poet laureate. Him always in a black tuxedo and her in long, flowing, glittering gowns. Their hairstyles changed over the decades, but their solemn faces and stoic poses did not.

Perhaps behind all the money, prestige, and family pedigree were two souls dancing in wild abandonment when they were alone. I closed my eyes, trying to reconcile the cold, humorless, distant version of Dr. Wayland with another possible side of him – a young man who wrote flowery love poems to his teenaged flame and future wife. I tried to imagine him whispering sweet nothings over rose bouquets and chocolates as a teen and her promising him an heir, a son to carry on his family's notable legacy, the promise fulfilled with Evan's birth.

Nope. I shook my head. Couldn't see it.

Nothing about Dr. Wayland's sunken demeanor and gray bushy

eyebrows and white stiff ear hairs spoke poetry and love and rose petals and chocolates to me.

But what did I know?

I was flipping through the years of Mrs. Wayland's life, trying to make sense of her and him, trying to see if I'd missed something that would reveal more clues of their love and passion, when the buzzing restarted—this time with a vengeance.

Louder, stronger in its reverberations, I scrambled to leave the scrapbook in its original position on the shelf, remembering to leave it on the page on which it had been open. I didn't want to leave any evidence of my snooping before I got out of there.

Forget trying to figure out what the noise was. The chainsaw sound was so loud and vibrational, I could only believe that it would not be long before someone else came to the room. Indeed, I could hear Mrs. Wayland's heavy footsteps nearly dashing down the stairs.

Still standing on the bookshelf ladder, I used a foot to push me and it back to its original position.

In retrospect, perhaps the ladder had been cooperating with me up to this point because it somehow sensed I was a woman with child, and it was willing to give me grace as I balanced on its creaky bottom rung.

In additional retrospect, perhaps the antique ladder was more for decorative purposes and not meant to be treated as some type of high-end playground ride that glided on its track with a strong push from my foot.

I heard the crack before I felt it. I tried to grab hold of a shelf but only managed to grip a loose basket filled with craft feathers, which was connected to a series of other baskets holding a hodgepodge of supplies.

"Selena."

My name sounded as sharp as thumbtacks coming from Mrs. Wayland's lips. She rushed into the room, grabbed her purse, did something to quiet the noise, then pulled her handbag close to her bosom.

I was sprawled on the floor, covered with sequins, silk flower petals, craft sticks and cotton balls. Multi-colored feathers floated gently in the air all about me. I watched one purple feather in particular meander through the chaos and finally land next to a pair of pale green pumps. I followed the stockings that rose out of them to the hem of the suit above it. Slowly, I turned my head and eyes up toward the towering figure before me, thinking of how to address the anger and hatred I expected to see in return.

"I'm sorry for the mess, Mrs. Wayland." I let out a nervous chuckle. "And for breaking your ladder. I was looking for...some cotton balls for my ears." I grabbed a handful that had landed in my lap. "Evan snores and, and—" *Oh goodness, did I really just say that?* Now there would be more contempt on her face at the unflattering remark about her son. "I mean cotton balls for Evan. I'm the snorer, and, and—"

"Here, let me help you with that." Once again, the anger I had braced myself for wasn't in her eyes. Instead, fear.

Pure unadulterated fear.

I marveled at her uncharacteristic clumsiness as she rushed through the falling feathers, stumbled through the scattered supplies, and grabbed a fistful of cotton balls.

"Here, Selena." She dumped the cotton balls into my lap. "And listen, dear—" Her voice was two pitches higher than usual, and her smile was just as forced— "anytime you need something, please let me know. I'll be glad to get it for you."

"Thank you, Mrs. Wayland." I stood with her assistance, then surveyed the massive damage and mayhem I had caused in her private space. "I am so sorry about this mess, but don't worry. I'll clean it up." I reached to scoop up some feathers. "And that sound—"

"Oh no, Selena." The high-pitched version of her voice continued as she gripped her bag tighter. "Please don't lift a finger. You are a guest in my home." No mention of the noise we'd both heard. "I don't mind cleaning this up at all. Don't worry about a thing, including this old ladder. It's an easy fix for my husband. It's happened before. Why don't you go see what Evan is up to? He might need help with something."

"Evan is right here, and I don't need help with anything. Looks like *you* need a hand here. Good morning, Mom." My husband, who seemed to have appeared from nowhere, bent to peck his mother's cheek before turning to me. "Whoa, what happened here? Selena, are you and the baby okay?" He bypassed my cheek completely and kissed my stomach instead.

"That's right, the baby." Mrs. Wayland gasped with such emotion, I recalled I'd seen a playbill in her scrapbook showcasing her starring role in a fifth-grade stage performance. She barely seemed to have noticed Evan's jovial greeting. "Are you okay, Selena? Falling like that. You need to go rest right now. Evan, help her to your room. She needs to get off her feet."

"Oh, Lena, you fell? Yes, let's get you off your feet," he gasped, noticing the cracked ladder rung. I saw the instant alarm on Evan's face, but even more than that, I noticed Mrs. Wayland— despite the sudden dramatic concern she had expressed over me and the baby's well-being—had not loosened her grip on her handbag, nor reached to clean up one single sequin or craft supply. Although the buzzing had been silenced, that lady was not taking any chances of anybody discovering her mystery possession or me attempting to ask any more questions. I wondered if Evan noticed her standing frozen as he ushered me out of the room.

What am I talking about? The man thinks Kiona Tandy wants to be my new best friend. He obviously is oblivious to the secrets and motives of the women around him.

"Are you sure you're okay, Selena?" His concern was genuine.

"I'm fine, Evan."

"Good, good. Don't scare me like that." He patted my back and brushed my forehead with a kiss. I smiled, catching a whiff of his cologne as he pulled me closer to him while we headed down the hall. With one easy swoop, he picked me up and cradled me to his chest. I remembered our wedding night and how he insisted on carrying me over the threshold into our deluxe honeymoon villa suite in St. Martin. The sweet memory carried me away for a moment—away from the strange, unsolved mystery in Mrs. Wayland's purse and the fear in her eyes—and I closed my eyes as his heartbeat melted into my ear. I didn't even notice we had bypassed the main stairwell that would lead to the guest suite, which had become our temporary living quarters, and were heading instead to a rear staircase that led to the mudroom.

"There's a large chaise in the garage. I'll lay you there, and you can listen to me play my clarinet. Just wait until you hear my new composition. I've been working on it all morning."

I shot up and out of his arms so quickly, he nearly fell trying to regain his balance. I struggled to regain my bearings.

"Just don't forget we need to get ready for our date with Neeka and Peyton later this evening." The only words I could blurt out. I knew our current circumstances had completely taken the bite out of my blackmail, but it was still worth seeing the fear on his face.

I was tired of being the only distraught party in this marital contract. I wondered then what I could do to fully get back the upper hand, the only hand at the moment I wanted to have and to hold. *The wise woman builds her house. But the foolish pulls it down with her*—I know, I know.

Look, I guess if I really was trying to play the game God's way, I would have been kneeling and meditating in that makeshift prayer closet I'd found instead of snooping around Mrs. Wayland's craft room.

Don't look at me like that. What closets have *you* been in and out of today?

I know.

I need to stop worrying about everybody else and do right myself.

28

The Betrayal

Growing up, the Inner Harbor was one of my favorite places in Baltimore. Tourists from every corner of the world would fill the massive pier, eating outdoors at seafood and chain restaurants; waiting in line to gain entrance to the National Aquarium or the Maryland Science Center; standing around the outdoor amphitheater looking at jugglers and fire-eaters; sitting on evenly spaced benches around the water's edge, watching the water taxis and private boats meander along the dark brown ripples.

Now, the once bustling shopping buildings in the center of it all were mere skeletons of their former selves. Largely vacant with just a few remaining stores and restaurants, the two Harborplace pavilions that anchored the corner of Light and Pratt Streets felt nearly abandoned on the water's edge, the lifeblood of eateries and souvenir shops drained and gone from its corridors. Passersby now flocked to other sites around the Harbor leaving at least these two buildings alone in their slow death.

The setting matched my mood.

. From our perch at the outdoor amphitheater that sat between the pavilions, I had a near uninterrupted view of the whole span of the Harbor, from the larger-than-life guitar overhead the Hard Rock Café at the Power Plant to the left of me, to the enormous flag flying over Federal Hill far to my right. The water in front of me was murky green. In the distance I knew the familiar Domino Sugar sign and Francis Scott Key bridge were standing duty, two Harbor landmarks that assured weary boats the dock was just around the bend.

Evan and I both sat in silence waiting it seemed for the other to make sense of our ever-changing predicament or offer a game plan for the evening ahead, something, anything.

Neeka and Peyton would be arriving soon.

I could see the Bay Queen waiting at her dock, ready to escort her guests to the outer edge of the Harbor's waters before circling back. I knew from prior experience the sunset cruise would offer all the crabs and drinks one could consume, and the calypso band would give the excursion a festive feel, the perfect soundtrack for the partygoers who would no doubt fill both decks. Some attendees would be dancing and laughing with old and new friends; others would be quietly sitting outside, perhaps cuddling or sipping wine, while enjoying the soothing panoramas of the water at twilight.

"I guess we should get going." I finally broke the silence. The Bay Queen sat a few minutes' walk away from where we sat and was due to depart in the next twenty minutes.

Evan didn't budge.

"They'll be here any minute. We're supposed to meet them at the ramp."

Wearing khakis and a light blue buttoned-down shirt, Evan looked lost in his own world. He sat with both elbows resting on his spread-apart knees.

"Evan—" I stood and patted his back— "we need to go." I swung my handbag strap over my shoulder and turned toward the steps.

"Peyton was my first roommate at Maryland."

I turned around and studied my husband who still hadn't budged. He wasn't looking at me either; rather, his eyes were fixed on a passing sailboat that had the name *CLARITY* in large block letters on its hull. A man and a woman sat close together on board, looking like they were laughing. They were too far away for us to hear their gleeful sounds, but from the way the woman threw her head back and opened her mouth in a wide smile, I knew they were enjoying the Saturday evening far better than Evan was.

Torment.

That was the look on his face.

"When my parents helped me move into my dorm room my first day of college, he was already there, unpacked, sitting on his bed watching *SpongeBob* and reading a biography on Jackie Robinson. I knew right then we were going to be brothers for life."

He looked at me now, and the expression on his face was one I had never seen on him before. Fear? Agony? Resolution? I couldn't tell.

"And we *were* brothers," Evan continued. "Freshman year we did everything together: went to games, hung out at the student union, ate dinner at South Campus. We even talked about pledging a fraternity together." A loose smiled formed on his face before slowly fading. "And then sophomore year, he had to transfer to a college back home in Baltimore. Moved back in with his mother to help her with his little brother. Dead now. Dominic."

There was a brief moment of silence, then: "We kept in touch through all that, though, hanging out during school breaks when we could, playing pick-up games, talking about the successful black men we would be in a few years. Me a lawyer, him an accountant. It wasn't until the end of my sophomore year that we began to lose contact. I think about a year or so went by without a single word between us.

"Then he calls me out the blue one day the summer before my senior year to tell me he'd dropped out of college, moved to Vegas, and gotten married there. He'd started some clothing brand business and was hanging out with celebrities and athletes. He wanted me to come to a big party he was throwing. Said it would give me an open door and connections toward my entertainment law goals." Evan shook his head. "Even then he was looking out for me. I went to the party. Flew out there for a weekend, and my boy had made it big. Had a massive, nice house, too. Seemed like everything was perfect for him. I was shocked when at that party his new wife, Kiona Tandy, kept making eyes at me. I was embarrassed, mad even, at her flirting with me every time he turned his back. I knew Peyton deserved better. They had only been married a couple of months at that point. I didn't go anywhere near her, I didn't say anything about it, and that's how I was going to keep it."

We were both quiet for a few minutes. Evan still stared at the sailboat of the laughing couple, now gliding leisurely out of view. I had an eye on the Bay Queen and the approaching groups and couples heading her way. Still no sight of Neeka.

"Then next thing I know," Evan blurted out, "Peyton's business took a downturn, he was back in Baltimore, and Kiona's suddenly a student at Maryland. Somehow Kiona and I both end up as teaching assistants together for a sociology class. It was my senior year. I was stressing over the LSAT and getting into Georgetown, and there was this impossible professor who really seemed to have it in for me. And then there was Kiona, by my side, hugging me, encouraging me, letting me lean on her shoulder when nobody else was there for me." A momentary pause. "It was wrong, Selena, I know, but I really thought I was in love with her." He paused again before continuing.

"I barely talked to Peyton for the nearly year and a half Kiona and I were together. He knew nothing about our relationship. Yeah, part of that time, I was with Celeste—you know, the ex-girlfriend I told you about? But I was with Kiona, too. It was a mess. Celeste suspected something was up. That's why she broke it off." He sighed, shook his head. "And then, Peyton calls me one day, angry, upset, telling me his beautiful and perfect wife had divorced him and that she was taking the little bit of money he had left after his business failed. She'd managed to get the proceeds from the sale of his home and his cars, nearly everything he owned. And—" he paused— "she'd told him she was pregnant with another man's child."

Evan dabbed a corner of one eye with his thumb before continuing. "I was shocked myself because she hadn't told me anything about either the divorce or the pregnancy. She told me the next day, though. Had her finalized divorce papers and a sonogram framed and wrapped in a gift box when we met for dinner. I was shocked, really. I wanted to hurry up and marry her, thinking it would somehow make everything right.

"The only thing my father had ever said to me about relationships was to not ever dishonor the family name or finances by having a baby outside of wedlock. I won't repeat the actual words he said to me. So, when Kiona told me she was pregnant, all I could think was I needed to marry her right away. Didn't want to mess up the family tree or cause inheritance issues, and all that. And Peyton...we barely talked. We'd drifted apart over the years. I was surprised I'd even heard from him when I did. Kiona never told him about us. I guess I thought I could hide the whole affair and child from him for a while and would deal with it if and when I had to. I don't know what I was thinking. I wasn't thinking. I was reacting. I was...panicked." Tears filled his eyes.

"You know," his voice dropped to a whisper, "I actually prayed with Peyton on the phone that night he called to tell me what Kiona had done to him. He was so devastated. He told me he was going to find out who the other man was and hurt him bad. I got all Jesus-y on him and told him to forgive and let God deal with it. I told him to let her go and move on, that finding the other man wasn't worth it. He took my advice, Selena. I talked to him maybe one or two more times before he moved on without a trace. Even his mother didn't know where he was. That night we saw him with Neeka was the first time I had seen him in years. We hadn't talked in years, but we had a strong bond once upon a time. I can't have him finding out about me and Kiona, Selena. It would crush him to the core. He's been through enough in life. Finding out what I did would devastate him. And I can't pretend to be all at ease around him." He shook his head, biting his lip. "I can't do this tonight, Selena. We can't do this."

We.

A sigh louder than I knew I could give passed through my lips. "Evan, I promised Neeka we would be here tonight. I'm not going to back out of plans with my best friend, especially since we're already here."

Really, this was ridiculous. *We.* I had nothing to do with his betrayal. Another sigh escaped. This time I could feel heat rising from my forehead, and my nose began to itch.

"Selena, please." His words begged, but his tone sounded strong and steady. He stared me straight in the eye. "I understand Neeka is your best friend, but I'm your husband. When it comes down to it, your husband should be your first loyalty. My feelings should matter more to you than anyone else's. The Bible says we're one, Selena, but how can we enjoy our oneness if you are more concerned about your best friend than your God-ordained union?"

"Oh, so now you're getting all *Jesus-y*, as you put it, with me?" My nose really itched now. "What about all that loyalty business on your part when I told you I didn't want you anywhere near Kiona? And do my feelings matter more to you than your mother's? And—"

"Okay, let me stop you right there before you go down the wrong road about the woman who is currently housing you and the friend who wanted to plan your baby shower *and* is standing up to her superiors to let you work from home."

"Oh, stop." I couldn't take his foolishness one more second. "Just shut up. Before I even get to your mother, let's talk a little bit about this so-called *friend* who I already told you will not be anywhere near my baby shower. I saw that half-naked picture of you and Kiona in your garden of evil. After what you just shared with me, do you really not see why I would have a problem with you being around her? She's sneaky and conniving. You have to know that she didn't just end up on the University of Maryland campus and in your sociology class by accident. You two had an illicit relationship that was not deterred by the fact that she was married. Am I really to believe you being married to me is going to stop you from indulging yourself with her again? And if you're supposed to be worried so much about your spouse's feelings first, why are you so adamant I protect your mother's feelings from the truth about you and Kiona?"

"That's different," he yelled. "Stop twisting my words around. It's not about my mother's feelings, it's about mine—how *I* would feel if she found out."

"Well, what about how *I* feel? Do you ever think about that? Does it ever occur to you how unhappy you are making me with all your past and present dilemmas involving your mother and your ex? Where do I rank on your list of loyalties?" I yelled back.

"For real though…" His voice was calm again. "You've turned this conversation into a completely different subject. We were talking about tonight and what to do about Neeka and Peyton. I said I don't want us to meet with them. The bottom line is this: I'm your husband, you're a Christian woman, and the Bible says you're supposed to submit to me. So, what's the problem?"

Oh. No. He. Didn't. No he did not go there, to one of the most misused and abused passages of scripture on marriage. Did I really need to explain to him that when Paul wrote for wives to submit to their husbands, he started the whole thing off saying believers should be submitting to *each other*, and finished with saying husbands were to be treating their wives the same way Christ treated His church? And in case you missed the type of treatment Christ gave his church, let's review: Jesus *died* for His bride. He gave up His entire life, denied Himself—His feelings, His will—completely. He became a total mental, spiritual, and physical sacrifice to provide for His church what she needed. That's the kind of love Paul said a husband should be showing and have for his wife. So many people skip right over that and the 'each other' part.

Christ wasn't in this relationship for Himself. He was in it for the love he had for His bride, to act in her best interests, and to perfectly submit to and please His Father's will. Christ's bride is a gift from His Father. He's only going to do right by her. If my husband was truly sacrificing himself to meet my needs and to please God, okay, sure, I wouldn't have a problem going along with his ideas. We'd be on the same page, serving, supporting, and submitting to each other as partners together in Him, right?

Well, I was certain there was nothing about God in Evan's whole equation. Past hidden sin plus present not coming clean equals continued stress, fear, and general unhappiness. And now his secret formula was multiplying and giving me grief. Like a farmer who plants an apple seed and gets back a whole tree of apples, I felt like Evan and Kiona's seed of sin had blossomed into a whole orchard of bad fruit that was spoiling my marriage, my happiness, and now my relationship with my best friend.

"Evan—" I took his hands in mine, stared him straight in the eye. "Yes, you are correct. I am a Christian woman, although I'm not going to pretend I'm perfect because we both know I'm not. However, I can't go along with you down a road that leads away from

Jesus. I'll be praying with and for you as you figure out how you're going to address this situation with Peyton. You know how I feel about you and Kiona spending time together, but I see all I can do right now is tell you my feelings and pray you make decisions based on pleasing God. But just so you know, I'm not one of these women who will stay around as you run around. I've got too much respect for myself and too much trust that God can bless me with His best, not your mess."

"Dang, Lena. I sound so stupid and wrong right now, don't I?" Evan closed his eyes for a second and shook his head before opening them. He looked straight ahead, as if he couldn't bear to look me in the eyes. "I mean, listen to me, Lena. I'm out here quoting scriptures like I know what I'm talking about and acting like the exact kind of man I don't want to be. I've done nothing but get you upset and put you in a hard place because of my own shortcomings. You deserve better than this. I'm sorry."

A few seconds of silence ticked between us before he continued. "Selena, I'm not cheating on you, and I have no plans to ever do so. I've been down that road of infidelity, and I already know the pain and problems that wait at the end. I never want to put you through what Kiona and I put Peyton through. As far as what to do about him, right or wrong, I don't want him finding out, and I don't see how the two of us can sit and pretend to enjoy dinner with them tonight. Forget the whole loyalty and submission speech—I was talking out of my own selfishness—but please, let's just go back home. Not because I said so or as a test of your loyalty, I'm just tired."

"No." I held my ground. "We are going to dinner with them, and we are going to have a nice time."

"How? By pretending we're having fun? Isn't that being dishonest? Wouldn't our actions be like lying?"

I sighed again as I felt my ground shaking. He was right in a way. Even I knew our awkwardness that irritated Neeka at our last meeting would only resume—and probably intensify—onboard the Bay Queen. It was unavoidable that both Evan and I would be uncomfortable until an open and honest discussion about the past occurred. And of course, that would most likely lead to even more discomfort.

My wavering must have been evident as Evan seemed to jump right into my thoughts. "Just call Neeka and tell her we can't make it."

"So rather than lie in action, you want me to lie in word? What am I supposed to say to her? Can't we just pray about this?"

"Yes, we can pray. We will pray. Together. I just need some time. Please, Selena, give me your phone. I'll call her. Please, I don't feel like fighting with you anymore."

My marriage so far felt like it had been nothing more than a menu of choices with only "bad" and "worse" as the options presented to me. I gave Evan my cell phone. He scrolled my contacts until he got to Neeka's name. As he dialed, my eyes drifted from the water and the Bay Queen to a beaming woman approaching the ramp.

It was Neeka, and she looked beautiful. Her natural hair was free in a perfect curly afro with a white flower on one side. She wore a just-above-the knee-length white linen dress with chunky white heels and a plain white sweater, a cool contrast against her dark cocoa skin. Large turquoise beads hung around her neck and from her ears, and several white and turquoise bangles covered one of her wrists. Peyton, walking next to her, was quite the looker himself in a striped polo shirt and equally bright smile. Together, they looked stunning, happy, complete.

Perfect.

Although they were talking and smiling, I didn't miss the quick scans Neeka was giving the surrounding crowd, the slight worry lining her regally featured face. After Evan dialed, I could see her digging in her purse for her phone and the smiling hopefulness as she answered.

"Neeka, I'm sorry." Evan's voice sounded distant to me. "We're not going to make it in time. We couldn't find a close enough parking space, and Selena can't walk that fast in her condition, you know."

I could see her smile dropping, her shoulders tightening, the panic on her face. She and Peyton were waiting at the bottom of the ramp, and she began to frantically scan the entire Harbor for a glimpse of us. I wondered if she would spot us in the amphitheater. Evan must have had the same thought for he quickly added: "We're coming from one of the side streets near Federal Hill." She turned completely to her right, her back now to us.

"I know. I'm sorry," Evan continued. "Yeah, I know they are pretty strict with their departure time. I just don't think we're going to make it. Yeah...I'm so sorry. Blame me for this. Selena is too upset and out of breath to talk right now. We'll definitely pay you back for the tickets... Huh? Okay... I will... Again, I'm sorry. Tell Peyton we said hi."

They both hung up. I watched with great pain and nausea as Neeka waited at the bottom of the ramp until the last possible moment. Both she and Peyton were silent and unsmiling, and I could tell by the way her sweater now hung limply from her shoulders she was thoroughly dejected. Her joy at the night's promise had been deflated, and it was our entire fault. What kind of friend was I?

What kind of wife?

Evan and I watched as they finally boarded the boat, the last couple before the crew untied the ropes and moved the vessel out toward the bay.

"Thank you, Selena." Evan stood at last.

I don't know what bothered me more: the sudden smile he had on his face as he got up and talked of finding some burgers and fries, or the fact that he had lied to Neeka without a blinking eye or hesitant word.

29

The Bad Week Begins

I guess I really shouldn't have had high hopes for the following week, but I can honestly say I wasn't expecting it to go as bad as it did.

It started on Sunday, the Lord's Day, when I should have been in church. Instead, I was locked in the guest suite, deliberating painting my toenails while I could still see them. Evan was busy squeaking away in the garage with that darn clarinet. I didn't miss that he kept his cell phone on him at all times now and the text messages kept rolling in.

Evan was opting to go to the church his parents attended, where the service would be over in less than an hour. The music there wasn't my style, and he didn't push me to join them. My mother wanted me to attend morning services with her, but it was easy to get out of that. After all, I was over an hour away from our home church, and in my condition, I didn't feel like driving anywhere, even the halfway point my mom offered to pick me up from. I was still feeling nauseated—at least that's what I told her. Truth was,

I did feel nauseated, but not really from little junior or juniorette growing inside of me.

I felt sick from our lying to Neeka the night before.

I felt sick from watching Evan reorganize his mother's home office for me to begin working from home starting Monday. It was his idea, a feeble attempt at a peace offering to make me feel like the space was my own. Mrs. Wayland watched every single move the both of us did as we rearranged her private space for my use. Of course, she praised all of Evan's ideas of where to move the desk and the printer and criticized even my slightest suggestions about moving the computer and the file cabinets.

I felt sick every time I passed Evan's iPad where the picture of Evan and Kiona staring at each other in that steamy publicity photo served as the screensaver. "Gotta keep my dreams in focus," he had explained.

With the way I felt, I didn't even feel like going to church, although that's probably the one place that day I would have caught a break. However, the idea of running into Fran Delaney or any other woman from the Bible study made me wonder how much of a break I would have really had. I didn't feel like explaining myself or my situation to anyone, not even Sister Corrine Knight, the one person I believed truly had good intentions and cared for my soul.

So, I laid in the bed listening to everyone else shuffle through their Sunday morning routine to get ready for eleven o'clock service. I kept a plastic bag in arm's reach to grab if the bedroom door opened. Whoever the intruder, they'd see me, see the bag, hear me gag, and then quickly reclose the door, leaving me alone. Well, that was my plan, anyway, though I doubted Mrs. Wayland would care, Evan would come in, or his father even knew I existed. I pulled a pillow over my head and fought to get comfortable under the heavy down comforter. I felt sick, tired, disgusted, nauseated, guilty, and really peeved about it all.

I tried to go back to sleep, but sleep evaded me, so I'd sat up, yanked off all the covers, moved to the end of the bed, and grabbed some nail polish.

A heavy knock sounded at the bedroom door. I had just applied the second coat of Silver Raspberry on my toes, and a large span of white carpet stood between my robe and my half-naked self.

Wet toenails, white carpet.

Didn't sound like a good combination. Then again, it wasn't *my* white carpet, and I was feeling evil and also unwilling to let anyone other than Evan see just how big my thighs and butt were getting. So, I walked to get my robe, and I walked to answer the door without a single look down at my feet or any trail they were or were not leaving.

Okay, I walked on the back of my heels. I don't have a death wish, y'all.

"Good, morning, Selena." Mrs. Wayland had an unusually large smile on her face. I didn't trust it. "Since you will, unfortunately, not be joining Dr. Wayland, Evan, and me for service at our church, I'm asking you to keep an eye on the roast in the oven. Our Sunday dinner is going to be even more special today." She beamed. "All of my children will be here." I groaned inside at the thought of Evan's sisters staring me up and down as usual. Mrs. Wayland looked up dreamily at the ceiling.

Then her smile cut off, and she glared at me. This I trusted. "You *are* going to be able to tell if the roast needs to come out of the oven, aren't you? Maybe I shouldn't trust such an important part of the meal to you. I want this dinner to be perfect, Selena."

"Good morning, Mrs. Wayland," I chimed. I couldn't decide if I wanted to ignore her, insult her, play along, or just slam the door in her face. I smiled back at her. "I think I can handle taking care of the roast. What time do you want me to take it out? Or does it have one of those pop-out thermometers like a Thanksgiving turkey?"

She recoiled. "Exactly what I thought. You're not going to know when it's done. Don't worry about it, Selena. I'm going to stay here and finish the dinner. I don't want a disaster."

"You're already dressed, and you're going to church." Another nearly foreign voice came from behind her.

Dr. Wayland.

He wore an ash gray suit that complemented his grave face. Although he spoke, he didn't stop or slow his pace as he passed us in the hallway.

"Selena, take out the roast whenever you think it's done. Madelyn, let's go. Evan already has the car started for us. Come on."

"Yes, dear." Mrs. Wayland nearly jumped and ran behind the man.

Evan rarely talked about his father, and as I stood there thinking about it, I had rarely even heard the man speak. At Sunday dinners and special occasions—the only times it seemed I even saw him—he was always just a quiet fixture at the table, like a bowl of peas or an extra napkin ring. When dinners were over, he would disappear into a deep armchair in his den and watch golf on cable in silence. He was usually nowhere to be found when it came time to say goodbyes.

As I watched Mrs. Wayland skirt off under her husband's command, I wondered how much I should have tried to learn about my father-in-law and his relationship with Evan and his wife before I got married. How much of who he is—or isn't—makes Evan who he is and how he thinks? I wondered if the doctor had had any flings. And how would Madelyn have responded? Cover it up? Tell him off?

How much does your spouse's parents and their marriage spill into your own marital relationship? Seemed like a good question to ask Sister Corrine Knight and the women's group if I ever got the nerve to go back again. I wondered about a lot of things regarding Mrs. Wayland, Evan, his sisters, and the good doctor as I leaned against the bedroom door, listened to their car roar off, and welcomed the quiet and calm that came with being the only person in the house. And then I got tired of wondering and got back into the bed, remembering how sick, tired, pregnant, and nauseated I felt. This time sleep came.

30

The Fire

They were all looking at me. Evan; his mother; Dr. Wayland; his older sisters, Penelope and Tracey; and Penelope's three-year-old twin daughters, Tori and Topaz. The sisters' significant others, quite a few neighbors. The firefighters, the policemen, and for some reason I still don't understand, a man in a biological hazard protection suit. All were looking at me.

I had been dreaming about polish dogs, corned beef hash, and carnival rides when I heard the smoke detector go off. In a panic, I'd immediately begun to run toward the kitchen, but when I smelled smoke from where I was on the upstairs landing, I dialed 911 on the cordless phone Mrs. Wayland kept at the top of the steps.

I was half-asleep when I dialed, and it really did seem like the house was filled with black smoke and engulfed in flames. That's what I screamed into the phone at the operator, and, if memory serves me correct, I yelled something about the homeowner being a doctor and there could be some medical specimens that needed to be saved along with me.

Okay, I guess that explains the biohazard man.

When I finally woke up completely and ventured down the rest of the steps into the kitchen, I knew immediately my frantic phone call had been a mistake.

The raging fire I thought had overtaken the house was some flames confined to a pot of greens. Mrs. Wayland had made no mention of the pot, so there was that.

Anyway, if I'd known about the greens or even the fire extinguisher under the kitchen sink, the whole scene in front of me probably could have been avoided.

Of course, by the time I realized this, sirens were already wailing in the near distance, the flames had leaped from the pot to the wall behind it, and, as is consistent with the usual events of my life, the emergency trucks and Evan et al. converged in the circular driveway all at the same time.

The image of Mrs. Wayland jumping out of her husband's moving Jaguar and running across her massive front lawn screaming and holding onto her chest is forever sealed in my mind.

"Well, it looks like everything is under control here, ma'am." The fire chief spoke to Mrs. Wayland. "Again, I'm sorry about your kitchen. Our rookie here was ready to put out his first fire and got a little overzealous with the extinguisher. He got in here before the rest of us could get in to survey the place."

I stood dripping in a sea of white foam. Me, the stove, the counters, and every tray, plate, platter, and pan of carefully prepared food sitting on or near the oven. All of it and me dripped with white foam. I'd been blasted by the rookie along with the stovetop when I tried to save dinner. The wall behind the stove was black, and the overhead cabinetry was charred and warped.

"Your insurance will take care of the mess. As far as the food, again, ma'am, I'm sorry."

And with that, all the emergency personnel filed out followed by the nosy neighbors. I guess I was secretly wishing at least the three police cars that had come would have stayed. I was certain to need armed legal protection from the coming wrath.

"My dinner!" Mrs. Wayland let out a wail I had never heard a human make before. I think all of us had tears forming in our eyes the way the woman wept and twisted and contorted and cried. She shook against her husband and held Evan's hand. "My kitchen!" she moaned.

"Frederick—" Dr. Wayland motioned to Penelope's husband— "can you go to the patio and get the grill started? I'll grab some steaks from the freezer. That smoky smell has awakened in me a taste for something chargrilled. Tracey, help your sister find some vegetables we can put on the grill along with the meat."

"My perfect family dinner," Mrs. Wayland yelped again. "Ruined. My beautiful kitchen." And then: "Get her out of here. Selena, get out of my house right now. You are not welcomed here, you idiotic fool." Her outburst of anger was quickly followed by another mournful wail.

Dr. Wayland nodded sternly at Evan and Tracey's boyfriend Cornelius. "Take Mother somewhere until she calms down." The two jumped to duty and went to either side of a sniffling and shaking Mrs. Wayland. She let out a low moan.

"Madelyn." He spoke sharply. She immediately quieted and straightened as he continued. "We survived a kitchen fire before, dear, remember? Our first condo, on the lake, not long before we learned that Evan was on the way. A contractor came and fixed it up better than new. As I recall, that kitchen re-do excited you. You had revived life like I'd never seen. This will be no different. A fresh project to indulge your fancies, right dear?"

Her eyelids fluttered, and she looked ready to pass out in response.

"Evan, Cornelius, take her upstairs to rest," he barked. The two men assisted her away. And then the good doctor turned to me. "Selena, I suggest you find something else to do out of our presence today while our family addresses the inconvenient catastrophe you have somehow caused us."

With that, he was gone, leaving me alone in the white foam-filled kitchen with Penelope's girls, Tori and Topaz. They both wore the same red-and-white polka-dotted dresses, black patent leather shoes, and red ribbons tied around the single long braids that flowed down their little backs. They had what my mother and aunts used to call "that good hair," i.e., hair free of kinks, knots, and naps. I've always resented that term because didn't God make everybody's hair? And didn't He call all His creation good? Anyway, I'll get off my soapbox for a moment and get back to my story.

I stood alone in the kitchen with Tori and Topaz who were standing still as statues and staring at me with the widest pearly-white smiles I'd seen in a long time. They had their mother's bright eyes and impossibly long eyelashes. Penelope was a meteorologist for a major television station in well-to-do Northern Virginia. Her striking beauty on air had made her a popular spokesperson for events and products promoted in the greater Washington D.C. area.

Beautiful girls, yes they were, and I was carrying a child who came from the same gene pool. I smiled at the thought and became aware again of the baby kicking in my womb.

"You two are so cute." Looking at their precious faces was the only thing keeping me from crying at the moment. "You are absolutely beautiful little girls." I waited for them to say thank you, to move, breathe, laugh, something, anything. But they continued to stand as still as statues, smiling and blinking at me from underneath their long eyelashes. Eyelashes that were starting to irritate me. How could they see under all that fur?

It dawned on me then that they were in full pageant mode. I recognized the rehearsed pose in which they both stood as the same one I had seen when they were onstage at the Little Miss Magnificent Tulip and Lily contest I had the torture of watching earlier in the year. After singing, tap-dancing, twirling, and prancing around in preschool-sized bikinis and adult-sized make-up, the twins tied for first place.

"*Ummm*...at ease?" I wasn't sure how to get them to relax, and I was getting more uncomfortable by the second just standing there with them. Never had I found preschoolers so intimidating. I'd seen smiling doll babies with more life than these two. *What if I'm carrying a girl? Is this what Evan's family is expecting? Another perfect beauty queen?* The thought sickened me.

"Oh, there you two are." Penelope rushed in and saved the girls from the evil monster. At least that's the way she acted, the way she ran in, glared at me, and swooped them away with one arm. Their stiff bodies nearly toppled over like dominos at her gesture. I noticed then Evan's other sister, Tracey, watching me from behind the sliding glass door that led to the deck. How long had she been standing there? A quiet medical student working through her sub-internship at a hospital in D.C., I often wondered about her own take on her family. Our eyes locked for a moment, but I couldn't read them or her facial expression. What I could read was the obvious displeasure on Evan's father's face at my continued presence. The men were coming back in to finish preparing for the impromptu cookout.

"I'm leaving now," I murmured before anything else could be said or done. Before seeing if Evan would come to my defense or aid.

I guess a part of me didn't want to know if he would.

I guess a part of me already knew the answer.

31

The Bling

Now, I wish I could say things got better after that, but like I said earlier, the whole week was awful. After I left the Waylands' estate, I drove to my mother's house, hoping to crash on her sofa for the rest of the day and all of the night. Apparently, my father had to work overtime, and my mother must have had other plans after church that my brother, CJ, knew about because all I saw when I opened the door to their apartment was my brother's bare ashy behind staring at me from their sofa—you know the place I had planned to rest my hurting head?

Anyway, I had no questions or comments at that sight and was more than happy to close the door behind me. I'm still trying to purge that image from my mind. Yikes. I had nowhere to go and no calls from Evan.

Okay, I guess I just assumed the man would call to check on his pregnant wife at some point. So confident was I that he'd call, I parked myself in front of a grocery store, knowing that when he'd finally reach out he'd end the call asking if I could bring home some chips and dip and orange soda like nothing had ever happened.

But my phone stayed silent.

I sat in front of the market for two whole hours, waiting. Okay, I did go in twice to raid the hot food section. And three times to use the bathroom. Okay, and one more time to grab an ice cream sandwich to gnaw on. I was going to go back in for the olive bar, but the security guard began looking at me suspiciously. I opted to head back to my car before he started asking questions. I mean, what would I say?

When my phone still didn't come to life, I shut it off. If Evan wasn't going to call me, I wasn't going to give him the pleasure of me even having the capacity to answer. Made sense in my mind. With nowhere else to go, I started my car up and headed to the only other place I could think to go.

I headed to Neeka's.

I'd known Neeka since I was nine, when she moved into her grandmother's home, along with four of her siblings and three of her cousins, down the street from where I first lived in East Baltimore. I was intimidated by her initially. She was loud, bossy, and knew all the lyrics to songs I wasn't allowed to listen to, belting out vulgarities then snickering when older adults passing by overheard and gasped.

That first summer, though, her boldness worked in my favor.

A girl named Takoya Smith would push me out the way whenever I was in line at our neighborhood snowball stand. Neeka noticed and didn't say anything at first. Round about the third time it happened, Neeka simply sighed, grabbed a handful of Takoya's beaded cornrows and yanked her down to the concrete. Takoya's mother witnessed the whole thing and proceeded to yell at Neeka, which meant that Neeka's grandmother, wearing her trademark blue housecoat, pink slippers, and permanent frown that peeked under her hairy upper lip, immediately got involved to defend her family's honor.

Takoya's mom didn't know Neeka was Ms. Mabel Howard's granddaughter when she first yelled at her. That one unknown fact could have changed the entire course of my life in that moment.

While the two women went at it, Neeka calmly gave me a plastic spoon for me to enjoy my cherry snowball with marshmallow topping. "You like the same flavor as me." She explained the whole situation with those words and a shrug.

We'd been besties ever since, even when neighbors, teachers, and other friends didn't understand our connection. Even my parents had their apprehensions during phases of my growing years. But, like salt and pepper or peanut butter and jelly, Neeka and I were opposites who went perfectly together.

There'd only been two quiet times in our friendship. The first was for a few months in eleventh grade when Neeka had gotten mixed up with this senior named Twon. He had her whole attention for a moment, then she popped back up on my doorstep one random Thursday evening like nothing had ever happened. She never talked about what happened with him, and I never asked.

The second quiet time was now.

I wanted to believe that the slowdown in our calls and texts were solely due to her attentions on Peyton. However, I knew there was more to the story.

I had been avoiding her and hoping that she'd been too much in love to notice.

I pulled up to Neeka's Gwynn Oak apartment just after five p.m. When I cut off the engine, I didn't immediately get out of the car. After all, it had been less than twenty-four hours since Evan and I stood her and Peyton up for our planned double date. After listening to Evan lie to her so easily on my cell phone the night before, I hadn't figured out what I was supposed to do or say the next time I saw her. Tell her the truth? Continue to lie?

I felt so lost.

At five-twenty, I finally ventured out of my car and walked the three flights up to her one-bedroom apartment. When I got to the door, I heard loud, unfamiliar female laughter and gospel music—*gospel music*—on the other side. Since when did Neeka start listening to Tye Tribbett?

She's busy. And happy. Having a good time. I didn't even bother to knock. I turned to leave, but as I was doing so, her door swung open.

"Okay, good night." A heavy-set woman with a gold tooth and wearing a wavy wig was coming out. "I'm so glad I got to finally meet you, Neeka. You really are a blessing. Just remember Romans 10:13. For, 'Everyone who calls on the name of the Lord will be saved.' Glory hallelujah. Amen."

"Yes, Pastor Anderson. Thank you. Thank you for sharing with me. It was very nice to meet you." Neeka giggled in a voice I'd never heard from her before. I watched as the two embraced. The woman, Pastor Anderson, turned with a grunt and began to make her way down the steps with a black wooden cane encrusted with a large emerald in the handle. I nearly tripped over my feet trying to get out of the way before I was noticed.

"Selena?"

It was too late.

"Neeka," I said a little too loudly and with a little too much gusto, "how are you?" The other woman was already down the first flight of stairs, but several other voices, both male and female, filtered out of Neeka's apartment. She leaned against the frame of the partially closed door. A loud laugh bellowed from somewhere deep inside. Both of us turned momentarily to look before meeting each other's eyes again.

"His family. They're here. I invited them over and cooked dinner for him, his sister, his mom and uncle. That was his mother you just met, Pastor Anderson."

"You cooked? Dinner? Everybody's still okay?" I'd known Neeka to cook one thing in her life, and that was a pancake in Mrs. Brown's eighth grade home ec class. It was a long-standing joke between us, who was the worse cook.

"Shut up, Selena." Neeka playfully rolled her eyes. "Girl, I just roasted my first chicken, baked my first sweet potato pie, and made some skillet cornbread, and let me tell you, Peyton's sister was in there asking me for *my* recipes." Her smile turned devious, and she added in a whisper. "So, I'm winning."

"Well, good for you." And I meant what I said, trying not to feel bad that nobody had ever asked me for any recipes. Shoot, after the fire trucks and white foam today, I guess everyone would be begging me *not* to cook.

"It is good, Selena. Very good. Because I'm going to be cooking a lot more now. Good old-fashioned home-cooked meals. This wasn't just a Sunday dinner. We could have done that at his big old house in Reisterstown. No, girl, this was a special occasion I wanted to host myself."

And then I saw it. How I had missed, I'll never know. The size alone was enough to have sent her crashing through all three floors of her building. The brilliance could have blinded me if she had been holding her hand a different way.

On Neeka's left ring finger was the absolutely largest diamond I had *ever* seen.

"Oh, my goodness," I gasped and threw both my hands over my mouth. "He proposed?"

"Last night, onboard the Bay Queen. I know it hasn't been that long, but both of us know this is it. We've found each other. I wanted his family to come here to meet me so they could see me in my element and know Peyton got a real one."

I was shaking, and tears fell from both my eyes as Neeka beamed (mostly from that diamond) in front of me. She was right, she and Peyton hadn't dated long, but I could feel even in me that this was a meant-to-be union. "Oh, Neeka, I'm so happy for you. I am so, so happy."

She continued to smile, but a silence fell over her. She licked her lips. Tears glossed her eyes. "You were supposed to be there."

"I know, Neeka. I'm so sorry."

"You were supposed to be there. I'm always telling Peyton how precious a friend you are to me, and he planned the cruise proposal so you would be there for the most important moment of my life so far."

"I know, Neeka. Like I said, I am so sorry. You will never know how sorry I am. Something just came up. We... Evan and I couldn't make it in time. I'm sorry."

There was a long pause of silence between us. A titter of laughter and a gentle whiff of cornbread wafted out of her apartment and filled the narrow corridor.

"You have company." I smiled. "It's a special occasion for you, and I don't want to hold you up." I swallowed over the lump forming in my throat.

"Yeah, I guess I'd better get back inside. We're about to play a quick game of Taboo." Neeka had a flat smile on her face. I searched her eyes for meaning.

I turned to leave, and she turned to close the door, but just before she did so, she looked back at me.

"You know, I saw you. Last night. You and Evan sitting in the amphitheater. I know you're lying to me. I just don't know why." She gave me one last flat smile then turned away.

"Neeka, I—wait." I stopped the door. "I should have just told you. It has nothing to do with me. Evan—"

"It doesn't matter now, Selena." Neeka smiled, cutting off my too late and unprepared confession. "I've gotta go. I have company."

She still smiled but the door slammed square in my face.

32

The Reveal

I stayed at a hotel that night, wondering, waiting to see if Evan would call and check on me. Hoping, praying he didn't. I turned my phone off and on, off and on, afraid of what a call would entail, afraid of what the lack of a call would mean.

What was I supposed to say to him? What could he say to me?

My marriage. My life. Was a disaster.

At 11:59 p.m. my phone finally rung.

"I'm not going to let a day end without making sure you are okay. Selena?"

He called! "I'm not coming home tonight. We'll have to talk later." I hung up on him both angry and relieved to have finally heard from him. I shut my phone off for the rest of the night.

Did I say my week only got worse from Sunday? Let me continue.

Monday morning, I emailed Kiona stating I would turn in all my assignments en masse later that week.

That took care of trying to figure out how I was going to get any work done that day.

With nothing else to do, nowhere else to go, and a best friend who was not returning my too little, too late phone calls, my sights turned homeward.

As in *my* home.

I hadn't been to my house since the day I met Genevaise Zuzani and her entourage. The design team had promised to transform my humble home into an inspired masterpiece worthy enough to be featured in an upcoming edition of *House and Studio* magazine. I knew from the conversations I'd overheard and from the sketches at which I'd managed to steal a glance that the finished product was supposed to be some type of gritty urban design Ms. Zuzani had entitled "Cityscape Revised," supposedly a loose interpretation of my inner-city upbringing. I knew all of this as I pulled up to my end-of-unit townhome in Randallstown.

And still I was totally unprepared for what I saw.

It started with the door.

Obviously, our community must not have a homeowners' association because there was no way the exterior of my house would have passed any sane governing body's bylaws, I reasoned. Looking at the thick metal grates and bars that now made up my front door, I couldn't help but wonder if Genevaise and her crew mistakenly equated growing up in the inner city as being raised in a jail. That's a philosophical discussion for another day. All I knew was the metallic beams and bars theme on my front door continued on the windows and the shutters. Even the welcome mat was made from a shiny piece of aluminum-looking material. With the overwhelming shimmering glare coming from the front of my house, I couldn't help but wonder if a special zoning permit would be necessary for Evan and me to maintain our residence.

After figuring out that the numerical keypad on the front door was just for show—I could still use my key—I entered what use to be the living room of my house.

The entire downstairs had been transformed into one large open space. A spiral staircase of dangerously narrow metal steps had replaced the former stairway with its broken banister. Strips of cement painted a stark white alternated with a frosted plastic to make up the walls and flooring. The plastic had a translucent quality about it and blinking silver neon lights illuminated from within it throughout the entire room—yes, lights were embedded in both the walls and the floor.

In the front of the room, the plastic came seamlessly up from the floor into a molded clear sofa and two armchairs. The clear, hard furniture was dotted with octagonal white pillows. The coffee table was made out of a large manhole cover held up by stacked bricks, all painted white. In a similar fashion, two end tables consisted of octagonal mirrors on top of several rubber car tires, also painted white.

The kitchen and dining areas were a continuation of the plastic and white cement, with stainless steel appliances and fixtures built in. A large plastic ledge with more silver neon lights inside swirled around the back wall. Barstools made from white cement came up seamlessly from the strip of cement floor next to the ledge, much like the plastic living room set had been made from the floor beneath it.

Oh, and there were touch pads everywhere. The oven knobs, the sink faucets, the refrigerator doors, even the light switches were complicated-looking silver-and-black numerical devices with miniature screens and keypads. With the exception of the framed graffiti art that lined the walls and counters, I felt like I was in some kind of control room for NASA.

Before I could scream and/or cry at the sight of the sterile white, the gleaming silver, the bizarre lighting, the painted cement and the frosted plastic, several footsteps thundered in the hallway above me. From the tinny vibrations that accompanied each step, I couldn't help but wonder what type of material made up the flooring upstairs. Seconds later, I watched as first a set of black cowboy boots, then a pair of aquamarine patent-leather loafers, followed by worn hiking boots, then two orange-colored high heels, and finally four paws wrapped in beige slippers stepped carefully down the deadly looking metal spiral staircase.

"Yah, this is perfect," I heard a man say. "Ah, look, the beautiful one is here."

Yuri, the European craftsman, spoke from behind Moonlight, Xander Jauq'sahn, Genevaise and her cat Phillipe who all stood in the living room beaming at me. Well, not the cat. You know what I mean.

Anyway, they were all smiles and grins as I stood in the center of the room ready to puke.

"Oh yes, what a nice surprise to see you, Selena," Genevaise gushed. "We aren't quite done. We still have much work to do upstairs, but the downstairs is just about completed. What do you think? Incredible? Oh, yes?"

"Beyond your wildest dreams?" Yuri growled in a seductive whisper as he shook his long blond mane over his bulging shoulder.

"*Ummm*, that's one way of putting it," I said with a forced polite smile. I was numb, exhausted, spent.

"Tell me, oh yes, what you think of the design. Please be honest. The more descriptive you are, the better your quote will read in *House and Studio* magazine. Xander, get out a pen to record her first reaction." Genevaise seemed intent on getting a truthful response from me. I had no intention of letting her down.

"Well, let's see." I studied the room, trying to decide exactly where to start with my feelings about their "design." "Where do I begin? Okay—"

"A moment, please." Xander cut me off with a single raised hand. "I am still getting out my pen." He pinched his lips into a frown, then pulled an ink pen out of his stiff red Mohawk before beckoning me to resume. "Continue, please."

I've always been fascinated listening to British accents come out of the mouths of people of color, but something about Xander's tone and overall mannerisms annoyed me. I directed my opening statement to him.

"As I was about to say, right now I feel like I am on the set of a wannabe *Star-Trek* movie knock-off, ready to be beamed up into a flying saucer. The only thing missing from my kitchen is a space suit and some packets of freeze-dried astronaut food, like the kind I used to get from the Maryland Science Center on field trips in elementary school. And what's the deal with the floor? I mean, plastic flooring with lights blinking inside? What is this, the International Space Station?" Now I was mad. My words came out in a breathless explosion. "This is supposed to be my house."

"Oh yes—no." Genevaise looked stunned, her hand held flat in the air above Phillipe as if while petting him she had been frozen mid-stroke. "It is supposed to be 'Cityscape Revised.' You only see science fiction in the design?" She looked horrified. "But what of the framed graffiti, the manhole cover coffee table, the abandoned car tires?" She pointed at each as she spoke. "Do you not get the raw isolation? The desolation? The purity in the painted white of it all? The cement?"

"Yes, let's talk about the cement." My hand was on my hip, my head was shaking, my index finger moving like a baton leading an improvised composition of cacophony. "I am having a baby. *A baby.* Do you really think it's a good idea for an infant to be crawling around on concrete? Look at the seating in my dining launch pad, or whatever you want to call that eating space you created. Concrete chairs? Seriously? Are you trying to give my child a brain injury?"

"Inter-na-tional Space Sta-tion." Xander scribbled without looking up. "Should abbreviations be used for the article?"

"Xander, please." Genevaise looked frantic. "It is not a space theme. It is 'Cityscape Revised.'"

"Cityscape, my behind," Xander quipped. His perfect British accent sounded a little off as he frowned in disgust. "I said myself this concept was all wrong. Nobody wanted to listen."

"You said no such thing." Yuri joined the battle. "The cement was your idea and yours alone."

"Yes, I said a touch of cement here and there would add an appropriate urban emphasis. I didn't say anything about pouring a second foundation and calling it a floor." Xander retorted. "And the plastic with the lights blinking on and off inside? I'm sorry, but, amazingly, I must actually agree on something here with my sister and call it what it is, tacky."

"Your sister?" Yuri gasped. "Just because you share the same skin color as the beautiful one does not make her your sister. We are all brothers and sisters." He suddenly turned to me, and his voice dropped two octaves lower into a sultry whisper. "Selena, I have felt a most unique bond with you since the moment we laid eyes on each other. I know you are married, but surely you must feel the spiritual connection that forever links our poor souls, lost together in the cosmos. The state of confusion in this house is only a symbolic analogy of the love we were destined to never share." He dropped his head and eyes in a dramatic, solemn fashion.

"Oh, pul-eaze!" Xander's British accent was gone. Completely. "You want to talk about confusion?" His voice was an angry, yet sorrowful roar. "I can tell you about confusion."

"Peace, peace. We must renew balance." Moonlight's first words of the entire exchange. He had been standing quietly to the side with his eyes closed. He stood now on one foot in a yoga tree pose. "We are at a moment that calls for meditation." His words were soft.

But even Genevaise wasn't in the mood to meditate. Her eyes were on Xander, her face continuing to contort in horror. "Xander

Jauq'sahn? What happened to your accent? Your lovely British accent? What is going on? Oh yes, what is it?"

"I can't take it anymore," Xander screamed in agony. In great gulps of sobs, in a torrent of tears, his words poured out. "I can't take it anymore. Not you. Not me. And definitely not this confusion. I can't keep living this lie."

"Lie?" Now even Moonlight looked troubled. "What lie do you speak of, Xander?"

"Stop calling me Xander Jauq'sahn," he screamed and threw his hands over his ears. "My name is really Alexander Jackson, and I'm from Kansas City. I've never even been to London. I don't know who I am or what I am. Everything about me is a lie, and I don't even know when the lies began. Oh, God." And then he began to cry uncontrollably.

"Lies? All these lies?" Moonlight's horror grew. "I cannot work under such untruthful circumstances. My balance has been destroyed. Goodbye, Genevaise." And he was gone.

"Moonlight, please wait, oh yes," Genevaise Zuzani called after him, dropping a startled Phillipe with a violent thud on the floor. The cat immediately looked at me and hissed. Genevaise didn't notice. "No, no, Moonlight. Do not go. You are my divine muse. Please."

She ran to the door, but Alexander Jackson, still crying, beat her to it and pushed past her. I could still hear his sobs as he ran alone down the street. Probably still running somewhere.

"Moonlight! Xander—I mean Alexander, whoever you are—please wait. Come back. Both of you. Please." Just before she went out the door, she turned to me. Fire burned in her eyes. "You. This is all your fault. You have no understanding of the finer points of design, and now, I have lost my design team. I am *ruined*." Her deep voice reverberated through the room as she stormed out.

Yuri looked at me with a solemn expression, then his lips curled into a mischievous smile. "Come back with me to Europe. We will be lovers, yes?"

"Get out of my house."

His face dropped, but even as he crossed the threshold, he blew me a kiss. "Parting is such sweet sorrow. Goodbye, my love."

And then it was just me and the cat.

The cat and I.

I looked at him. He looked at me.

"Who is going to fix my house?" Now it was my turn to cry.

As if in response, he bore down on his haunches.

"Oh no you don't," I yelled at the feline. But it was too late. Phillipe had already done his business—both number one and number two—on my floor. Without a look back, he slithered out the door. As I stood there examining the mess in and of my house, I couldn't imagine that my life could get any worse.

33

The Association

Of course, it did.

The minute I closed the front door behind Phillipe and turned to tackle the horrific smelling mess he'd left on my cement floor, a knock sounded behind me, strong and authoritative.

"The cat left already," I yelled as I swung the front door back open, assuming it was Genevaise and ready for more heated words.

Wrong.

"Cat?" A black woman of about fifty years old stared back at me over square black wire rims. Her eyeglasses looked more expensive than my car, and her hair was molded into sharp, hard finger waves. She wore a fuchsia suit, matching fuchsia shoes, and more gold jewelry on her neck, ears, wrists, and fingers than I ever imagined one person wearing. Or owning. "See, I told you there was a touch of ridiculousness in this house." She spoke to another woman standing beside her.

"More than a touch from what I can see." This other woman was as short as she was wide and let out a loud, unflattering cackle of a laugh. Her hair was pulled back in a gray-streaked and stubby ponytail. Despite her laugh, there was no humor in her dry, patchy face.

"Hello," she said in a less than warm greeting. "My name is Alfeena Rorick."

"And I'm Delores," the first woman chimed in.

"And we are the president and the vice-president of the Greater King Courtyard Terrace Homeowners' Association. Are you the homeowner of this..." Alfeena cleared her throat, "fine establishment?"

Oh. I had incorrectly assumed there was no HOA. I groaned inside as I nodded in shame. I knew where this was going.

At least I thought I knew.

"Good," Delores said, glaring at me over her glasses, "because we have here the lien on your property along with the notice for the date you must vacate. Normally this would just be mailed to you or left in your mailbox, but this situation called for a face-to-face delivery. Can you sign our receipt that you received the notice?" She dangled a little yellow sheet of paper in front of me and offered me a pen. "Right here on the dotted line, please." She tapped a fuchsia fingernail impatiently next to a typed "X."

"Huh? Vacate?" I stared at the two women in disbelief. "*Ummm*, as I am the homeowner, I don't see how you can force me to vacate my property. Which you do not own. Because I am the homeowner. The deed was transferred to my husband and me from my parents. I don't recall seeing anything about an HOA or the right for you to put a lien on my home." I crossed my arms in unison along with Alfeena. I could see this was going to get ugly.

"It is not our fault or concern if you did not pay attention to the documents you signed when the deed was transferred." She held up a form that did indeed have my signature and Evan's. "You fully agreed to accept the *entire* bylaws of our covenant. We followed our end of the agreement and gave you sufficient notice to change the exterior of your home to meet the voted upon guidelines. However, since you have ignored all three warnings mailed to you informing you of your blatant infractions against our covenant, we are within the legal right to assume ownership of this property at the end of this week. Sign here, please." Delores tapped again at the dotted line.

"Wait a minute," I said, glaring, "we never even saw any mail from you. What are you talking about?"

Alfeena took out another sheet of paper and read the dates and times certified and notarized letters had been sent to our address.

"All three letters were confirmed delivered and signed by a—" She squinted. "Yuri Boyko."

Spiritual connection? Whatever. That man didn't even pass along my mail.

"Okay." I sighed and shook my head at the unsympathetic duo. "I am very sorry. There's been a huge misunderstanding and breach of communication. I can't stand the way this house looks myself and have every intention of fixing this problem. Obviously, it won't happen before this Friday, but I'm sure you—"

"The letters we sent you clearly gave a timeline, and you blatantly ignored even the deadlines for a simple response of acknowledgement," Delores interjected.

"But Friday? That's unreasonable. I'm telling you I never received those letters, and it would seem you could give us more time to work this—"

"Clause 131(b).79k, paragraph z94 of the Greater King Courtyard Terrace Homeowners' Association states that if a homeowner has refused to respond in writing to three attempts at resolution offered by the association, the board members may unequivocally take over the deed and title of the home in question at a date voted upon and agreed to by the board members. We voted for this Friday, and you signed this agreement back when you accepted the deed for this house. This is a contract recognized by law, and my brother is the councilman for this district. Now if you don't sign this receipt acknowledging you have accepted this notice, according to clause 131(b).79k, paragraph z95, we have the right to take over your property immediately."

"Wait a minute! Can't I—"

"You signed. It's done." Alfeena eyed me curiously. "You're with child. I don't want to put you out of your house today." A slight vibration of sympathy sounded in her voice.

Slight.

"So, even if you don't sign the receipt right now, we'll still give you until Friday. Come on, Delores. It smells like cat crap in here." They turned to leave, and once again I was alone.

It was only Monday, and I was forsaken, friendless, practically husbandless, and now on the verge of experiencing homelessness. I thought about and had a new appreciation for Job in the Bible. That poor man was stripped of everything—children, home, finances, friends, and health. Look, I know I'm nowhere near the high standard of righteousness Job exhibited that made Satan want to get permission from God to test him, but Lord knows I'm trying to do right. I go to church regularly, I don't steal, and I haven't cussed out Kiona or Mrs. Wayland.

Yet.

Why, oh why has my life taken such a turn for the worse? I mean, Neeka, who has never said anything about trying to pursue God or living holy seems to be getting a better deal than what I'm getting. She's engaged to a brother who's both handsome and well-off.

And a homeowner.

And sane.

I know. There's no point in wallowing in self-pity or drowning in a sea of jealousy. That's not pretty or productive. But am I not allowed to have just two minutes of self-reflective grief?

Then again, wasn't I the one who wanted to get rid of the house by any means necessary? I guess I need to be careful what I pray for.

Prayer.

I made a mental note to study the book of Job once I resumed my daily quiet times. Maybe that's my problem. I hadn't been spending time with the Lord as I should. Not that doing so would keep the problems away, but at least I would have a better hand at knowing how to deal with my trials if I was truly in tune with the Most High who promised sufficiency. The deluge of emotions I felt was overwhelming.

"God, help me with what is happening all around me, and prepare me for whatever is next." My prayer was simple but sincere in its plea.

The only bright spot in my life was the child kicking in my womb. I smiled at the sensation.

My smile was cut short by the realization that kicking was not the only thing I felt going on with my uterus.

34

The Complications

Preterm labor.

To make a long story short, it's the Friday now of what has been the worse week of my life. On top of everything else that had happened on Sunday and Monday—call it stress, call it dehydration, call it whatever you want, all I know is I began to feel a tightening sensation in my abdomen right after the homeowners' association subcommittee left my front door. I immediately went to see my doctor and was given both a verdict and a sentence.

The verdict was preterm labor. For some reason, God only knows why, the baby wants to come way too soon. *Don't rush it, Boo-Bear. Enjoy the good life while you can and get as strong and ready as possible for what comes next.*

The sentence was complete bed rest.

The good news is I have been granted a temporary leave of absence from all activity and can now get the most rest I have ever had in my life. The bad news is I have been granted a temporary leave of absence from all activity and can now get the most rest I have ever had in my life.

I have to stay in the bed until the baby comes.

Months from now.

So, here I am, back in the big fluffy king-sized bed at Mrs. Wayland's house. When I called Evan from the emergency room on Monday, you would have thought I had last left the Wayland Estate to buy bread or for some other harmless reason. There was no mention from him (or me) of the fiery circumstances of our last exchange. In fact, there was no mention of anything else—Kiona, his clarinet, his mother, our house—just rightful concern for our child. I was certain Genevaise had said something to his mother, but he didn't bring it up.

It was a nice but scary moment.

I wish we could talk—really talk.

But the conversations we needed to have were too frightening, so I enjoyed the fragile peace our mutual silence allowed.

Now, as I lay here sinking in billowy soft sheets, down comforters, and pillows, eating snacks and meals from a silver tray, with a television remote, laptop, phone, word search books, and novels all within reach, it seems nearly everyone has forgiven and forgotten the fact that I ruined Sunday dinner.

Okay, I know that's an understatement. I completely destroyed Mrs. Wayland's kitchen. Thankfully, the outdoor kitchen off their main deck and the appliances and counterspace in the basement bar area could fill in while they began the arduous task of clean-up and repair.

"Selena, here's your lunch."

Madelyn Ernestine Wayland stormed into the room without knocking, a snarl on her lips, hatred in her eyes.

Remember, I said *nearly* everyone had forgiven and forgotten.

"I fixed you a ham, turkey, and cheese sandwich. I heated up the lunchmeat first since the pregnancy book I'm reading warns about the dangers of contracting listeriosis." She slid a rolling tray to the bedside. I wondered if it had been nabbed from the hospital where her husband worked. "I'm going to give you the book when I finish reading it so you can do something productive with all this free time. We will reserve time to discuss the disaster at your house. And mine. "For now, focus on your rest. I don't want you getting riled up trying to come up with some pathetic excuse to explain your actions. We must keep Evan, Jr. safe. That is the only thing that matters right now."

"Thank you, Mrs. Wayland." I tried to sound as gracious as I could as she turned and left the room. I mean, the woman's kitchen was destroyed. It didn't burn down, but whatever the firemen did to treat the non-fire completely saturated and ruined the expensive wood finishes and rare stone countertops. Not to mention the carefully planned, lovingly prepared home-cooked meal.

And there was the whole disintegration of her favorite design team that was sure to cause some waves and ripples in her circle.

Anyway, I looked down at my heated lunchmeat sandwich and said a quick grace. Mrs. Wayland's concern over "Evan, Jr.," as she continually called my baby, kept me from worrying the food was poisoned or something like that. I figured I was safe in this house—at least until my due date. After that, anything was possible. I shuddered. With all the baby books and articles Mrs. Wayland had been reading, I did have some idea of what possibilities lay in my future once the baby came. Seemed like Evan's mother had motherhood plans of her own, and those plans appeared not to involve that much of me.

One thing looked certain. Evan, baby, and I will probably still be at this address come February. I groaned anew every time the realization resurfaced. Evan had made no move or suggestion that he was looking for another job, still squealing away on his clarinet in his father's garage, and I had successfully been placed on temporary disability with my job, resulting in only a portion of my usual pay. What other housing options did we have, especially now that I couldn't do anything but lie here in the bed and fill in word search puzzles, and my space-age home is currently about to become communal property for the home association? I finished my lunch and drifted into a restless sleep.

"I could have had his baby."

A voice, low with a rasp I'd never heard in it before, nudged my ear and caused my eyes to flutter open. I would have thought the voice a dream but my eyes came into focus and settled on the curvy frame filling the doorway.

Kiona.

"What? What did you say?" I struggled to pull my head up from my pillow. *And why are you here?* Was I dreaming?

"Oh, you're awake." She stood frozen in the doorway. "I just said...I said...I ...should have brought a pastry. But I didn't." A forced smile formed on her lips. "I brought this." She thrust out a hand and held up a slender vase holding a single white rose.

I took her presence and the flower to be an offering of surrender, an unspoken truce she wanted to initiate between us.

But I knew better.

I held my breath and nodded for her to come in as I continued to pull myself up to a semi-sitting position in the mound of pillows that surrounded me. *Does Kiona know how much I know about her past with Evan? Would Evan have told her what he's shared with me?*

The thought of such an intimate conversation between them was unbearable. I swallowed hard. Then again, she'd been quick just now to change her words about almost having their baby. Maybe she didn't know I knew her secrets.

I was too exhausted to explore.

"I also brought along some magazines for you to read," she said in a chipper tone. "Latest editions of *Vogue* and *Essence*." She set the vase on a night table and gingerly laid the magazines next to it. Then she crashed down into a heavy white armchair close to the bed. A leather tote bag on her shoulder collapsed on the floor. She kicked off her shoes and pulled back her hair. I could smell her perfume. Smelled like peaches, vanilla, and evil.

"Oh, Selena." She let out an exaggerated sigh, pulled her knees up to her chin, and began playing with her French-manicured toenails.

My Grandma Verdine used to tell me if you have nothing nice to say, to say nothing at all.

I continued to sit in complete silence.

Kiona reached for the remote and clicked on the TV. Fred from *Sanford and Son* filled the screen. He bantered back and forth with his son. Kiona and I had only caught the tail end of the joke, but for some reason Kiona let out a loud wallop of a laugh. She clapped then had the nerve to slap me on the shoulder.

"Oh girl, these classics are too funny," she shrieked, all giggles and snorts as the contemplative look on her face dissipated into a smirk.

"Kiona, what do you want?" I didn't even crack a smile.

She looked at me a second, a smile on one corner of her mouth, then stared back at the television. Another round of studio laughter filled the room before she spoke again.

"Perhaps I could be your baby's godmother."

A laugh started somewhere deep in my belly, rolled up through my chest, and landed in my vocal cords as more of a gasp than a chuckle. The nerve of this woman.

"I'm serious, Selena," she said, closing her eyes as if to steady herself before looking at me with a look of sincerity I didn't know she was capable of. "I know our friendship has gotten off to a rather shaky start, but I'm hoping we can turn a new leaf and begin to build a better bond from here on out. If not godmother, I'd love to be play auntie."

Her words, her smile, even her tone suddenly sounded well-rehearsed. No, of course I didn't trust her, but I decided to play along until I could figure out what she was up to.

"That's a very nice offer of you, Kiona," I answered back with a big, fake smile of my own, "but my best friend Neeka will be both my child's godmother and auntie."

She nestled back in her chair, seemingly pleased with my response. I wondered at this, as if she'd purposely brought up an impossibility to make whatever else she'd come to propose feel possible. She took back the *Essence* magazine and started flipping through the pages as she spoke again.

Why had Mrs. Wayland even let her in? Maybe this was her attempt at punishing me, I gathered.

"You know," Kiona blurted, "I really have been wanting to thank you for trusting me with Evan. I really mean it when I say my role in his act is good for my creativity. That's all I want, to have this outlet to express my true self. I'm not naïve. I know you see me as a threat, but I promise I'm not. I have a man—Dylan." She gazed off into space, her smile turning into a sensual grin. "He is absolutely wonderful." She snapped back into attention. "Anyway, I need you to continue to trust me with him and give your blessing on our act together. It's genuine. It's pure." She blinked with long lashes.

"Mmmm-hmmm." Try as I might, I couldn't hide my suspicions. *Forgive me, Lord, if I'm not taking the right attitude. I don't doubt your ability to change people; I just one hundred percent question her sincerity.* If she noticed the sarcasm in my tone, she pretended to be oblivious.

"Trust me, please, because I need to trust you with something." She sucked in a deep breath as if about to say something of great importance.

"What is it?"

She put down the magazine and began fishing in her tote bag. After a few seconds, she found what she was looking for. She cupped a small piece of paper in both of her hands before gingerly laying it into my lap with a nervous smile.

"*Ummm*, what is this?" I picked up a receipt, torn on one side and wrinkled in the middle. Some words and numbers were scrawled on the back.

"That," she said, giggling with a snort, "is the answer to *all* our dreams."

"It's a phone number and a string of words." I squinted and frowned. "Coconut Shrimp. Fruit basket. Tuesday. Park Hall. Kiona, what is this?"

"The phone number." She tapped a fingernail on some digits in the middle of the scribbled notes then snatched the receipt away before I could make more sense of them. "Selena, I was able to speak to Razi's manager, and he agreed to let him sing a song at your baby shower *in person*—not just some pre-recorded video like at your wedding rehearsal dinner."

"What? Huh?"

"Girlfriend, I *need* to plan your baby shower. I most definitely can book Razi as a special guest. It's already done."

Every sentence she said made me queasy. "What does this have to do with anybody's dreams?" My patience was gone.

"Listen, Evan lost his job due to Razi's case, right? This will give him a new audience with Razi *directly* and a chance to present himself better. Please, Selena, let me plan this shower."

"What's in it for you?" I narrowed my eyes. "What about this shower and Razi is the answer to all *our* dreams." I didn't trust this woman for two seconds, but I needed to know her end game to stay two steps ahead.

Kiona leaned forward, a broad grin snaking across her face. I noticed for the first time a slight gap in her bottom front teeth. "So, listen—"

"*Knock-knock.*" Mrs. Wayland rapt on the bedroom door, her voice a singsong of cheer. "Can I interrupt you two lovely ladies? I just want to clear up Selena's lunch dishes. I won't disturb you long," she chirped.

Kiona snapped back in her seat, a quick tremble on her lips turned into an elaborate smile. "Oh, Madelyn, you must have used that gift card I gave you to Sephora. I recognize that fragrance you're wearing."

"Kiona, you are such a sweet doll." Mrs. Wayland beamed as the two began discussing some new line of products I'd never heard of, and from the sound of it, was beyond any price range I dared imagined. I wanted to ask Kiona again about her plans and this dream she was pushing. I wanted to know why she'd dropped the whole thing the moment Mrs. Wayland came back in the room. I remembered the lies Evan had been keeping from his mother. Did Kiona have her own set of distortions and untruths she was also keeping out of Mrs. Wayland's view?

Kiona and Mrs. Wayland were made for each other. Tweedledee and Tweedledum. And I was Alice lost in this wonderland of lies and betrayal, phoniness and duplicity.

They were so intertwined in conversation, I don't think they even noticed they walked out the room together.

My dirty dishes still sat on the tray.

I needed some kind of breakthrough, an advantage, anything to pull me out of the rabbit hole into which my life had plunged.

35

The Secret

The advantage came.

And in a way that left me feeling like the Cheshire Cat.

Knowledge is power. I was in the third grade when I first heard that phrase. We had a new principal, Mrs. Dalia Lipscomb, and she was determined to turn my low-scoring, low-income elementary school into a model of school success. It started with assemblies, or Power Rallies as she called them. We chanted the phrase over and over, watched it demonstrated in skits, sung it in songs, even learned an interpretive dance movement to a cheer she composed based on those simple three words.

Classrooms were renamed PowerZones. The computer lab, with its three working computers, was dubbed the PowerLab.

Knowledge is power. Knowledge is power. The more I know, the further I go, 'cause knowledge is power.

I was holding fast to that mantra. Being on bedrest had left me in a place of powerlessness I had never known or imagined. Besides the frequent home visits by a nurse who administered injections in my backside and helped hook me up to a uterine monitoring system meant to keep ahead of the preterm contractions, life carried on about me, and I couldn't participate. There was nothing I could do about employment. Whatever was going on with my house in Randallstown was out of my hands and in Evan's, which gave me no comfort. He refused to keep me updated on the developments with the homeowners' association for fear it would upset me and trigger contractions. I couldn't even make my own peanut butter and jelly sandwich or pour myself a glass of water from the kitchen. With the exception of getting up to go to the bathroom and my doctor's appointments, I was forbidden to get up at all save for a quick shower once a day.

The only power I had was knowledge, and the only thing I knew for certain was Kiona had set wheels spinning to a plan even Mrs. Wayland wasn't privy to.

I wondered if Kiona knew Evan had shared some of her past secrets with me. I wondered if she knew I had a direct connection to her ex.

Well, somewhat direct.

Neeka still wasn't returning my phone calls, and Evan's confession didn't seem like the type of thing to leave on a voice mail, you know?

My mother had been pulling extra shifts at the convenience store, determined to have extra money on hand for her grandbaby. My father wanted nothing to do with the Waylands, which meant I never heard from him—which I guess wasn't new, just more noticeable. And my brother? Only God knew where he was or what he was up to these days.

If it wasn't for the occasional kick in my ribs and gelatin-like bounces that rippled over my belly, I would have truly felt all alone.

Anyway, the days were beginning to crawl into weeks, and besides the pending birth of my baby, my gut told me something big was about to go down. There was nothing else for me to do but bide my time before everybody's truths had to come out. So, swimming in a sea of baby name books, word search puzzles, magazines, and a halfway finished latch hook project of a pale green seahorse (I had decided the nursery's theme would be Under the Sea before I realized my baby didn't even have a nursery), I wasn't surprised when my big break finally came.

What did surprise me was it had nothing to do with Kiona.

One day—a Thursday afternoon to be exact—right after watching some afternoon talk shows, the entire direction and nature of my relationship with Madelyn Ernestine Wayland changed.

She busted into the room as usual with my afternoon snack, face drawn in total disgust at my presence. I hadn't asked for a snack of any nature. She'd decided on her own accord, after reading some pregnancy book, I needed a daily cocktail of bananas, peanut butter, flaxseed, spinach, and yogurt blended together. Trapped in my own temporarily twisted taste buds, the taste (and texture) of the smoothie didn't bother me; therefore, I didn't fight her demand that I drink it "for the baby's sake."

She came into the room as usual, and I gave her my usual response: a curt nod, a quick smile, and a subtle roll of the eyes.

As was our accepted routine, our rehearsed dance with each other if you will, she ignored my greeting and plopped a bed tray with the tall glass adorned with fresh pineapples and strawberries on the shrinking space next to me on the bed. My reading material and craft projects were taking over.

"Really, Selena?" She eyed the baby name book I was thumbing through with a frown. "I don't know why you're wasting time trying to find a name for my grandbaby. I thought we already decided he will be named Evan Jr., and in the small chance it's a girl, which I think is highly unlikely as our family is due for a grandson, I think the name Evaline will be proper for a member of the Wayland family. Evaline Gertrude Wayland. A nice combination of Evan and Madelyn, and Gertrude was my grandmother's name. Excellent choice, do you not agree?" She looked up into her dream world with a distant smile on her mauve-painted lips.

I had been here long enough to know no matter what day of the week, what time of the day, Mrs. Wayland didn't venture out of her bedroom without a fully made-up face and wearing expensive jewelry and shoes. I also had been there long enough to know better than to say what I said next.

"Actually, I have some other names in mind I'm considering. D'quintonio or Jontavion if it's a boy. Tierellini or Aja-Monae if it's a girl." Those were not the names I had listed on a piece of paper for Evan's review, but I *wanted* the woman to dare challenge me about what constituted a "proper" name for a member of the Wayland family.

We eyed each other, and I waited for the firestorm that promised to follow. Instead, I heard a familiar loud buzzing noise. Mrs. Wayland's face contorted in horror as that same mechanical, chainsaw-grinding, dying animal buzz— the one I had heard coming from her purse when Evan and I first married and then again from her craft room that weekend we first moved in—grew louder and louder.

"Oh, dear." Mrs. Wayland gasped as the buzz increased in intensity. Did I mention the noise came this time from somewhere deep in her bra?

"Uh, Mrs. Wayland, is everything okay?"

Instead of words for an answer, a piercing, high-pitched siren filled the room, replacing the buzzing sound. A smile froze on her face, and she began to slowly back up from the bed toward the door as if neither one of us were hearing the ear-scraping noise. She began patting, then clawing at her bosom as she walked backward, her smile still frozen in place. She'd almost made it out the room when the unimaginable happened.

A voice boomed out from her breasts, "Madelyn Wayland, please report your location."

With shaking hands, she dug through her bra and pulled out a cell phone, a plain black phone with no case. I'd never seen it before. Definitely not her gem-encrusted iPhone. With a look of pure defeat, she pressed a button on the side, swiped the scream and spoke.

"I'm home." Her voice came out barely above a whisper. "This thing malfunctioned again. I'm resetting so you will see my coordinates." She pressed another button, and both the siren and the buzzing stopped. When the screen darkened, she pushed the phone back into the narrow space between her breasts.

"*Ummm...*" Really. What was I supposed to say?

"You must not tell a soul," Mrs. Wayland hissed. "Not Evan, not Kiona, not your mother, nobody. Please, Selena."

"Tell what? I don't know what just happened."

"I–I had some minor legal problems and must...wear...a tracking device."

Uh, come again. "I don't understand."

"I'm...on...home detention. However," she quickly added, "a reasonable judge allows me to use this phone app instead of one of those ridiculous ankle bracelets as long as I stay within an hour of my home. Those were the terms I was able to negotiate." Her voice was small and hoarse, barely above a whisper as she shifted on her feet. Her eyes darted around the room.

"You have to stay within an hour of your home?" I had questions. So, so many questions. "How were you going to go to the ski trip baby shower Kiona talked of planning? The Poconos is, what, three, four hours away?"

"My sentence would be over by then. It's really a minor issue. And, like I said, I was able to negotiate the terms myself. With the right offer, I can make any deal work." She did her best to hold her head high, but even she knew her own words spoke against her. She gave up and collapsed in the armchair beside me.

"What did you do, Mrs. Wayland, to be on home detention?"

She cleared her throat. Then, cleared it again. "Shoplifting." And then, as if to explain, she added, "And I'm in therapy as part of my...requirements."

"Kleptomania? You have kleptomania?"

I widened my eyes as I felt myself taking control of the conversation about her inability to control her sticky fingers.

"It's only, well mostly, ever been small things." She shuffled in her seat. "I most obviously can afford everything I've ever taken. It's ridiculous they are holding this against me, but after the fourth time I was caught, I guess they thought I needed help."

Caught four times? I tried to picture Mrs. Wayland on one of her many shopping trips to Tysons Corner, stuffing an expensive plate or wine flute or high-end cosmetic or silk blouse in her coat. Or down her shirt. Clearly, she was an expert at hiding things in her chest area.

I couldn't picture it at all. I frowned. I didn't want to picture it at all.

"Four times?" I could not help but say it out loud.

"Well, y-yes. Four times. As an adult." She stumbled through her words, clearly free-falling. "I suffered a bit more with this...ailment when I was younger. But those...missteps are completely off my record. I spent time at a...special...juvenile center when I was sixteen to address it. I became entangled with the wrong crowd and lost my way back then. Selena, very few people know about the dark times of my life, so I'd appreciate your silence on this matter. I am much better now."

"What did you take this last time?"

She cleared her throat again. "Meatloaf mix. From the supermarket. I told you. It's an issue I'm addressing in therapy and with medication due to an imbalance of serotonin in my neurological system. I am not a real criminal."

That tracker hidden in your teats says otherwise, I wanted to say. A hush filled the room as I tried to process this new development and she tried to figure how to reassert herself after this admission.

But there was no ladder back up to her throne, and she knew it.

"Listen, Selena, you must not tell anyone. It's been hard enough having to deal with this device as it frequently malfunctions."

"So... That's the buzzing I keep hearing?"

She nodded. "Yes. I didn't want to use my own personal phone... for obvious reasons. So, they gave me this one. Apparently, the last person who had it made this ringtone. I can't figure out how to change this dreadful noise." She took the phone back out from between her breasts and gave me a hopeful look as if I was going to touch that thing and fix her problems.

Listen, I don't have good facial control, and I was feeling all kinds of disturbed. Whatever my face was saying, she read it real quick and slowly pushed that thing back into its dank hiding place.

"Please, Selena, I beg of you, please don't tell *anybody* about my...indiscretions. The only other person who knows about this is my husband." Tears glistened in her eyes. "Vanessa doesn't even know. I usually hide the phone when we go on our shopping trips. I keep it in my purse, but it's been malfunctioning so much lately, I've had to keep it on my person." There was no anger or accusation in her tone, just fear and panic. "So, do I have your word, Selena? Do you promise not to tell anyone about this?"

Look, I'm tired of making deals and hiding secrets. That's what I was thinking. *I do not want to be a part of anybody else's schemes or misguided dreams. I've had enough of lies and blackmail, trickery, deceit, surprises...*

"Perhaps I can get you another pillow, Selena." Mrs. Wayland's smiling offer broke through my thoughts. "And didn't you say lasagna is your favorite dish? And cherry pie your favorite dessert?" She began plumping the pillows around me and organizing the clutter that was on the verge of swallowing me. "Why don't you write down a list of any movies you want to watch or books you want to read, and I'll be sure to order those as soon as possible. Please, don't hesitate to let me know anything you need to get little...Domino...D'ominee...Aja-mayo...here safely." She pulled the comforter up to my chin like she was tucking in a preschooler.

"Mrs. Wayland, you don't need to—"

"Oh, please call me Maddie. That is what my dearest friends call me," she blurted with a panicked smile.

"Really, there's no need to—"

"A dinner!" She clapped. "That's what we'll have to honor you. We'll invite your mother and father, your friend Neeka. How is your brother, CJ, these days? Oh, and, what's his name? Kunta X, right? He can come. I'd be happy to meet him and go over the account I still have available at Wood and Beams."

"Mrs. Wayland—"

"Remember, Maddie, please."

I didn't have the energy for this. As fascinating as it was to see Mrs. Wayland eager to cater to my every whim and desire, I was through with making deals with the devil. Besides, having this information about Mrs. Wayland's gangster side was much too valuable to waste by telling just anybody. I needed the right moment for revelation. "Mrs. Way...Mrs. Mad... Maddie... Look, I don't need a special dinner. I just want a healthy baby, a happy home, and a drama-free—"

"Baby shower." Mrs. Wayland clapped again.

Hold on. Did she just say something about the baby shower? Maybe...

"Kiona never stopped planning it. It's supposed to be a surprise, but tell me everything you've been wanting in a baby shower, and I'll personally see to it you'll get exactly what you want." Her eyes sparkled with either tears or insanity, I couldn't tell, but I knew this might be my one chance to put Kiona and her schemes in her rightful place, once and for all. And with Mrs. Wayland on my right side.

"Kiona is not allowed to plan it, attend it, or even imagine, think, or speak about it."

"Of course."

"And I want all of my friends and family to be a part of every detail."

"Done."

"And," I cleared my throat, feeling more power rising within me, "most importantly..." I paused for effect. "I do *not* want Kiona Tandy anywhere near me or *my* Evan."

Silence.

Okay, maybe the *my Evan* part had stepped over the line, but these reins were new in my hands and awaiting to be cracked.

Mrs. Wayland stared and blinked at me as I waited for a response.

"Maddie?" I didn't stutter this time.

More silence.

More blinking, more staring.

And then the buzzing began again. She quickly pulled out the device and pressed several buttons to silence it. "Okay." Her voice was weak as fear filled her face anew. "No more Kiona anywhere near you, your baby shower, or...your Evan."

As she turned to leave the room, the crush of defeat weighing heavily on her posture, I knew there was no need to rub my victory in her face. *Love your enemies. Pray for them which despitefully use you. Turn the other cheek. Humility. Self-control. Patience. Temperance.* I knew about the fruit of the Spirit and the higher standards God expects us to live out even toward those who can't stand us. I felt in that moment God had given me a rare chance to show Mrs. Wayland the magnitude, reality, and strength of His love, grace, and forgiveness; to be a living example of the Christ in me so her life could be changed for the better, and our relationship could take a turn for good and not be based on blackmail or any other power struggle. Here, at this moment, I had a chance to have a genuine sit-down, woman-to-woman conversation with Mrs. Wayland, knowing I would have her full ear and attention. This was my chance to be a better Christ-follower, to give God glory.

I knew all of this. I guess that's what made my decision at that moment all the worse.

"Oh, Maddie." I smiled as she turned back toward me.

"Yes?" She looked so afraid.

"Just so you know, I like my lasagna with extra cheese and garlic bread made with fresh basil."

"Yes, dear."

"And I also like cheesecake—with fresh strawberries."

"Of course."

"That's all."

"Yes, dear." She closed the door quietly behind her, and I listened to her soft footsteps disappear down the hall before I flipped on a home remodeling show on the HGTV network. Besides putting Mrs. Wayland in her place and getting rid of Kiona once and for all, I was determined to use Mrs. Wayland's "indiscretions" to get my house fixed to *my* specifications.

Look, I told y'all a long time ago to pray for me to do right. Ain't my fault if you haven't been doing so.

36

The New Year

Well, I have to admit. The next few months in some ways were the most relaxed of my life. As the keeper of the Wayland clan's darkest secrets, I held the reins of power from the bed of my sustained rest. It was a king bed, but I truly felt like the queen. I called Mrs. Wayland "Maddie" as she insisted. The family thought it was a term of endearment that grew from our seemingly growing bond. She served me breakfast in bed, lunch at noon, my favorite dinners at night.

She even tried to keep my mother happy when my mother was able to visit. She'd scoop my mom's bean casseroles into her best dishes and place them and vases of fresh flowers from her garden on trays, no hint of criticism or disdain in her words, tone, or face. This only grew my mother's suspicions, and she refused to engage me in any conversations of substance, certain the room was bugged, no matter how much I tried to convince her otherwise. I missed having real talks with my mommy, but at least I got to see her.

The tour dates for Evan-Essence kept getting pushed back, partly because Kunta X kept having something to take care of, he said. Largely, I knew because Maddie, determined to keep me happy, convinced her son he should probably stay closer to his pregnant wife while she was having a difficult pregnancy. Kiona had no say in the matter.

Evan's godmother, The Honorable Judge Vanessa Grant, had managed to arrange a judicial clerkship for him, part-time, an opportunity that arose from the sudden departure of an intern at a circuit court. The part-time hours gave him freedom to keep playing his clarinet. The money would help keep us afloat and build our savings as we determined our next housing arrangements. And would also pay for the lessons he secured by reaching out to one of the YouTubers he followed.

I didn't pick fights over his clarinet obsession, mostly because Kiona sightings had become rarer, also because the peace and quiet was welcome. Kiona's name came up less and less.

As a bonus, I'd heard nothing else about baby shower plans in a hall or on ski slopes with Razi.

By all accounts, life looked good. Evan's godmother had used her legal knowledge, prowess, and position to keep the ownership of our spaceship house tied up in the court system. It was likely to be months before that chaos sorted itself out, months I needed and welcomed as my pregnancy successfully continued. The baby in me was getting bigger and stronger every day while the contractions of my preterm labor still struggled to be held at bay. I was eating well, entertained with books and binge-watching shows, and indulged in an environment of peace and beauty.

But the peace was surface deep. I couldn't sleep at night.

Indigestion and heartburn weren't what kept me up after Thanksgiving dinner at the Waylands. The nonstop piano playing and singing by Evan's twin nieces wasn't what disturbed my sleep on Christmas night.

Evan and I only talked about safe topics: baby registries, the weather, the latest viral videos.

Mrs. Wayland only smiled in my face and served me because she feared the knowledge I had that could destroy her world—not because she truly respected and admired me.

And...Neeka and I had only had five conversations since the day I'd knocked on her door. Five. Nothing really said. Nothing really done.

I'd lost the heartbeat of my marriage, my pride of good character, and my best friend.

Was I really the woman I wanted to be as a soon-to-be mother, a wife, a daughter-in-law, a friend?

I was numb inside. Empty. But determined to keep up the charades I played because what else did I have?

***

"Three, two, one... Happy New Year." Horns honked, champagne glasses clinked, and the familiar notes of "Auld Lang Syne" blared from a television. Polite cheers and shouts of glee echoed through the house.

The Waylands were hosting an intimate gathering to usher in the new year. I listened to the chatter as Evan sat in an armchair beside our bed. His dress shirt was unbuttoned at the top, his pants a little looser on his frame. He looked how I felt: worn, ragged, exhausted.

And it was only 12:01 of a brand-new year.

"Thanks for staying here with me, Evan." I reached out a hand as I lay on my left side—doctor's recommendation as my body still fought against too early contractions.

"Of course. I'm not going to bring the new year in without my wife." He grabbed my hand for a quick second, rubbed the back of it, then let go. "Happy New Year, babe."

He stood. He left. I was alone in the room again as he joined the festivities on the main floor of the house. It was a new year, and we seemed no closer to effectively talking with each other. I didn't know what was on his mind, and he didn't know what was on mine.

Who knew marriage could be so lonely?

I looked around the empty room. I knew my parents were at their church's watch night service and that my mom would be dropping off her black-eyed peas later in the day. I imagined Neeka was dressed up in her finest, out somewhere with her fiancé, smiling at the promise of the new year and all the upcoming joys it held for her.

With the stroke at midnight, I was officially eight weeks away from my due date. Anytime I moved or stood or walked, the contractions would stir. The baby was fine. I just needed to be still and to rest for my body to cooperate so he or she could make it to my due date in late February. And I needed the rest of my life to come together to properly welcome my baby into the world.

"Now what, Lord? What about me? What do I do from here?" I whispered. It was my first prayer of the year. In truth, it was my first prayer in a while. And it was all I could get out. I tried to imagine myself in His presence, but there's no way He could be happy with all the blackmail, secrets, and lies.

A soft knock sounded at the door.

"Come in." I pulled the heavy down comforter up to my chin as the door was creaked open.

"Happy New Year, Selena. I bought you a slice of cake." Tracey, Evan's other sister, the middle sibling of the Wayland family.

"Thanks, Tracey, or should I say 'Dr. Wayland,'" I said with a fake formal accent. "How nice of you to think of me." I gave her a genuine smile as I eased up to a sitting position and took the plate from her. We'd had no real conversations over the years. I was surprised to see her in the room and even more surprised as she sat down in the armchair Evan had vacated.

"I'm not a doctor yet. Just a few more months of med school and then my final board exams."

"That's impressive. Sounds like we both have life-changing moments to look forward to this year." I patted my belly instinctively. She smiled then looked down and took a deep breath.

"Listen," she said, taking another deep breath, "we haven't had a chance to really get to know each other well, but I've seen how my mother has warmed up to you—or at least to the idea that you're going to be the mother of her favorite grandchild. Tori and Topaz don't stand a chance next to Evan's child." I didn't miss her rolling eyes. "Speaking of whom," she continued, "I also see how patient you've been with my brother. Lord, I know he's special. I'm so sorry, honey. The Razi case is the first time he's publicly failed. If you weren't in his life, I don't know he would have even found the ground he needed to land on, even if that ground at the moment is looking like quicksand."

"Quicksand?" I snickered. "Feels more like scorched earth with his clarinet screeching across the smoking desert of our lives. I can promise you this was not the sod or the soundtrack I imagined when I said 'I do.'"

Thankfully, she laughed along with me. "Selena, you are such a pure, beautiful soul. I mean that. No matter what anyone says, you're good for him. You're good for our family."

"I... Thanks for saying that." I swallowed hard, feeling the sudden weight of being the blackmailing guardian of the Wayland clan's secrets.

And only I knew just how dirty my hands were playing in this untested soil.

"Thanks again for the cake, Tracey." I reached for the fork to look like I was ready to begin eating. I wanted her to leave so I could be alone in my shame and guilt. But Tracey stayed planted.

"Selena," she grew serious, "I know because of your condition you only leave the house for your weekly OB appointments. Your delicate state is why I'm going to share this with you." She took in a deep breath and let out a loud exhale.

I felt my forehead wrinkle. "Share what?"

"I don't think your system is set up for big surprises right now, so I'm just going to tell you." She looked over at the closed door, and when satisfied nobody else was near or coming in, she continued, "You're having a surprise baby shower today. It's not going to be here. You're going to be asked to get up and go somewhere, and there will be a big party. As I am the medical person on the shower planning committee, I didn't think it would be right to let you walk into a situation that could send your body into shock." Footsteps sounded in the hallway. She paused until whoever it was headed down the stairwell. "Nobody knows I'm telling you this." She lowered her voice. "And there's been a lot of back-and-forth about keeping it a surprise. So, just act surprised and keep my cover."

Another secret to keep to protect another member of the Wayland family.

I was so over it.

"Shower planning committee?" The only words I could get out as I realized my heartbeat had picked up its pace. "Who exactly is on this committee?" I held my breath.

"Some of our family, some of yours, your friend Neeka. We wanted to make this special for you. They all figured since you're able to get up once a week to go to your appointments, you'd be okay getting up this once to go to…the shower. I just don't want you to go into labor."

"So, I guess it's safe to assume there's no skiing involved."

Tracey stifled a laugh. "Oh no, I can assure you, Kiona Tandy has nothing to do with the plans. My mother knew better than to add that skank to the guest list."

"Tracey," I said, gasping, "does your mother know you talk like this?" I couldn't help but snicker.

She sobered. "My mother doesn't know the half of me. Or any of her kids, I'd say. And I think it's safe to reason we don't know the half of her." She looked me dead in the eye. "You're getting close to her. If you ever find out something I can use against her to get her off my back, I'd appreciate it."

The whole family had issues.

And I had married into it and was about to give birth to another one of their blood.

"I–I don't know what to say." That was the truest thing I'd said all year, all twenty-five minutes of it.

Tracey got up and headed to the door. She wiped some confetti off her shimmering top. "I have your back. Just act surprised today and cover mine."

37

The Surprise

I barely slept the rest of the night. When Evan came back in the room around two a.m., I closed my eyes to keep from having to address him. Not that it mattered; he got in the bed with his back to me and never turned around.

At five a.m., still awake, I sent a text to Neeka: Happy New Year!

I was encouraged to know she'd made it onto the baby shower planning committee, but who knew if she'd done so willingly or out of deference to my mom or some final act of loyalty toward me.

She didn't return my text. Then again, maybe she was out partying or perhaps passed out from partying or just spending time with her fiancé.

Kiona's ex.

It was too much.

After thinking, weighing, and knowing I couldn't continue with this charade of fake communication and maintaining secrets and lies; after tossing and turning as much as was possible with my irritated uterus; after wrestling with my soul, my fears, and my conscience; after praying and asking God to forgive me for where I'd fallen short and to fix it all, I finally fell asleep, just before six a.m.

***

"Selena, wake up. Selena." Evan's fingers poked and shook my shoulder. "Selena."

"Wha— Who…" I mumbled, rubbed my eyes, and tried to sit up and adjust to the brightness as Evan rolled the drapes open. Bright afternoon sun, which had been hidden by the room-darkening curtains, flooded the room. "What time is it?"

"It's almost 1:30 in the afternoon. You looked so tired this morning, I let you sleep. You'd think you were the one up all night."

His dress clothes from the night before were off and draped on a dresser. Now he wore a light blue sweater, jeans, and boots. A casual ensemble but not casual enough to spend a lazy day at home.

"Going somewhere?" I asked, still trying to orient myself to the new day. It was still January 1, I reminded myself. Had my mom dropped off her pot of black-eyed peas yet? I felt a tightening sensation across my abdomen and quickly laid back down. "I need some water. Dehydration isn't good for holding off these contractions."

Evan grabbed a water bottle from the mini fridge that had become a fixture in my bedrest suite. "Here you go, babe." He handed it to me. "And as far as going somewhere, we both are. Just got a call from Dr. Nelson. She saw something in your last set of labs that makes her want to check you out. Now."

"On New Year's Day? She's open?"

"Not her office. She's on rotation on the OB unit over at the hospital today."

"We have to drive all the way to downtown Baltimore? That's almost an hour away."

"I know," he acknowledged. "She said it was a bit urgent or she would have waited until your Thursday appointment."

Dread and panic—sensations that had easily dropped by to visit me throughout my pregnancy—started knocking on my chest in the form of heart palpitations.

Then, I remembered Tracey's midnight visit. The surprise baby shower. This must be it.

But what if it's not?

I took a deep breath and decided to hope for the best. "Give me a moment to clean up and get dressed. I'll be ready in about twenty minutes."

"Do you need help?" He held my arm as I pulled myself to a sitting position on the side of the bed.

"I'll take my time. I'll be okay. Thanks, Evan." *It helps to know you even care*, I wanted to say, but didn't.

Half an hour later, we were on the BW Parkway, driving toward downtown Baltimore. I had on my favorite maternity top under my winter coat, a silk multi-colored blouse. I'd paired it with blue jeans to match my husband's.

"Fancy today." He'd nodded at my shoes, beige wedges that offset my colorful top. I'd last worn them with my Easter suit.

"I felt like being cute-cute. Not too often I get to go out these days, you know?" I looked out the car window, grateful he couldn't see my face, and also that I'd opted not to put on my full-face make-up. Just lip gloss and mascara. I didn't want to raise suspicions that I was on to the surprise.

But what if this is real? What if Dr. Nelson does think something is wrong? And if Evan was lying, boy was he doing it well.

A little too well for my comfort.

I closed my eyes and rested my head on the back of my headrest, trying my best to tune out the ripples of contractions that continued stretching over my belly. The car was quiet. No music, no laughter, no talking. *Will it always be this quiet between us?* The single question repeated over and over in my head as I drifted off to sleep.

"Selena, I have to make a quick stop."

I woke up to Evan's voice and tried to make sense of the scene in front of me.

Our house. The old house. The broken down, beat-up dwelling that had been the starting place of division for us from the first day of our marriage. The place that had been renovated then litigated.

The metal bars and grates and all the other weird outdoor designs from the Zuzani crew were missing. Odd.

Evan hopped out the car with no explanation and used a key to enter the door. He shut it behind him. I guess his godmother had gotten everything worked out. *Did we still own it?* Did I even *want* to own it? I had no idea what was going on. I waited for five minutes, trying to understand. Finally, I got out of the car. We were parked right in front of the front door, so it was only a couple wobbly steps from me to get to the door. Before I could reach for the knob or knock, it was swung open.

"Surprise!"

It wasn't a shout, more of a muted cheer, as if the very words would send me tumbling over. A crowd of smiling faces, balloon bouquets, and the smell of barbecue meatballs and fried chicken greeted me. Still groggy from my nap in the car, I tried to get my bearings.

"Huh?" I looked back at the parking lot for our development, noticing for the first time extra cars lined the opposite end of the lot and a small side street. "Huh?" I rubbed my eyes, asking again.

"Here, Selena, sit." Neeka was in front of me, guiding me to a velvet chaise longue that sat under a window in the living room.

As I looked from face to face at the people who filled the newly opened floor plan, I didn't have to fake my astonishment. I wasn't just shocked at who was there, but also at the apparent and dramatic transformation of my home. From my seat in the living room, I saw hardwood floors, beautiful crown molding, and a calming shade of blue on the walls. The dining room had a modern crystal chandelier. The kitchen had new white cabinets and quartz countertops.

And stainless-steel appliances that looked like they actually worked.

And everywhere I looked, I saw new furniture.

My house had new, plush, coordinating furniture in shades of earthy brown and light blue. Light fixtures and window treatments straight from high-end catalogs. Bookcases, shelving, accent rugs—and was that a new gas fireplace? For the first time ever, my home looked like it could be featured on an HGTV special. The transformation was breathtaking.

"The concrete, the manhole cover coffee table..." I mumbled.

"Gone. Yes, all that hideous stuff is gone," my mother sounded from a matching velvet sofa opposite me. I didn't miss the tightening lips of Evan's mother as my mother continued. "I know what kind of décor my daughter would dream of having, so I picked these furnishings out myself."

"But we footed the bill," Mrs. Wayland managed to blurt out.

"Seventy-five percent of it," my mom corrected. "Your dad and I took care of the rest, Selena, namely this living room set and the nursery."

"That's right." My father nodded next to her, a cup of red punch in his hand. "There's a brand-new nursery with everything off your registry in the middle bedroom upstairs. We took care of it."

"Half of it," Mrs. Wayland interjected.

"Hey, everyone," Evan jumped in. "It's not a competition. We're all family here, and we're all celebrating the upcoming arrival of this child." His stiff posture and careful tone told me all was not yet calm and settled despite the festive green and yellow balloons and cheery banners that filled the space. Cousins, church members, and long-lost friends sat and stood around the sanely updated living, dining, and kitchen areas with a continued awkward silence. I noticed

Sister Corrine Knight on a folding chair in the kitchen. She gave me a quiet, smiling nod, as if knowing what I needed. It seemed like an invisible line had been drawn down the center of the room with everyone picking a side to stand on. My people and family on one side; Evan's parents and siblings on the other. Neeka and her beau, Peyton Anderson, seemed to be the only ones who'd not gotten the memo of the battle lines.

Or maybe this tension was all in my head. Oh, the horror, the torment of hidden lies and things left unsaid. *This isn't how I want my child to enter the world, Lord. This isn't the example of marriage and family I want displayed to the world.*

"Wow, everyone's here." I smiled and tried to think of something else to say that would break through the awkwardness.

Evan knelt next to me. "I did this all for you, babe. I wanted to get this house right for you. I did a good job in court representing us. There are no issues, no liens, and the homeowners' association has no more complaints. You would have been proud of me. Your mom and my mom worked together to do the rest—the work, the design, and the décor."

He looked worn down and beat— though I now knew getting this house together had to be part of the reason for his exhaustion, especially if both of our mothers were involved. I also knew the secrets motivating the actions and adding to the weight.

God, I want to be free. I want us both to be free.

"And, listen," Neeka spoke again to me next, "I know you haven't heard much from me lately, but that's mainly because I didn't want to blow up the whole surprise for my best girly. You know I can't keep secrets."

And I can *keep secrets, and things are all blown up.* A tear escaped from my eye, and Neeka wiped it with her pinky. Evan narrowed his eyes at me. I gave him a quick smile to reassure him I had no intention of messing up this moment revealing his past messiness.

"*Awww*, you're so surprised. Good. CJ—" Neeka turned to my brother and barked— "where's the music? Let's get this party going." Neeka grinned as music and chit-chat began to fill the room. Peyton came beside her.

"Girl, I have so much to catch you up on," she continued while gnawing a buffalo wing. Her smile was genuine. She was truly happy. "February 14. Mark the date. I don't care if Peyton and I have to get married next to your bed with a bridesmaid gown laying across your big belly, you are going to be in my wedding."

"You know I wouldn't miss it. I'm happy for you. And, Peyton, you obviously are a great man to have won over my Neeka."

Evan, watching from across the room, breathed hard. I could see his shoulders move up and down, his chest heave in and out. I knew he wondered what we were all talking about. His mother studied him from across the room then stared at me as he stared back at her. I could almost hear her questioning in her mind if I'd said something to her son about her that had him looking upset.

It was all too much as I tried to nod to the music, laugh along with the games, eat the food I was certain my aunts had prepared, and *ooh* and *ahh* at the multitude of presents—baby outfits, diapers, gear, and more. I did a pretty good job of staying calm, considering. The contractions didn't spike as I reclined on the chaise longue and told myself to exhale slowly.

Maybe I really could manage the mayhem and hold on to the secrets that were uncomfortably but effectively keeping the peace. Maybe this new strained reality was survivable. A smile, though uneasy, pulled on the corner of my lips as the cake was set to be cut.

And then there was a knock at the door and all hell broke loose.

38

The Crasher

Kiona Tandy.

She stood in the doorway with a smile. Despite the chill of the January air, her coat flapped open in the winter wind to reveal a tight, short, goldenrod yellow dress. Cleavage, hips, legs, lips—every voluptuous curve of her body had been highlighted, emphasized, and underlined.

"Evan! Selena! Congratulations!" she squealed as she stepped in, oversized gift bags dangling from her wrists.

But nobody was paying attention to the squeals, the curves, or the gifts. Like me, all eyes were on the person standing next to her.

Razi.

In the flesh.

A chorus of screams and gasps filled my living room as everyone seemed to tumble over each other, cameras and scrap papers in hand to request autographs from and selfies with the superstar.

My brother, CJ, serving as the DJ for the event, cut the gospel music he'd been playing to blast one of Razi's upbeat songs, a collaboration the crooner had done with a rapper from South Florida. CJ's head nodded to the bass of the beat.

"Ladies and gentlemen, the one and only Razi," he said, beaming. "I don't know how he got here, but we're going with it."

As I tried to make sense of the chaotic scene, and my mother tried to get CJ to lower the volume just a bit, another commotion on the opposite side of the room caught my ear and pulled my entire attention.

"Kiona? What are you doing here?" Peyton stood frozen in the corner, a meatball on a toothpick held mid-air.

"Kiona?" Neeka did a double take, her eyes darting back and forth between her new fiancé and his ex-wife. I knew she instantly understood who this stranger was. Neeka stepped closer to Peyton and grabbed his hand before another word was said.

"Peyton?" Kiona looked shocked for all of half of a second, then she shrugged and headed for the buffet table in the center of the dining room. Razi, stuck at the doorway, continued grinning for selfies with the party guests, all oblivious to the real threat of danger unfolding across the room.

"I'm Selena's boss," Kiona explained to a stoic Peyton, an air of triumph in her tone. "Evan told me about the baby shower, and I wouldn't miss it for the world. Congratulations, Selena," she shouted over the music. "It's a wonderful feeling carrying Evan's child, isn't it?" She winked at me before sucking a meatball off a toothpick.

"What does she mean by that?" My mother had picked up on the conversation. "Evan, is this woman pregnant? And did you really invite her to my daughter's baby shower?"

"No, no, no. Absolutely not. Impossible. I can assure you she is not pregnant." Evan tried to keep his voice low. "And I didn't invite her. I must have mentioned the shower in passing—a long time ago—but never did I invite her, Mrs. Tucker. And, again, Kiona is absolutely not pregnant. At least not by me. That's not even possible.

Nothing has happened between us. It's all a big misunderstanding. Right, Kiona? Right?"

Kiona shrugged and piled a large spoon of pasta salad on a paper plate.

"Kiona," Evan demanded, "Why are you here? Why are you doing this?"

"Doing what?" Kiona whipped around to face him.

My brother, his lips pursed, started lowering the music.

"Doing what exactly?" Kiona asked again, putting down the plate she'd started making. "Standing up for my dreams? Standing up for myself? Am I just supposed to sacrifice what I want and disappear again? I did that for you years ago. I'm not doing it again."

"Kiona, please. Not here. Not now." Evan let out a weak, nervous smile as eyes started turning toward them and ears began to perk.

But Kiona was ready for her moment.

"Why not here and now?" she shouted. "I gave up my baby's life so you could marry this...her." She cut her eyes at me before turning back to him. "I gave up my baby. Am I supposed to give up my dreams, too? Razi is here. I got him here. Let's show him our act. You owe me this. You owe me at least this, Evan." She snarled, then with wet eyelashes, she threw a half-sorrowful look at Peyton. "I'm so sorry about everything, Pey-Pey. I was lost back then." She narrowed her eyes. "But now I'm found."

"Wait, Evan, that was you, man?" Peyton's voice was two octaves higher. "You're the man who got my wife pregnant and broke up my marriage? You? My so-called best friend?"

The room went full gasp and then silent.

"*Awww*, shucks. This about to be some *Jerry Springer* ish." My brother CJ cut the music completely, grabbed a folding chair, sat down, and swung his head in the direction of my breaking life.

Razi's pen stopped mid-signature on the napkin my thirteen-year-old cousin Donesha had held out for him. "Oh, my," I heard him mumble.

I'd been sitting in silence, my heart thudding in my throat, my stomach swirling. I tried to sit up from the chaise, but my body wouldn't let me move. I realized a hand had been resting on my shoulder the entire time since Kiona showed up. The pastor's wife, Sister Corrine Knight, kept a steady hold on me. I tried to breathe.

Evan was frozen in silence, too. My mother muttered something under her breath.

"Yes, Peyton." Kiona seemed to be the only person who could talk out loud. "When you started your business in Vegas, you promised to help me reach my dreams to be a star. Then you and your business failed. That's when Evan came along. With his entertainment law plans, I knew he could help get me to where I belonged. He fell in love with me, and I couldn't resist. I should have known and did better, but he said all the right lines. Everything was perfect. I got pregnant with his baby, and we had a wedding date set. We were on our way to happily ever after and my dreams coming true. And then... Selena."

"Now that's a lie." I couldn't hold back anymore. "You transferred to his college and went after him. Evan was wrong for what he did, but you are not going to pin your dirty plotting on him. You are not some victim here."

Why, oh why, was this the first thing out of my mouth? Of all the things I could have said, here I was playing defense attorney for my dingbat husband who couldn't even win a case over song lyrics.

I wanted to kick myself.

And apparently so did Neeka. She glared at Evan and then looked with shock and sorrow at me. "Selena, you knew all this? Why didn't you tell me? I can't believe you knew about Kiona and this whole situation—and that Evan was involved—and you didn't tell me."

The look on her face. The pain in her eyes. Then the anger burning in them. At me. At Evan.

At Kiona.

Everything in me broke.

"Oh, yeah." My brother rubbed his hands together, then got up and started pushing furniture back. "Excuse me, *beep beep*, everybody back up. Give these people some room. It's about to go down in here. Watch out for the pregnant lady."

"Selena!" Madelyn Ernestine Wayland's sudden shout jolted the entire room. "Are *you* the reason Kiona and Evan broke up? What happened? I never understood why things ended so abruptly between them. And to know there was a baby involved—my beautiful little grandbaby." She clutched her hands over her heart.

Hold up. Did this lady just miss the whole Kiona-was-married thing?

"Are you kidding me?" My mother must have read my mind as she tried to stand. "My daughter had nothing to do with your son being a homewrecker. How dare you raise your voice like that to *my* Selena while *your* little Evan was out there being a ho." At first, I thought my dad was trying to pull my mom back down, but then I realized he was using her shoulder to try and push himself up, too.

Dr. Wayland, who'd been sitting quietly in a wingback chair in a corner eased to a stand, glaring at my father.

"Oh, I got you Pops." CJ glared and nodded.

I closed my eyes and opened them, wishing this was all a dream. People had out their cell phones, cameras pointed, videos on. And not at Razi. My whole family was about to become the next viral sensation. This wasn't a shower. It was a storm, a deluge of destruction and if things went further, there'd be too much irreparable damage to clean up and repair.

Or was it already too late?

"Enough." I shouted. "Mom, Dad, no. Stop. CJ, be quiet. And,

Mrs. Wayland, if you have any questions about your son, you need to ask him, not me."

"Selena, no. You tell me what happened," Mrs. Wayland screeched. "This entire situation reeks of you. I will not let you and your family degrade my son's name. I don't know all what happened with Kiona, but I know my son. He's not some awful adulterer. There's a big misunderstanding somewhere in this whole convoluted story, but I will not let you, Selena, nor your low-class family drag my son down one second more. The gutter is what your people know. Not mine."

My mother had murder in her eyes as she took two steps toward Mrs. Wayland.

"Okay, enough. Stop," Evan boomed as he rushed between our mothers and stretched out his arms. "Mom, no. Selena did nothing wrong. This is all my fault. I wasn't honest, and the results of my dishonesty are what we're seeing in this room today. I've hurt the people I love most, and it's had me losing my mind trying to hide it. Selena knows that more than anyone." He shook his head, shut his eyes for a second, then reopened them and stood tall.

"Look, I messed up, man. Peyton, I messed up. No excuses. I'm sorry. It was me. Yes, I'm the one who's responsible for ending your marriage to Kiona. I'm forever sorry. Mom, I'm sorry. I never told you I got a married woman pregnant because I didn't want to disappoint you. I didn't want you looking at me differently as I know you always will now. I'm sorry. Selena, I'm sorry for putting you in the middle of this, for not telling you sooner and imprisoning you to my past. Please know I do truly love you. You alone have my heart, always."

He turned back to Neeka and Peyton. "Neeka, please don't hold anything against Selena. Please. This is all on me. I put my wife in a terrible position. You've been a good friend to her. I'm the one who failed. Everyone, I've failed. I'm so very sorry."

He turned to my parents. "Mr. and Mrs. Tucker, I'm sorry." He turned back to me. "Selena, I'm sorry, I've failed."

"Oh, stop it." Kiona's voice slapped the room. "Evan, you and I together were not ever and can never be a failure. I will always—"

"—Be a distraction I don't need in my life." Strength and certainty grew on Evan's face. A part of me was like 'too little too late.' Another part of me, the part that still dreamed of my happily ever after and wanted my marriage to survive, was intrigued and impressed. "Kiona," he continued, "I was wrong to you and for you. I was selfish and I didn't handle things the right way between us. I apologize. For it all. That said, our friendship is not sustainable. I love and value my wife too much to have you in my life even a little. Considering our past, I don't want even the appearance of evil in our present. It's time for you to go."

"But our act—"

"—Goodbye, Kiona." Evan held firm.

Kiona froze then shook her shoulders as if clearing the space around her. She then turned toward the superstar sensation still standing near the doorway. *Lordy, the man was still there.*

"Razi, this is for you." She closed her eyes and tilted her head back as if to start singing.

"Not interested." Razi cut in before a single note sounded. His phone was in hand, and he was typing vigorously on it. I imagined he was summoning his manager, security team, shoot, maybe even an Uber, the armed forces, or Jesus Himself to come get him out of my house and away from the scene that had unfolded in front of him.

"But—" she said, pouting.

"—Not. Interested." He didn't even look up.

The room stayed silent save for a loud slurp of punch from my brother.

Kiona scrunched up her face. *"Hmpfh."* She began buttoning up her coat, her long painted fingernails clicking on each metal fastener. Then she turned toward the door. I held my breath as her punched heels echoed on the hardwood floor as she left my home, my life.

Forever.

I felt it in my bones, in my spirit.

And, as if to confirm my gut feeling with an 'amen,' she turned around to face us when she got to the door and said, "Evan, don't expect me to help you anymore with your stupid act. Once you realize the mistake you are making by pushing me away, no begging or pleading will ever bring me back. And, Selena, I have much bigger plans than that off-brand radio station you're stuck with. You will never have the privilege of seeing me in that place again to make it worthy. Sorry for your loss, love. You are on your own there now. I know who I am and what I'm worth. I have options waiting for me in Atlanta. Razi, when you are indeed ready to witness greatness, call me. You have my card."

With a huff and a puff, but not enough to blow my house down, she left with a slam of the door.

Gone.

The room broke out into applause. Even Razi joined in the clapping.

"Nothing like being back home in good old Baltimore," he said, grinning. "I get the best material and inspiration for my music when I'm here."

A little alarmed, a little comforted, I exhaled, and a few of my cousins and some church members chuckled. As warm air from my lungs rolled out of my mouth, I realized how long I'd been holding in so much. I was ready to breathe again.

Or so I thought.

The party wasn't over.

39

The Song

"This—" Mrs. Wayland cut through the applause and giggles—"this is all just terrible. And, and..." She looked at me, *glared* at me. "I know in my heart this is somehow all your fault, Selena. I'm sure of it. You've been nothing but a terrible influence on my son since the day he met you. Maybe Evan and Kiona could have worked this out years ago without you getting in the way. I would have already had my grandbaby and you, you wouldn't be anywhere near my family. My son may have made some mistakes, but you've only brought him lower. Razi, I'm so sorrowful and ashamed you've had to witness such ghetto behavior."

"Now, you listen—" My mother pointed her finger.

"No, Mrs. Tucker, I've got this," Evan interrupted. "Mom," he said, turning to his mother, "you're not going to talk to Selena like that. Ever. She is my wife and the mother of my child. You may not respect what I've done, but you are always going to respect her."

Mrs. Wayland frowned. "Evan, you've lost too much since you've been with her. Your job, your common sense, your dignity. I'm your mother, you need to listen to me. She isn't a good influence on you. She's not good for you."

"I don't get it. Why are you so against Selena? What is it about her that has you so mean and bothered?" Neeka. Her voice was one degree above a whisper, the weakest I'd ever heard it.

But she was there for me.

Even in her tears, her pain, her anger, she was there for me. A friend. A true friend. A friend I hadn't even shown myself to be. The shame I felt pierced beyond description.

"Evil company corrupts good morals." Mrs. Wayland turned up her nose. "I learned that the hard way. If you let low-class people get too close, you end up—" She blinked in a flurry. I knew what she'd stopped herself from saying.

You end up sixteen and sent away to juvie jail and spending the rest of your life hiding secrets about your past and your imperfections.

But that past and those imperfections didn't belong to anyone else. Even if she'd gotten mixed up with the wrong crowd or hooked up with the wrong person, those problems in her past—and in her present—were her own. And if her penchant for stealing really was a mental disorder, she needed to stay with getting help.

And, for the record, there was nothing *low-class or criminal about me and my loved ones.*

I thought all of this. Knew I could say all of this. It was right there in my grasp and on my tongue to say something about her "other phone" and the "app" it carried, the secrets of her thieving ways, the legal problems she'd be horrified for anyone to know. Why couldn't that alarm malfunction right then?

I could put this woman in her place once and for all.

Right or righteous.

I looked up at Sister Knight. I recalled her vlog I'd watched on YouTube some time ago. I hadn't been able to see an application for my life when I'd watched it, but the message gushed up within me now like a geyser of living water. Sister Knight gave me another shoulder squeeze and a reassuring smile, having no idea the choice I had in front of me.

Here was a chance for me to use some wisdom to build my house. I'd been blackmailing, wheeling, and dealing left and right. That wasn't me. That wasn't the me I wanted to be.

I looked around my living room, the newly done dining room and kitchen, the people in in it—family members, church members, friends, and some people I had no idea who they were. And Razi. I looked at the new furniture, the curtains, the stainless-steel appliances, the absence of cement. This house had been through a lot. This house and I had been on a long, twisted road—a torturous route that winded around my parents' issues, my own fears, poor communication, bad starts, quick fixes, and weird pit stops. It had finally come into its own after a shaky united front to make things right.

My house wasn't broken anymore. It was renovated from the floor up, the ceiling down. No need to tear up my home and the people who stood in it with my words. I didn't need to boost myself up on a shaky ground of spite. In Christ, I was better than that.

I looked at Mrs. Wayland who was both trembling in anger and looking small in her fear. In her boldness, I guess she'd forgotten I knew her secrets. But it didn't matter. I wasn't going to out her. Not like this. There'd been enough drama in my house for the day. For the past several months. It was time to honor the rebuild.

"I forgive you," I whispered. She hadn't asked, but my heart answered. I let go of any scheme or intention to expose her. I let her go and left her with God for handling. *It is a dreadful thing to fall into the hands of the living God*, a verse from one of my quiet times reflections, Hebrews 10:31, pierced my thoughts and made me shudder. *Yeah, I'm going to get out of the way and let God deal with her.* It was a quiet moment, but one I knew would echo personal victory in ways I could not imagine.

Starting with feeling free.

"Hey DJ man," Razi broke my moment of reflection. I was shocked—and embarrassed— he was still there, but there he was, the one and only Razi, now standing center in my living room acting like part of the family. Maybe that was a good thing. Maybe this whole scene would really end up inspiring his next hit.

So, yeah, basically, I did not at all foresee what happened next. None of us did, not even Razi.

"I've got a song I want to sing," he continued to my brother, "and I need you to play the track. This song has never been released and might never be. The lyrics got tangled up in the courts," he said, winking at my husband, "but Evan, I'm rooting for your redemption both with your wife and with what you can do with my contested song lyrics one day. Seems fitting to sing it here for this occasion. Track ten, my man." He handed my brother his phone to hook up to the speaker. A jazzy piano run was the intro. Razi lifted his voice and began to sing:

We were young when we first met
I was Romeo to your Juliet
You stole my heart, I stole your mind
Two thieves who had to serve time

Hold up. These words were familiar. The scrapbook I'd found in Mrs. Wayland's craft room had those same words, I recalled. But why would the scribbled poem on the chocolate candy wrapper I'd seen be both at the center of Evan's butchered copyright case and coming out of Razi's mouth? I tried to make sense of this as the singer's smooth vocals continued.

Sentenced to live forever apart
Different paths, lonely hearts

Until years later your broken home
Led me back to you, and we were again alone
Me ready to repair what was lost
You willing to pay the highest cost

"Wait—" Razi abruptly stopped singing as the music continued. "I'm sorry. I always forget the chorus." As he wrinkled his face and tapped a finger on his chin, a loud burp sounded from my basement doorway, and a new voice began slurring in rhythmic rhyme.

"My calloused hands did so much more
Than simply fix your walls and floor
I took a home that was broke and shoddy
And resurrected it all with the help of your body
Oh the sweetness of our secret rendezvous
When I fixed up your home, your heart, for you."

Kunta X.

"Wait, you know the words to this song, Mr. X?" Evan stepped forward. "How do you know the words?"

Kunta X took a swig from a silver flask. I wondered how long he'd been drinking in my basement. I imagined he'd come early to the home with my father and the two had stayed out the way and in the basement while the women of the family came and set things up. My father had come upstairs in time for the celebration because he knew better. Kunta X had probably just arisen from his stupor.

"It's my story," he spoke, "my life, my words you see.
And now that I hear it sung from the lips of Razi
I ain't even mad he stole those words from me.
I sent my poem with chocolates to a long-lost lover
But left a draft in a studio I cleaned where they were discovered.
Hearing them now sung brings up such sweet memories.

From my youth, of my truth, of a woman who wanted all of me
It's my true love story and it ain't rated 'G.'
The Broken House was the name of the poem I had planned
But then I heard it sung at the studio as *The Handyman*.
So let's just say this 'handyman' knows how to fix all that is broken-
Houses, hearts, and some things that will remain unspoken."

He let out a drunken giggle and another burp.

"*The Broken House?*" my little cousin Donesha muttered. "More like *Need to be Housebroken*, the way he's smelling."

As my aunt Cookie tried to quiet her child, Evan shook his head.

"I still don't get it," he said. "The plaintiff in the copyright suit was named Kenneth Robertson. He didn't even show up, and I still lost the case."

"Madelyn, you look faint." The first and only words uttered by Dr. Wayland.

Indeed, she did. All eyes turned to her. I wondered how long she'd been standing there frozen, mouth agape, eyes fixed on the drunken poet who smelled like pee, fart, and liquor.

Who'd just shared his rhymes of a long-lost forbidden love from his youth.

"Kenneth?" she finally whispered. "Kenneth Robertson?"

Kunta X's eyes widened and glistened as he came almost to a full stand.

Almost.

"I haven't heard that colonizing name since I was a wee little laddie.

I go by Kunta X now, and it's great to see you again, my dear Maddie." He winked.

In all the drama of the past few months, it occurred to me they'd never actually crossed paths.

"We met at...at—well, when we were teens, very young." Mrs. Wayland's voice was a broken whisper.

"And met again when you needed some home repairs done." The Poet flashed all of his teeth in a wide smile.

"Wait, Kenneth Robertson?" Evan's oldest sister, Penelope, spoke slowly. "Isn't that the name of the contractor who fixed our old condo? You know, the condo where we lived right before we found out Mom was pregnant with Evan? She kept his business magnet on the refrigerator for years and used to smile at it saying that contractor had gifted hands."

Mouths began to drop open as the rest of the room started putting two and two together... Or should I say one and one?

"We survived a kitchen fire before, dear, remember? Our first condo, on the lake, not long before we learned that Evan was on the way. A contractor came and fixed it up better than new. As I recall, that kitchen re-do excited you. You had revived life like I'd never seen. This will be no different. A fresh project to indulge your fancies, right dear?"

I looked at Dr. Wayland who had uttered those words the very day I'd messed up their kitchen. At the moment, his eyes were piercing Mrs. Wayland's.

"Interesting," my mother muttered as she looked from Evan to Kunta X and back.

Evan's other sister, Tracey, looked at me. "Checkmate," she mouthed.

Evan's newborn picture, that dead rose petal, and that single line of poetry on chocolate candy wrapper paper in Mrs. Wayland's scrapbook page? I'd misread the line as *Forever a part*. It was really *Forever apart*. Mrs. Wayland had spent her lifetime "forever apart" from her one true love and her only connection to him.... was Evan.

I'd be willing to bet they met
When she was "away" at sixteen
And then they were reunited

Just before Evan came on the scene.
The timeline is suspect
Oh, what a home project...
A home renovation
Appears to have led
From a fire destroyed kitchen
To a fling in a bed.
Sounds like more than a cabinet upgrade was done
Had Maddie messed around and given the handyman a son?

The way the rhymes and the truth were flowing in my head? Whew, child.

"Well, this took an unexpected turn." CJ.

Mrs. Wayland stood in the center of the room but no longer on a pedestal, and she knew it. The spotlight must have been pretty hot because girlfriend was sweating.

"Harold, let's go." She frowned, trying to regain some dignity.

The good doctor didn't budge. He stroked the salt-and-pepper hairs on his chin, a chin that had no resemblance to Evan, as neither did his eyes, his nose, his ears, or his hairline. Indeed, the only thing Evan shared with the man was beautiful rich, brown skin.

"Vanessa." Mrs. Wayland cut her eyes nervously at her dear friend the judge.

Honey, if Evan's godmother was the judge, the whole room was the jury, and the Honorable Vanessa Grant was not about to leave us alone with our deliberations.

Or with our judgments.

Right or righteous?

I took another deep breath and opted to keep building up my home, my family.

"Nobody is perfect," I said to Mrs. Wayland. "You're not. Evan's not. I'm not either."

"At least we see where Evan may have got his homewrecker skills from," my mother muttered. I respectfully cut her with my eyes.

"Look, we all have done things we're not proud of. None of us is perfect." My eyes swept the whole room. "No need to keep holding on to pride and secrets and lies. That's why we're where we are right now. We're all together in this. Who in this room truly has a lifetime of clean hands?" I nodded at my parents, my brother, the Wayland sisters, and the rest of their clan. I looked over at Neeka. Her arms were crossed, anger still seared on her face.

"We all want the same thing. Happiness, peace, and freedom. Neeka, you and Peyton want it and deserve it. Mom, Dad. Mrs. Wayland. Everyone in this room. Evan, I want us to be happy together, to be able to really talk with each other, to not let anything, any person, or any situation get in the way of us. I want our friendship back. No, I want it even stronger. Transparency. Authenticity. That's why I can say all this in front of everyone. We said our vows publicly, so I'm not going to hold back now on what I really want with you. I want us to be able to truly talk with each other and truly share our lives so nothing and nobody can get in our way."

Evan looked at me and nodded. He looked over at Kunta X, pain and questioning on my husband's face. Then Evan looked away from him and walked over to me and grabbed my hand. There was warmth in his fingers, in his thumb massaging the back of my hand. I saw in his eyes the man I knew he could be. I held his hand tighter, letting him know we were together, no matter what new twists would spring up in our life stories. We looked each other in the eyes, breathed on the same beat. The union and intimacy of that pure moment was such that I knew we would act on it as soon as it was safe to do so. In that moment, I could tell he'd heard all I'd just said. Really heard me—my words, my unspoken prayers, my willingness to do whatever was on my end to make things work.

I'd chosen a path of love—not spite, not secrets, not shame—and it allowed my voice, my vulnerability to be heard by the one who loved me back. I'd trusted this man enough to marry him. Now, I was going to trust God enough to keep us together with happiness, peace, and freedom.

"We're a team, Evan," I whispered. "We are imperfect people in a perfect union, and I promise before God I will do all I can to be a woman who builds up our house, and I'll build it on a firm foundation of openness, honesty, and truth."

But I could only hold up my end of the bargain, and he knew it.

"And, Selena, I'll be a man who makes our house worth having." He nodded at me again, strength like I'd never seen in him taking over his eyes, his posture, his very voice.

"So sweet." Razi, who'd moved from near the door to taking a seat by Donesha, dabbed his eyes with the napkin my little cousin had wanted him to sign.

I didn't miss her frown.

"Y'all been through some things." Neeka looked at me, a frown of her own on her lips as her arms slowly uncrossed. She reached out a soft hand to her fiancé's face. Tears filled his eyes as he glared at Evan who looked back at him with tears of his own.

In the impossibility of the moment, I knew a journey of healing had begun. It would not be immediate or easy, but our love and commitment to truth and authenticity had set the stage for growth and reconciliation, perhaps.

As the room slowly came alive with chatter, laughs, and chairs scraping on the floor, I didn't miss Sister Corrine speaking to some ladies near us.

"See how quickly the air can begin to clear when real communication happens?" I heard her say. "Entire homes and families have been broken down and destroyed when people insist on holding their secrets, when husbands and wives don't talk, when friends aren't open and honest. Getting things out in the open can clear things up immediately. We can't control what happens afterward," she said, glancing over at Mrs. Wayland, who'd sunken into a dining chair in the back of the room, alone, "but we can at least be free."

"Amen," I agreed silently, grateful God was answering prayers I'd prayed long ago. Though I'd stopped my daily meetups with Him, He'd never forgotten my cries. He'd never abandoned me. The past few moments had been uncomfortable but necessary. "Thank you, Lord, for a new chance to get my house in order, in every way."

"This is the best baby shower I've ever been to." Razi's eyes were glistening. "I've gotten so much material, I'm about to have another breakout record. And listen, Kenny, or should I call you Kunta, I'm sorry. A young'un at my old studio told me he wrote those lyrics. This was way back when I was just trying to make a name for myself in East Baltimore. He gave me the words, and I added the melody. I guess he was just trying to get his name on my record. You have real talent that no one can take from you. I hope you hold true to that. And, Evan, my man, I wouldn't have known who truly penned those contested lyrics if you'd never taken—and lost—my case. Great work. I'm going to remember this. I'm going to remember both of you, Evan and Kunta X. Madelyn, you should be proud. In your own way, you've bought us all together."

Mrs. Wayland let out a small moan. Blank face. Silence. Her husband and daughters had moved to the other side of the room. There was work to be done yet, but that was not on me.

Evan, who still held me, was about to say something when Neeka stepped in, seeing the look, the sudden strain on my face.

My stomach had squeezed and tightened into a taut ball.

"Selena, are you okay?"

"It's been too much." Evan's sister Tracey was right behind Neeka as the squeezing in my abdomen tightened even more, taking my breath away.

"Evan, start your car. Better yet, call 9-1-1." Tracey was in full medical mode as she put a hand on my stomach and stared down at her watch. "Selena, we need to get you to the hospital right now."

40

The Ever After

February 13. The day before Valentine's Day.

We hadn't even made it to our first anniversary, and yet the past months had dramatically changed our lives. Evan and I now talked, laughed, and prayed together. We'd become best friends again, cooking partners, workout pals, reality TV-show binging buddies, and, yes, the parents of a cherub-looking beautiful brown child. No more secrets, big or small, between us or the ones we loved. We talk things out—with each other, not at each other, and not just surface conversations either.

For as much as we converse and laugh, my favorite moments are just lying next to him, both of us awake, listening to the wind whirl around outside, aware of each other's company, alive in each other's quiet love.

And can I tell you what that level of unity and intimacy does for sex? *Mmm*, child.

Wait, let me calm down and finish my story.

While my baby shower had enough drama to land me in the

hospital, the skilled doctors and nurses of Baltimore Metropolitan Hospital talked my uterus into holding on for another month. Yes, it meant staying in the hospital bed the entire time, but it was worth every long second, every tasteless meal from the hospital cafeteria, every visit one by one from family members and friends who kept me company.

One of those regular visitors became Mrs. Wayland. She didn't say much, usually spent her energy fussing with the nurses over what they needed to be doing to keep me comfortable. I think I was waiting for an apology of some sort. Hasn't come yet, but there's humility in her eyes and pleading in her smile.

We'll get there, I believe.

My son, Kaleb Evan Wayland, entered the world four weeks early on January 29. He looked like me but with Evan's hair and my mother's chin.

And Kunta X's eyes.

But that's another story for another day.

Though Kaleb was nearly six pounds, the doctors debated putting him in the neonatal intensive care unit since he was born a month early. That debate lasted only five hours. They kicked him out the incubator and put him in the room with me. I got to put him in the car seat for the ride home the same day I was discharged.

So here we are, this, the eve of our first Valentine's Day as husband and wife, a family of three, nearly two months' shy of our first wedding anniversary, standing on the brand-new and furnished deck of our home in the middle of winter. Looking up at the trees in the backyard.

Trees.

"No, the string lights should go over that branch," I shouted down to CJ. He groaned but listened, moving the ladder to where I pointed. I could hear his footsteps crunch on the snow as I looked again at a picture on my phone that was serving as inspiration for the elaborate lighting idea. The screenshot was from a new website for landscape designs, Zu's Views.

I had to admit, for as ludicrous as her inside décor had been, Genevaise Zuzani had some good ideas for exteriors. She'd restarted, a solo business, rebranded, and refocused on backyard designs. Not surprising, considering my home's interior at one point had all the makings of an outdoor city street.

"Those lights are perfect for the soulful wintry wonderland theme tonight." I held up the picture and compared it to the ambiance we were creating in the backyard. The hint of the passing flurries added a bonus of drama and intrigue. "I love it." My voice was a whisper, but it reverberated deeply inside of me.

For all that happened between Neeka and me, I was ecstatic my place was the venue for her wedding rehearsal dinner. Yes, my house really was a showcase, hon. She and Peyton were choosing to splurge on a ten-day Mediterranean cruise for their honeymoon and focusing on plans to build a custom five-bedroom home out in the rolling green of pricey Woodstock, Maryland. Before she went bigtime with her deep-pocketed man, she wanted her nuptial celebrations to be small and intimate, attended by only those near and dear to her journey. Using my home for the dinner was Neeka's own way of letting everyone know we were still best girls.

My entire downstairs had been transformed once more for the intimate celebration. Red and white roses, silver branches and white lights filled the interior. All the furniture had been replaced with linen-covered chairs and a long table, elegantly set and ready for the five-star catered dinner. Lines of poetry from Kunta X were written on bits of musical composition paper as part of a silver, glittery centerpiece. A saxophonist was setting up to serenade the event.

Evan's clarinet was packed away in the third bedroom while he focused on fatherhood and rebuilding his law career. He had an upcoming interview with an arts foundation in need of legal counsel, thanks to a good word by Razi.

The highlight of the evening set-up was where we stood at the moment. The draperies covering the sliding doors to the deck were pulled back to reveal the dramatic backdrop of twinkling and snow-dusted trees.

Neeka's plans leading up to a perfect, cozy wedding were coming true. I was her sole bridesmaid, her matron of honor, and her niece and nephew were flower girl and ring bearer. Her future mother-in-law, Pastor Anderson, would be the officiant.

Evan was respectfully keeping his distance, only there to help put together the room before the bride and groom made their entrance. The pain of bitter betrayal was going to take more than a couple of months to recover from—if ever—but Peyton didn't argue against Neeka insisting on having the wedding rehearsal dinner at the home of her very best friend. Smart man he was, knowing what battles to pick with his beloved.

The view, the backdrop of trees is what she wanted as we worked toward restoring trust and rebuilding our friendship to be even better than what it was before. We would grow from here, like those trees. Strong, not easily toppled.

"Selena, look at the sky." Evan stood next to me, a brisk breeze whipping over our heads as final preparations were perfected. I wrapped the blanket tighter around our baby son, snuggling my nose into his lavender lotion–scented cheeks before looking up to the setting sun where Evan pointed. The day was ending, readying to prepare for a new day to begin. Kaleb let out a slight coo and gurgle.

Listen, I don't know what the future holds. Shoot, I haven't even made it to my first anniversary. I hadn't figured out my long-term career goals and neither had Evan. Plus, there was still some work to be done in the basement. And a pool to plan for the summer.

But, I've learned each step of my life journey is just that, a step. Along the way is forgiveness, communication, authenticity, trust in each other, and trust in the One who brought us together. I've learned to embrace the good moments when they come because there will be others that may be a bit harder to bear. I've learned to catch bubbles gently, stand firmly when needed, and keep sharing my thoughts, my heart, and my truth.

In this moment, the evening sky was a perfect blend of pink, orange, and purple over the treetops. My husband's arms were around me, his black, nubby elbows covered. My baby is here and healthy.

I'm a mom.

And Mrs. Maddie (as I'd settled on calling her to respectfully remind us both how we'd gotten here), is fussing at CJ for not using the extension cord she'd bought for the occasion. She would be leaving out with Evan before Neeka and her beau planned to arrive.

Nonetheless, our families are trying to unite, on their own terms and timetables.

My best friend is about to start her own journey of holy matrimony and I—for once—will be the advisor, the guide, the shoulder to lean on, the cheerleader. The prayer warrior.

Sometimes, it's not about what you do or don't do—if you are right or wrong. We can't control other people and their decisions and reactions—even when it's our mate.

Especially when it's our mate.

At the end of the day, we've got to trust, hope, pray, and believe and try to be players on the same united team with God as our coach. God remembered my prayers even when I got off track, and He allowed a victory that brought us all back to Him. And, we can know that no matter which way the day goes, the sun will set in the west and a new day—a new chance to enjoy new moments, to try and get it right—dawns in the east.

Even if trees block the view.

My peace isn't in Evan.

Thank God.

It's in the promise that my life and times are in God's hands. And that is enough.

Are life and my marriage and my hopes and dreams perfect?

Uh, that would be a hard no. However, I can still look up at the sky next to Evan and appreciate the grace in the moment.

"Beautiful." I lean more into the crook of his arm while pulling our little bundle closer to my chest. "Everything is beautiful and happily enough."

THE END

Other Books

STAY TUNED FOR...
Heartbroken: Madelyn's Story
Unbroken: Neeka's Story

OTHER BOOKS BY LESLIE J. SHERROD
Like Sheep Gone Astray
Secret Place
Losing Hope
Without Faith
Sacrifices of Joy
Sweet Violet and a Time for Love
The Man of My Schemes